CHASED BY

LOVE

THE RYDERS

LOVE IN BLOOM SERIES

MELISSA FOSTER

ISBN-10: 1941480438
ISBN-13: 9781941480434

CHASED BY LOVE

Cover Design: Elizabeth Mackey Designs

WORLD LITERARY PRESS
PRINTED IN THE UNITED STATES OF AMERICA

A Note to Readers

I have been excited to write Trish Ryder's story since I wrote Cash and Siena's book (FLAMES OF LOVE, The Remingtons). Trish is just as feisty as I imagined she'd be. Growing up with five brothers made her strong and independent, and the perfect match for uber-alpha rock star Boone Stryker. I hope you love them as much as I do!

To ensure you never miss a release, sign up for my newsletter: www.melissafoster.com/news

If this is your first Love in Bloom book, then you have a whole series of loyal, sexy, and wickedly naughty heroes and sassy heroines to catch up on. The Love in Bloom big-family romance collection is comprised of several family subseries (40+ awesome books). You can jump into the series anywhere. All Love in Bloom books can be enjoyed as stand-alone novels or as part of the larger series. The characters from each family appear in other Love in Bloom subseries so you never miss an engagement, wedding, or birth. For more information on the Love in Bloom series including a downloadable book list, family tree, and more, visit: www.melissafoster.com/LIB

Melissa Foster

For my readers

Chapter One

"I'M GOING OVER. Should I go over? Tell me I shouldn't. Or should I?" Trish Ryder clutched her cell phone, pacing inside her trailer on the set of her latest film, *No Strings*. She'd been trying to study her lines all night, but her co-star, famed rocker Boone Stryker, had a full-blown party going on at his trailer, and she could barely think past the noise.

"It's midnight and you have to be on set in seven hours," her best friend, Fiona, reminded her. "*You're* the star, so yes. Get your ass over there and pull a diva."

Trish stopped cold. "But I'm *not* a diva!"

"Of course not, but you know that's what his groupies will think, which you do *not* care about. Right?"

"Right." She nodded curtly, but she *did* care. She cared a lot, and Fiona knew that about her. She'd worked hard to keep a professional reputation clear of

1

any diva attitude or impressions, and she didn't want to blow it for a self-centered rock star making his film debut.

Fiona groaned, and Trish heard her friend's fiancé, Jake Braden, say, "Give me the phone."

"Do *not* give him the phone." Trish paced again. She adored Jake. Not only was he an amazing stuntman, but he treated her bestie like a princess. But Jake, like each of Trish's five brothers, had the protective alpha thing down pat, which meant he'd want to take care of this *for* her.

"Like I have a choice?" Fiona giggled, and Trish heard them struggling over the phone.

"Trish?" Jake's tone made her name sound like a command she should salute.

Trish Ryder saluted no man. "No, it's Mary Poppins."

"Okay. Well, listen, Mary," Jake said without missing a beat. "March your pretty little ass over there and tell the guy to straighten up. If he gives you any crap, call me back, and I'll come to the set and knock some sense into him."

Of course you will. "Thanks, Jake, but I can handle it. I just wasn't sure I wanted to stir up trouble. He's already messed up so badly, the whole crew knows the film's on thin ice."

"Even more of a reason for you to set him straight," Jake said. "You don't have to be a bitch. Just be your normal, confident self. He'd have to be a real dick not to rectify the situation."

She sighed, and heard Jake pass the phone back to

Fiona. Maybe they were right. She was a well-respected actress, and this *was* Boone's first film. Maybe he simply wasn't up to speed on film-set etiquette. Obviously, since in the span of a few weeks he'd missed the preproduction meeting, showed up late to the set, and screwed up too many scenes to count.

"I'm back. You okay?" Fiona asked.

"Yes. No. I don't know, but I'm going over. You guys are right. If I'm awake all night, I'll be the one messing up tomorrow, and I don't need the director upset with me."

After Trish ended the call, she set her phone down beside a copy of *Rolling Stone* magazine. A picture of Boone, shirtless, graced the cover. She'd read the article. She'd read every article about Boone taking on the role in *No Strings*, and they all said the same thing. *Boone Stryker is everything fantasies are made of: warm brown eyes that say "help me," "do me and you'll never forget me," body ink indicative of a troubled soul, and an insurmountable dedication to his craft.*

They left out *self-centered asshole with no respect for anyone but himself.* And based on his behavior, she wasn't even sure he had that.

Well, guess what? It's time to grow up.

Her phone vibrated with a call from her eldest brother, Duke. She groaned. *Damn it, Jake. You've got a big freaking mouth.* Sometimes being a little sister sucked—even at almost thirty years old. She let the call go to voicemail. She wasn't in the mood to deal with her overprotective eldest brother, who was ten years her senior. When would he learn that having ovaries didn't mean she needed looking after?

She stormed out of her trailer, assaulted by the sounds of rock and roll coming from across the lot. Groups of scantily clad women and shirtless men, smoking and drinking, created a buffer between Boone's trailer and the rest of the world. Trish stood and watched for a moment, trying to spot Boone among the mass of swaying bodies. She couldn't imagine living with groupies around all the time. It was no wonder he showed up late and was never prepared. How could anyone deal with this and concentrate on anything?

She tossed her hair over her shoulder and lifted her chin, squaring her shoulders like she wasn't nervous at all. She was an actress. She could do this, and Jake was right. There was no need to be a bitch. She'd act calm and cool, and hopefully Boone would respond reasonably. *Cool. Yeah, right.* She didn't usually have trouble with confrontations, but the badass rocker struck chords she'd never had tweaked before, and he did it with little more than a glance, which was horribly embarrassing. She couldn't deny the rush of heat that consumed her every time their eyes connected. Unfortunately, as hot as their chemistry was off set, when she and Boone were acting, he became cold, like he didn't want to feel the heat. In an effort to keep the situation from becoming even more uncomfortable, she'd kept her distance when they were off set. She hated that this would be their first *real* interaction. But that was on him, she decided, and set out across the lot, hoping to get this over with as quickly as possible.

The smell of cigarettes, weed, sweat, and sex hung heavily in the air. She pulled her arms in close, turning sideways to fit between less-than-accommodating people, and weaved through the drunken mob toward his trailer. She scanned the crowd for Boone, trying to ignore the way men and women were eyeing her up. She was used to being looked at, and she wasn't generally judgmental, but the groupie vibe and raunchy smell made her feel like she needed a shower. Stat!

"Hey, babe," a long-haired guy said as she squeezed between him and a busty brunette.

She forced a smile and pushed past, making a beeline for the trailer door. It seemed ridiculous to knock, given the scene she'd just waded through, but she knocked anyway. No one answered. She knocked again, louder, and when no one answered, she tried the knob. Locked. *Perfect.* The asshole was probably passed out naked with a harem of women. An icy chill rushed down her spine. *Yuck.* She pushed her way back through the crowd, determined to give him hell tomorrow, regardless of how it affected the movie. This was bullshit. How could he sleep with all that racket?

"Trish?"

She startled at the sound of Boone's voice coming from the direction of the parking lot and spun around. He had the most sensual voice she'd ever heard. It didn't matter if he was singing or acting, it affected her every time. It was deep and rich, and somehow rough, demanding both attention and intimacy. She tried to steady her racing heart with a few deep breaths as she drank him in. He held his guitar case in one hand and sported a half-cocked smile. He had beautiful full lips, and despite everything, the mere sight of his perfectly bowed mouth made hers water. His faded T-shirt clung to every muscle in his insanely defined chest. Lust chased frustration up her body. She had the inside scoop on his selfishness and *still* she wanted to fell him like a tree and devour him limb by perfect limb.

She swallowed a puddle of drool, drew her shoulders back again, and set a hand on her hip, hoping to mask her attraction. His smile turned smug, and his eyes lit with a spark of intel that made her gut twist. *Bastard.*

"Did I wake you?" She might not have been able to mask her attraction, but every word she spoke was laden with sarcasm.

He ran a hand through his hair and sighed, as if he were bored with the conversation. Or maybe with life.

"Wake me?" he said with an arched brow. "I just got here."

She glanced at the crowd and pointed to her ears, indicating the blaring music there was no way he could miss, and glared at him. "You just let your groupies run wild like this while you're not even around?"

He strode toward her, his piercing dark eyes sucking her right into his vortex. He stopped when they were toe to toe, filling the air with his confident arrogance and making it hard to breathe, much less concentrate.

"I had no idea they were partying. I'll shut it down. But for the record, no. I don't let my *groupies* run wild." His gaze roved over her face, and she narrowed her eyes, hoping he couldn't see the way every sweep sent waves of heat to all her best parts. "You went over there?"

"Some of us take this movie seriously. I can't prepare with that noise going on all night."

Boone raked his eyes down her body, causing her to nearly combust. A sinful smile curved his lips as his eyes began a slow stroll north, over her hips, lingering on her breasts, and bringing her traitorous nipples to attention, greeting him like a long-lost lover.

"Pretty woman like you shouldn't scowl so much." His rich voice slid over her skin like a caress, leaving goose bumps in its wake.

God, she hated herself right now.

Unwilling to give him the upper hand, she flashed a haughty smirk and returned his assessment with a lecherous leer of her own, drinking in every inch of his athletic build, from his bulging biceps to the ripped abs evident beneath his clingy shirt, all the way to the formidable package at the juncture of his powerful thighs. She lingered there, brazenly licking her lips.

He leaned in close—so close she thought he might kiss her. And damn it to hell, she wanted him to. Lust and challenge pulsed between them, thick and alive like a third heart. She shifted her eyes away and noticed a gorgeous platinum blonde standing in the shadows behind him. Embarrassment and something that felt far too similar to the claws of jealousy dug into her.

Her eyes shot to Boone, but before she could say a word, he said, "I'll take care of the noise," and stalked away with an arm around the blonde.

**

"JESUS, BOONE," HONOR said in a hushed and excited tone as they approached the crowd around his trailer. "The two of you looked like you were going to detonate. And I mean that in the hottest way possible."

Honor reached for his guitar, and he handed it over without responding to her comment. Yeah, he knew all about the sparks igniting between him and his gorgeous co-star, but he also knew how he was messing up the movie for her, which was why Honor West, one of his oldest and closest friends, had come to see him tonight.

As they approached the crowd by his trailer, the group of women stumbled toward them. Boone held up his hands. "The party's over. Everyone out." The women stopped in their tracks, their shoulders drooping along with their eager smiles. The string of pleas and promises that followed fell on deaf ears. Boone was sick of dealing with groupies who didn't give a hell about anything other than their ten minutes of fame. They'd sell their souls for the chance to brag about partying with the band or sleeping with a rock star. He'd given up sleeping with groupies a few weeks after he'd started, and he'd given up partying with them a short while later. About the time he got sick and tired of being treated like a commodity.

"Sorry," he lied. He'd made a mistake telling Benny, the bass player for their band, Strykeforce, he could stay with him for a few days. When Benny had taken off, he'd left his groupies behind. Boone had gone to meet Honor after filming, mistakenly assuming they'd leave. He made a mental note to call his manager and have them amp up security.

When everyone finally cleared out, he sank down to the couch in the trailer beside Honor. "Remind me to give Benny hell."

"You always give Benny hell. He's not going to change. He'd forget his head if it weren't attached. Luckily he's a creative genius. Like you." She rested her head on his shoulder. "Besides, Benny doesn't matter right now. You do. Are you going to be okay with this role? Do you want me to change my schedule and stick around?"

"No, but thanks for coming out and talking me off the ledge." He scrubbed a hand down his face, wrestling with the guilt and anger the movie had unexpectedly dredged up. Or more specifically, the emotions Trish dredged up every time she was in character as Delia, his character Rick Champion's strung-out girlfriend.

"We've all come a long way from the ghetto," Honor said softly, her pale green eyes soft and supportive. "Can I say that? The ghetto? I hate being politically incorrect. Benny told me to stop calling it that and call it the 'projects,' but we didn't grow up in the projects."

He sighed. "Fuck political correctness. The place was a ghetto. Don't let anyone else tell you where you grew up. That kind of stuff pisses me off. Like the people out in LA don't want to believe places like that exist, or giving it a more acceptable name like the 'projects' makes it seem better. Like being poor is contagious."

"Says the man who hides his hometown every chance he gets." Honor tucked her white-blond hair behind her ear and smiled, softening the truth.

He gave her a deadpan stare. "To protect my mother." At least with his success his mother and youngest brother, Lucky, didn't have to live a life of poverty, even if they'd chosen to remain in the area where he'd grown up.

"I know. I'm just giving you crap. Anyway, I'm proud of all of us, and I know Destiny would be, too. She'd want you to do well in this movie. She'd want all of us to be happy. You know that."

All of us. There was one less of them now. He closed his eyes and rested his head back against the cushion, remembering all the years they'd struggled. Boone's parents had married at seventeen, when his mother found out she was pregnant with him. They'd been poorer than dirt when he was growing up, and lived so far from the right side of the tracks he wasn't sure there was a right side. But what their family had lacked in money, they'd made up in love. Honor and

Destiny hadn't been as lucky. Destiny had turned to drugs to escape her druggie parents' abuse, and Honor had turned to Boone and their tight-knit group of friends.

"I know you don't blame yourself for Destiny's death," Honor said softly. "But you have to find a way to let her go. That's why you keep seeing her when you're doing those scenes with Trish."

"She was your sister. She was *our* sister," he said adamantly. Even though Trish's role was one of a girlfriend and he'd never had that connection with Destiny, the emotions she unearthed were the same. He'd felt helpless watching Destiny lose herself in drugs. "I'll never let her go."

"You know what I mean, Boone. We all loved her, and we all miss her. None of us will ever really let her go, and you know I don't want you to forget her. I'd never want that. But this movie is bringing you back to the darkness we *survived* years ago. I'm just worried about you."

He opened his eyes, meeting her compassionate gaze.

"You've got so much on your plate with Lucky, and your mom's recent health scare, and now Jude using again. I know you wanted to challenge yourself, but maybe this isn't the right time. If this movie is too much for you, maybe you should back out of it."

Between bailing his cocky youngest brother out of trouble, trying to convince his drummer, Jude Birch, to get his shit together, and his never-ending worries about his mother's health, he was practically drowning. But he was a man of his word, and he had no intention of letting anyone down.

"I can't do that. Even if I could, I never would. You saw how upset Trish was. You read the papers. This is her shot at an Oscar, and they've been pimping me out as the lead for months. If I bail, the movie will tank, and she'll get screwed over. I'll figure it out." He pushed to his feet and reached for Honor's hand, helping her up.

"You have too big of a heart. You always have." Honor hugged him. "If you refuse to put yourself first, then I think you should take my advice and tell Trish what's going on. She might be able to help."

Boone laughed and headed back toward the bedrooms. "I think she's doing all she can to keep from killing me on a daily basis."

"Since when have you sucked at reading women?"

"I don't suck at it. Turning a woman on and being liked by her are two very different things. I just need to get past seeing Destiny every time Trish is in character. Talking tonight helped. I appreciate it." He kissed Honor's cheek, opened her bedroom door, then headed for his own.

"You could always picture her as a fat, ugly guy instead of a hot chick you'd like to see naked."

Boone shook his head and closed his bedroom door behind him. He'd have to give Honor hell in the morning before she left, because now he couldn't stop picturing Trish naked.

Chapter Two

TRISH LAY ON the concrete floor in an abandoned warehouse, covered in dirt and grime. Her tattered dress was bunched around her bruised and battered thighs, her hair was a mass of greasy tangles, and her arms were tracked with angry red marks. She stared up at the ceiling with unseeing eyes, barely breathing, waiting for Boone to say his lines. She was nailing her role as Delia Ellis, rock star Rick Champion's heroin-addicted girlfriend, in the gritty indie film about a reclusive musician that made it big. She'd starved herself down to a dangerous one hundred and six pounds, which was well below her healthy weight at five nine, but it was worth it. Trish was an A-list actress, and this role should finally put her in the running for an Oscar. But they'd been filming for weeks and Boone had yet to make it through a single scene without screwing up, which meant delays the producers couldn't afford.

Boone paced a few feet away, his rapid breathing and heavy footfalls the only sounds on the set.

Come on. Three lines. You can do this.

She knew he had it in him to evoke the intense emotions needed for his scene. When she'd learned they'd secured Boone for the role, she'd jumped at the chance to work with him. Not only was he hotter than sin, but he also wrote all of his own music and lyrics. His songs were soulful and torturous, and Trish had immense respect for his musical talents. But the ability to parlay those talents to acting seemed to evade him.

Regulating her breathing when all she wanted to do was shake the hell out of her co-star was a definite test of her acting abilities. She couldn't even shift her gaze to see what Boone was doing without breaking character, leaving her stuck, silently willing the six-two rock god not to screw this up for both of them.

Boone crouched beside her limp body. Tension and angst billowed around him like a storm cloud threatening to burst, perfect for the scene where he finds his strung-out lover on the precipice of death.

Hope rushed through her. *You can do this. Please do this.*

"What do you expect me to do now?" Boone had the lines right, but his tone was off. *Again.*

Disillusioned and upset, it was all Trish could do to remain still, and when Chuck Russell, the director, yelled, "Cut!" for the millionth time, his tone told her he was nearing his own breaking point.

Chuck stalked toward them, and Trish pushed to her feet beside the shirtless, brooding musician. The muscles in Boone's neck and broad shoulders bulged, corded so tight it had to hurt. Tattoos snaked beneath his collarbone, across perfectly muscled pecs, and down each impressively defined arm. He crossed his arms, watching Chuck close the distance between them. Chuck was a burly, barrel-chested man in his late fifties, with thick hair that always appeared windblown. His shoulders were rounded, like a grizzly readying to pounce, and he set a dark stare on Boone. Boone didn't flinch. His left hand was tucked against his ribs, his right palm turned upward, fingers extended and slightly curled in a quizzical pose, which matched the knitting of his thick, dark brows. His hand gesture and pleading eyes relayed, *I'm sorry, but...*with no excuse at the ready.

You've never needed excuses, have you?

Trish wanted the film to succeed not only because of her chance to finally take her career to the next level, but also because the story was intense and real. It was a story worth telling, one that many artists could relate to, which was another reason she thought Boone would do well in the part.

"What's the problem, Stryker?" Chuck's voice echoed off the rafters. "This is a pivotal scene. You're supposed to be on the brink of the most important moment of your life. You're about to leave for stardom. You're on a high, the biggest high you can imagine, and then your world comes crashing down." He waved at Trish. "She's fucking up *everything* for you and you *love* her. You're tortured, stuck in a fathomless position that's gnawing at your gut. We need to *see* that. *Hear* it. *Feel* it."

Trish knew Chuck was referring to her character, Delia, but she wondered if Boone did. He couldn't possibly think he meant *Trish* was getting in his way of acting, could he? Boone's jaw clenched, accentuating his perfectly bowed lips. Last night there had been a moment when Trish had fantasized about sinking her teeth into those perfect lips. *A momentary lapse in judgment.*

"Right," Boone said flatly. "I'm working on it. But these lines don't feel right."

Ohmygod. Wrong answer.

"You should have been *working on it* for months," Chuck snapped. "Every time we have to reshoot a scene it costs us money we don't have. And this is a *Chuck Russell* film. We do not *improvise*, so get that out of your head. I don't care if you love or hate the lines. You stick to the script." He shifted a fed-up expression to Trish, and her stomach plummeted.

"We'll get it right," she assured him. She'd promise her firstborn if that's what it took to make sure this movie didn't get canceled. She glared at Boone, hoping he'd read, *Shut the hell up and let me handle this.* "Give me a few days to work with him. I know we can nail the chemistry. I know he can do this."

Boone shot her a quizzical gaze.

She'd deal with him later. Right now she needed to get Chuck to believe she could make Boone take the film seriously, and she wasn't entirely sure she believed it herself. "You know I can do this, and I know he can do it."

Chuck's eyes darted between the two of them. Boone had a death stare locked on Trish, but she didn't care. She was sick and tired of repetitive roles that didn't test or stretch her acting skills. She'd been ready to take a hiatus when she'd read this script, and the gritty part had spoken to her from page one. She wasn't about to let an arrogant musician mess it up for her.

Chuck pointed at Trish. "You have ten days to pull this shit together. From this moment on, the two of you are Siamese twins. Wherever he goes, you're there." He waved his finger at Boone. "Where she goes, you go."

"We'll get it right," Trish assured him, at the same time Boone said, "What?"

"You're damn right you will," Chuck said to Trish, clearly ignoring Boone's complaint. "Or you're both off the film."

"Wait. What? Both of us?" She scowled at Boone, who was grinding his teeth together, eyes locked on Chuck.

"You can't take her off the film because I suck," Boone complained.

Chuck crossed his arms, eyeing them both with more than a hint of arrogance. "I'm the director. I can do anything I want. Siamese twins. I want you both at the farmhouse in Hurricane, West Virginia, by tomorrow night. Ten days of getting into character should give us a perfect film."

"You want us to *stay* at the next location for ten days? What about this scene?"

"We'll come back to it. The farmhouse," Chuck reiterated. "Ten days. No crew, no bullshit. Get there and fix this." He eyed Boone. "No doubt you know music. She knows acting. If you have a lick of sense, you'll listen to whatever she says."

Trish scowled at Boone as Chuck walked away. Then she ran after Chuck. "We don't need to live together for ten da—"

Chuck stopped short, and she nearly bumped into him.

"Trish, we *know* you can pull off your role." He shifted his gaze to Boone, who was ambling toward his trailer like he hadn't a care in the world. "But he's the one the fans want to see as Rick Champion, and it's going to take a fucking miracle to get him to perform well enough to pull this off. I want you to hammer the character into his head."

"And if I don't pull off a miracle, I lose my shot at this incredible film because he's too much of a dumbass to take it seriously?"

Chuck's expression softened. "You know the game. The fans make or break these kind of movies. He's been pimped as the lead in every media outlet for months. If he doesn't perform, the movie doesn't get made."

**

BOONE HAD THE innate ability to compartmentalize his life, and as he stepped into his trailer, he shoved the ten-day mandate into a mental compartment called *Not in This Lifetime* and focused on more pressing issues. Like the text from Jude. *Back off. I can handle this.* Like hell he could. His cocaine addiction had gotten out of control. It wasn't the first time, but Boone had thought the last time had been just that. The last time. He'd known Jude since he was a scrappy teenager busting into houses to feed his brothers. Honor was right; they'd come a long way from their meager beginnings, and they owed it all to one man. The man Boone was dialing up as he pulled a soda from the fridge. The only other person on the planet who might be able to get through to Jude.

He smiled as he read the note Honor had left propped up against his soda cans. *Good luck! Call me if you need an ear, and remember, talking helps. Talk to the hottie you've been trying to pretend isn't so hot.*

Harvey Bauer answered on the first ring. "Heard you bought yourself ten days in heaven with Trish Ryder."

Boone pictured him sitting back in his leather chair, his feet kicked up on his desk and a wise-ass smile on his face.

"How could you possibly have heard that already? They just handed down the prison sentence ten minutes ago." Boone took a swig of his drink and sank down in a chair, thinking about his gorgeous co-star and the way she'd looked at him last night—like she wasn't sure if she wanted to fuck him, kill him, or figure him out.

He was pretty sure *kill* was now highest on that agenda.

Harvey was quiet for a beat too long, bringing Boone's mind back to their conversation. He knew he'd screwed up, and not only was it screwing Trish for this movie—and the next ten days—but it would also reflect poorly on Harvey if Boone didn't nail this part. He pretty much owed Harvey his life, since he'd not only paid for Boone to attend Epson School of the Arts, where Boone's mother worked as a janitor, but he'd also mentored Boone, his brother Cage, and a number of their friends, and helped them build their careers from scratch.

"I've got a lot on my plate." Boone rested his head back and closed his eyes against the lame excuse. It didn't matter that it was true. Things could be a hell of a lot worse, and if anyone knew about having a lot on his plate, it was Harvey.

"Mm-hm." Harvey would never fall back on an excuse, which was only one of the reasons Boone respected him with the same vehemence as he'd respected his own father, and it was the reason Boone turned to him now.

"I'll fix it," Boone assured him.

"Hey," Harvey said casually. "You're not doing me any favors, but Chuck isn't screwing around. His assistant called me within minutes of Chuck giving you the directive."

"I said I'll fix it." Chuck had been after Boone to do this film for a long time, and he'd wanted to do the movie since he'd first read the script. He'd wanted a new challenge. Lately he'd felt creatively blocked. He was having trouble writing songs for the first time in years. He was sick of groupies, sick of the rock-star persona he was expected to live up to, and was ready for a change, but doing something like this came with risks. He wasn't an actor, and he'd known once he'd accepted the role that he'd have no choice but to sink or swim. If he sank, so would his reputation and the reputation of everyone else who was involved with the film. With the support of his closest friends and family, he'd finally accepted the challenge, and he'd thought he could pull it off. But he hadn't expected his life to implode at the same time. And now his worst fears were coming true.

He wasn't going to help anyone if he got himself fired.

"You always do," Harvey said. "So, what's up? You need me to ship a crate of condoms out to the godforsaken place you're going?"

Boone laughed, thinking about the scathing looks the chestnut-haired actress had given him. "I'm sure I won't be needing them. We'll be lucky if we don't kill each other out there." He'd been shocked when Trish had offered to help him, and as much as he appreciated it, he hated that now she was stuck giving up her time because of him.

"So you *are* going, then? Because Chuck's assistant said if you don't play well in the sandbox, you're out of the schoolyard."

"I'm not going for ten days, but I'll go and play nice. I need a few days at most. I just need to focus." He took another swig of his soda, hoping focus was all it would take. "Which is why I need you to visit Jude.

He's using again."

"Aw, hell, again? Have you talked to him?"

"For hours. I was *this close* to getting him to agree to go to rehab the other morning, and then he bailed on me. That's one reason the director is all over me. I was an hour late to the set."

They talked for a few more minutes, and Harvey agreed to track down Jude and let Boone know how their meeting went. After the call, Boone tossed his phone on the sofa, stripped off his pants, and headed for the shower. Someone banged on his trailer door. He cursed under his breath and reached for a towel as the door swung open and Trish stormed in.

"Do you have any idea how close he is to shutting down this—" Her eyes swept down his naked body. "You're naked!" She spun around, and her hands flew over her eyes. "Why are you *naked*?"

"I usually get naked before I shower. Why are you in my trailer?" Boone couldn't help but laugh at her reaction. She was still wearing her character's dirty dress, her hair looked like a rat's nest, and her body was covered in a layer of filth. She was tall and waif thin. Too skinny for Boone's usual taste, but he'd noticed her confidence and determination the first moment they'd met, and her feistiness was definitely hot.

She turned, her eyes going directly south. "You're still naked!" She spun around again.

"And you're still in my trailer." He casually wrapped the towel around his waist. "You can turn around and bite my head off now."

"Are you *clothed*?"

"You'll just have to take your chances."

She turned slowly. He had the urge to rip off his towel just to see her fly into another fit, but he refrained. He had a sister, and he knew the wrath of an angry woman, so he waited out her fury in silence. She put a hand on her hip and pursed her lips together. Her perfectly manicured brows knitted, as if she was trying to remember what she'd come there to say.

"I don't know what you're trying to do out there," she finally said with a huff of anger. "But I'm not about to let you screw this up for me, or for any of the other people who are pouring endless hours into this movie."

"Do you really think that's my plan? To screw this up?" He reached for his soda and held it up. "Want a drink?"

She rolled her eyes. "That might work on your groupies, but I'm not a groupie."

He eyed his soda. "Now you've lost me. What might work?"

She waved her hand in his direction. "You. Naked. Offering me a *drink*, which I'm sure is code for…Never mind! In case you haven't noticed, you've wasted enough of my time."

"Is that right?" She'd snarled, glared, ogled, and shaken her head at him, but other than last night, when she was pissed off about the groupies—as was he—not once had she actually taken the time to talk to him when they weren't filming. Not that this was talking, but at least she was communicating instead of holing up in her trailer. "And how is that?"

"How?" Her eyes widened. "First you don't show up for the preproduction meeting, and you don't even have the courtesy to warn anyone so we can reschedule. Then you show up late on not only the first day of filming, but several other times, too. And you obviously haven't studied your lines. It's completely unprofessional. I mean, I know *No Strings* isn't exactly a high-budget film, but it's disrespectful to everyone when you treat it like it doesn't matter."

He stepped closer, cataloging the quickening of her breathing and the spark of heat in her eyes that had nothing to do with anger. It was that spark that had his brain sliding down a slippery slope it hadn't slid down in far too long—and it was the heat brewing inside him that had him scrambling back to reality. There was no room in his life for another complication, and though he was used to the less-than-stellar reputation that came along with being a rock star—self-centered, driven by booze and sex, and light on intelligence—he didn't take her assumption lightly.

"Is that what you think? That this film doesn't matter to me? Just because I'm not the actor you hoped I'd be?" All of the tension from the last few weeks came tumbling forward and his words came out harsher than he'd intended.

A look of contemplation washed over her face.

"Taking on this role must have been a step down for an A-lister like you," he said with a serious tone. "Did someone force you to take a bum deal? To work with an unprofessional ass like me?"

"Of course not. I wanted this role. I wanted to work with you." She searched his eyes, determination and annoyance sailing through hers. A second later those emotions were pushed aside and replaced with desire so raw it drew Boone a step closer. Their chests grazed, and they both swallowed hard.

"Good to know." He'd known passion and he'd known lust, but the inferno raging between them had a dangerous draw, one that was proving hard to resist.

As if she'd read his thoughts, or caught herself reacting to him like a *woman* rather than a pissed-off actress, she narrowed her eyes and lifted her chin defiantly. "Because of you, we're stuck together for ten days in Bumfuck, West Virginia. You *cannot* screw this up."

"No shit, Trish. It was never my plan to screw it up," he said honestly. "I appreciate your offer to help me learn how to do this. We both know I can use it. But rest assured, I have no intention of keeping you from your life for ten days. I'll go for a few days, and then you'll be free from the likes of me."

She crossed her arms and shook her head. He'd obviously said the wrong thing.

"I don't know what it's like for you when you're on tour," she said angrily, "or who's the boss of your schedule, but when you're making a movie, the director holds all the cards. He *owns* you, and Chuck made it perfectly clear that we have to spend ten days together. So by cutting that time short, you are intentionally screwing with him."

Well, hell, what did she want from him? She *wanted* to spend ten days in Hurricane, West Virginia? He thought of Jude, whose life was on the line every day he refused to go to rehab. If Harvey wasn't able to convince him to go, there was no way Boone would leave it up to anyone else to handle. And if Lucky got into trouble, or his mother fell ill again, he'd have to leave to help them out. Then there was Trish, putting herself on the line for him, even if she currently looked like she might want to throttle him. There was no way he was going to promise her something he probably couldn't do.

He hated to be a jerk, but the truth was the truth, and he wasn't about to lie to make her feel better. And he needed to douse the flames between them or there would be no way in hell a few days alone would do a damn thing for his lack of focus.

"I don't want to screw this up for you, but unfortunately, *pretty little A-lister,* the world doesn't revolve around you *or* this film. Two days, three if we need it."

She threw her hands up and reached for the door. "I had a ton of respect for you before we started filming. Now I have no idea *what* to make of you."

"How could you? All you see is a guy who's screwing up your chance to make it big." He paused, letting those words sink in. "At least now we're even, because I have no idea what to make of you, either."

Chapter Three

TRISH SAT IN the rental car outside the West Virginia airport the next evening flipping through *Rolling Stone* magazine while she waited for Boone to get off the phone so they could get on their way. He was wearing a path in the pavement beside the car. She looked down at his picture on the cover of the magazine, wishing she had picked up something else to read, but she'd thought her Kindle would hold her over while they traveled. The darn thing had died ten minutes ago, so she was left with three choices: Find something interesting to look at on her phone, watch Boone pace, or read the stupid magazine. Too frustrated to read, she closed the magazine and watched him pace. His face was a mask of concern. He'd been distracted on the long trip from Los Angeles, and he'd taken calls from his mother and brother, but he'd let every other call go to voicemail. She wondered if it was the blonde she'd seen him with that had his rapt attention now.

She looked down at the shirtless picture of Boone on the cover of the magazine and her stomach fluttered. Fluttered! *Ugh!* Her stomach hadn't fluttered since she was a teenager. She couldn't afford those types of distractions. This was her only chance to get him past whatever was holding him back when he was acting.

Trish grabbed a pen from her purse, smiling as she pressed the tip to his picture and drew thick dark glasses around his eyes. When that only made him sexier—*the bastard*—she drew scars on his face, big and black with thick stitches like Frankenstein. *Nope. Still frigging hot.* She scribbled over his shoulders and neck, filling in every inch of his skin, and creating a jagged-edged black smock to cover his perfection.

She startled when he opened the car door, and shoved the magazine and pen in her bag.

"Sorry that took so long." He eyed her curiously, and his mouth quirked up as he settled into his seat. "Most people want me to take my clothes *off*, not put more on."

Trish followed his gaze to the magazine cover peeking out of her bag. *Crap.*

"About time," she snapped.

He lowered his chin and spoke a little quieter and somehow rougher. "Are we going to do this, or what?"

She blinked several times, fighting the ridiculous response, *Yes, please.* "We have no choice. Siamese twins, remember?"

"What's got your panties in a bunch?"

She rolled her eyes as if hearing him talk about

28

panties hadn't made her insides quiver. "What do you think?"

His jaw tightened as he drove out of the parking lot. "I said I was sorry the call took so long."

"It's fine. Let's just get going."

They listened to the radio as they drove. His phone vibrated a number of times. Each time he lifted it, glanced at the screen, then set it back down.

It vibrated again and she finally had to say something. "Aren't you going to answer that?"

"Nope."

"What if it's important?"

"Unless you want to wait on the side of the road for another half hour, I'll deal with it when we get there."

"So you're not answering because you don't want me to hear your conversation?" That piqued her curiosity.

"Bingo."

Her phone rang and she reached into her bag for it with a smirk. "This is how much I care about you hearing my conversations." She saw her brother Duke's name on the screen and silently cursed. Why couldn't it be Fiona? She could speak cryptically and Fiona would understand every word. Duke wasn't nearly as easy.

"Hey, Duke."

Boone slid a curious look her way. She gave him a see-how-easy-this-is smirk.

"Hey, sis," Duke said. "You didn't return my calls. Everything okay?"

"Sorry. Things have been crazy. Everything's fine. I'm on my way to Hurricane, West Virginia, for ten days, as per Chuck Russell." She purposely left out that it was just her and Boone, given her brother's propensity for worrying.

"They changed the filming schedule? I thought you were in LA for another month."

"Something like that," she said. "I spoke to Gabby last week. She said the wedding planning is done. You must be relieved."

"Very. I'd marry her tomorrow if she'd agree. Hold on a sec." She heard him talking with someone, and when he came back on the line he sounded rushed. "Trish, I've got to run, but I wanted to make sure you were okay. Jake Braden called and said you were having a hard time with Boone Stryker. Let me know if you need me. The guy's got a harsh rep. I don't want you going face-to-face with him alone, okay? Promise me you won't."

She eyed Boone, who was pretending not to listen, but she was pretty sure he was taking in every word. "Duke, you know there's nothing I can't handle." Her brother knew it was true, even if he refused to treat her as if he believed it. She didn't make the promise to Duke because she knew there was no way she'd keep it. But she assured him she'd call if she needed his help.

They drove down Main Street, where a massive bank with wide stone columns that looked like it belonged in the Deep South was built beside a one-story, old-fashioned diner, and just beyond, stand-alone shops varied in heights and design. Some looked more like houses, while others looked like brick-front office buildings that belonged in bigger cities. The wide sidewalk was illuminated by streetlights, and potted trees graced every corner, giving the quirky little town a welcoming feel.

They stopped for gas and groceries. The young cashier studied them as she rang up their purchase. "Y'all look familiar."

"Just passing through town," Boone said.

"Huh." She watched Boone swipe his credit card, then handed him the receipt. "I know who you look like. That Cuban actor. What's his name? Oh, I know! William Levy. My friend is gaga over him. But he doesn't have all those tats like you do."

Boone smiled. "William Levy. I'll have to Google him."

Trish stifled a laugh. William Levy was hot as hell, but he wasn't exactly a household name. She shouldn't be surprised Boone had no idea who he was.

"Where do people go for fun around here?" she asked the cashier.

"Fun? In Hurricane?" She laughed. "If you like playing pool or karaoke, you could try the Rum Hummer, but mostly people just hang out."

They thanked her, and while Boone put the groceries in the car, Trish went to use the ladies' room. When she came back out the car was unlocked, but Boone was nowhere in sight. She had no idea what to make of him, but the more time they spent together, the more curious she became.

He walked out of the grocery store a few minutes later with a little gray kitten snuggled against his chest, a litter box tucked under his arm, and balancing a full grocery bag against his side. Her heart melted a little at the sight. She took the grocery bag from him and peeked inside. Cat litter, kitten chow, and kitty toys. *Toys?* She just about liquefied.

He climbed into the car and settled the kitty on his lap.

"Did you get lonely?" she asked.

"Found him wandering around the parking lot. He has no collar, so I went inside and asked around. No one seems to know where he came from." He lifted the kitty and looked into its tiny little eyes. "I couldn't just leave him there to starve."

"So, you're keeping him?"

He put the kitty back in his lap, laying one big hand protectively over his fluffy little body. "Would you rather I gave him to a shelter? They kill animals when they're not adopted."

"No, of course not, but you don't seem like a kitty type of guy." She reached over to pet the kitten and their hands touched. Electricity sparked up her arm. He must have felt it, too, because when their gazes met, those sparks had nothing on the blazing heat their connection created.

She pulled her hand away, a little flustered. "What're you going to name him?"

He shrugged as he pulled back onto the road. "Hell if I know."

"That's not a very nice name," she teased, earning

her first-ever true Boone Stryker smile, and she liked it a lot. A whole heck of a lot. She wanted to fan herself. Instead, she rolled down the window and let the cool air wash over her heated skin.

"Too bad he's not a Siamese cat," she teased.

He laughed.

Darn it. She should have known she'd like that, too.

**

TRISH WAS RIGHT about Boone not being a *kitty* type of guy, but he also wasn't the kind of guy who could pass by someone—or something—in need. But he wasn't about to name it. The minute he did, it would be his forever and would be added to the list of things he needed to worry about. *Nope. No name for you, little buddy.* He'd find him a good home with someone who had less crap going on in their lives. Maybe he'd give him to his mother or his sister.

They set out to find the farmhouse. The GPS directed them to a narrow winding road that took them fifteen minutes away from any signs of civilization and forked at a wide creek. Boone stopped at the end of the road, having absolutely no clue which way they should turn, or even if they were in the right place.

Trish was busy texting, sitting cross-legged on the passenger seat, like she was completely comfortable with herself, which wasn't at all what he'd expected given how uptight she'd seemed. But then again, he'd expected her to dress the part of an uppity actress, too, and he'd been pleasantly surprised to see her wearing a pair of tattered form-fitting jeans shorts, a black scoop-neck shirt, and sandals. He'd also been surprised by the large colorful tattoo of a butterfly on her left arm just above her elbow and the hint of another tattoo peeking out from the collar of her shirt. They must have covered them with makeup when they were filming. And she definitely hadn't come across as the type of woman to wear a sexy black and brown leather wrist cuff like she had on today. The one that gave him ideas of other types of cuffs he'd like to see around her wrists.

"Take your pick," he said. "Left or right?"

"It's a right-handed society, so go that way." She eyed the sleeping kitten on his lap.

"Okay, but you should really stop checking out my crotch."

"You wish." She waved her finger toward the kitty. "I've seen what you have down there, remember?"

"Yeah, and I also remember the rather impressed look in your eyes when you got an eyeful."

"You're incorrigible."

"*Encourage* me, baby."

She smiled and it reached all the way up to her eyes. She had the most incredible hazel eyes, with varying shades of greens and browns. They vividly relayed her emotions, which drove home every scene she acted out. He already knew they also made it hard for her to hide her feelings. He stole another glance, taking in her high cheekbones and slightly pointed chin. She'd put her earbuds in. She'd listened to them on the plane, too. He was dying to know what she listened to. Her hair was tucked behind her ear, revealing a mix of stud and small hoop earrings from the lobe to the very top. She obviously wasn't as straitlaced as she appeared. She had a perky nose, and he'd noticed that when she was angry, she crinkled it a little, which made her look even cuter.

He felt a smile tugging at his lips. It had been a long time since he'd felt like smiling. He stole another glance. She was still texting, her thumbs racing over the screen. She was stubborn as the day was long. When he'd tried to carry her luggage, she'd insisted on carrying it herself, and when he'd tried to open the car door for her, she'd pushed past him and opened it. But then she'd been playful on the plane, stealing his snacks and pointing out women who were watching him. She made him want to escape the chaos in his own life. And it wasn't just because she was gorgeous. Gorgeous women were a dime a dozen in Los Angeles. Maybe it was because she'd given up several days of her time, and though she'd seemed upset yesterday, she hadn't made any snarky comments about it today. Or maybe it was because she didn't seem to have a shit storm following her around the way he did. Either way, she was getting to him.

After driving for ten minutes along the windy road, Boone was ready to head back to the frigging airport. "Are you sure Chuck didn't send us on a wild-goose chase?"

Trish was moving to the beat of whatever she was

listening to. He pulled an earbud from her ear, ignored her gaping jaw, and stuck it in his ear.

"REO Speedwagon?" He laughed.

She yanked it from his hand. "I happen to like them. And Journey, and just about any band from the eighties. Queen. Madonna. Phil Collins." She pointed to a dirt road. "Look. There's a house on the hill. I bet that's it."

"I didn't peg you as a music girl." Boone turned onto the dirt driveway and followed rutted tire paths through the thick grass and up the hill.

"I love music. I love all music, really, but nothing beats 'Can't Fight This Feeling' or 'Faithfully.' Oh, wait, maybe 'Keep on Loving You.' I do like that. I love Michael Jackson, too."

He parked in front of the old clapboard farmhouse and watched her as she shoved her phone into her purse.

"Stop looking at me. I don't care if you hate those bands."

He didn't bother to correct her and turned his attention to the house, wondering what else they might have in common.

The dingy, faded white siding was aged and weathered, with a few slats missing. Overgrown bushes blocked the windows to the left of the front door. Weeds and ivy snaked up the doorframe, reaching like invasive tentacles toward the slightly bowed roof.

"You've got to be shitting me." Boone looked at Trish, expecting her to complain, but she was already out the door and heading toward the house. He kissed the kitty's head and set him on the seat. "Wait here, little buddy."

"This is perfect," Trish said as he stepped from the car. "It's exactly as I'd imagined it would be." She was calf deep in grass and didn't seem to care, surprising him again.

"It is?"

She put a hand on her hip and glared at him. "Now I'm positive you haven't read the whole script, because this house is exactly what I pictured Rick and Delia's house would look like."

He had an excuse ready, but when he opened his mouth to set it free, it lodged in his throat. He'd never been good at lying, and sometimes he wished he could, like right now, because it would make things like this a lot easier.

"I knew it." She stormed up the front porch. "Why did you even agree to do this film?"

He caught her by the arm. "So what if I didn't have time to read the whole script? Is that a crime?"

"No, but it is unprofessional and disrespectful to the rest of us who really care." She glowered at him, but he saw through the anger to the doleful undercurrent, as if he'd personally let her down.

That bugged the shit out of him, and momentarily rendered him silent.

"I can't believe you," she seethed. "If I was in one of your music videos, I'd never treat it like it didn't matter."

"Trish—"

She wrenched her arm from his grip. "Save it, because whatever you have to say doesn't excuse your apathy for the project. You could have let the role go to someone who cared."

"Goddamn it. You're so sure of yourself, aren't you?"

She turned with a shocked expression.

"You're right," he admitted. "I could have let the role go to someone else. But just because it could have gone to a better actor—which it definitely could have, considering I'm not a fucking faker—doesn't mean it would have gone to someone who cares more about the story than I do."

She crossed her arms and stared at him like she was deciding if she wanted to believe him. He'd been picked apart by the press and public for a decade. Would it ever end?

"I'm here, in the middle of nowhere," he finally said in the calmest voice he could muster, which was about as calm as a winter storm. "If I didn't give a shit about the movie, do you really think I'd be here?"

Her eyes narrowed, hurt and anger warring for dominance. He turned and headed for the car, but not before seeing that anger had won the battle. Could he blame her? Anyone would feel the barb he'd tossed like *they* were nothing. Damn it. He hadn't meant it like that, and Trish didn't deserve it. Especially since *she* was the one who didn't need to be here. Fighting against years of his finely honed skill of blocking everyone but his family and closest friends out, he turned to apologize, but she'd already disappeared into the house.

Chapter Four

"I'M TELLING YOU, Fi, he's as arrogant and selfish as he is sickeningly sexy, and—" Trish groaned into the phone. She and Boone had moved through the house in uncomfortable silence, putting away their belongings and the food they'd bought. Every step felt like she was wading through a tension-filled swamp. She knew better than to take anything another actor— or wannabe actor—said or did personally, but for some reason his words stung. They shouldn't. She was nothing to him but someone to help him get through this role, and he was nothing to her. It was her ridiculous reaction that had driven her out the door and across the field to vent to Fiona. They'd been college roommates, and if anyone would let her rant, it was Fiona.

"So what?" Fiona said. "So are most of the actors you deal with."

"He's not an actor."

"Right, which is why you're there in the first place. Chuck was right to quarantine you two. You're the one who always says immersion is the only way to get into your character's head. You *know* how this game is played."

"I know," Trish relented. "I'm stuck with him for ten days, if he stays that long."

"For several weeks," Fiona corrected. "This is just to get him up to par. You still have to film the movie. And may I remind you that for years you have had his picture as the wallpaper on your laptop, and before he missed that first meeting you were over the moon about being introduced to him, much less working with him."

It was true. Trish had been like a swooning teenager, which was silly, because she'd known all about Boone's reputation. The sheer number of scantily clad women and men hanging around his trailer had reinforced the rumors.

"That was before he ruined my fantasy."

Fiona laughed. "Now we're getting to the heart of the problem."

Trish sighed and gazed at the farmhouse. Boone had carried the kitten the whole time he'd put things away. "You know," she said with a little less anger. "He could have lied to me about not reading the script."

"Yeah, I pointed that out when you told me."

"I know. I'm just thinking about it again." She'd been too upset in the first five minutes of their phone call to process anything, but now that she was calmer, the sweeter side of Boone returned to the forefront of

42

her mind. "He also nixed that party the minute I asked, and he thanked me for offering to help him with his acting. But there's something gruff about him, and how can anyone take on this big of a movie and *not* study their lines day and night?"

"Trish, you know the answer to that."

Fiona paused long enough for Trish to agree. There were plenty of great actors that weren't always prepared for the whole movie their first few weeks of filming.

"Remember how excited I was about filming here?" She headed back toward the house. "I dreamed about this house for weeks, and the minute we pulled up, I could feel it, Fi. It's so right for Rick and Delia."

"How could I forget? You texted about it nonstop, and now you're there, where Delia and Rick's world will come to life. You should just brush off the crap about Boone and dive into your character like you always do."

She thought about that for a minute. The house was absolutely perfect, from the creaking floorboards and cobwebs to the dented and scuffed old-fashioned appliances and the cracked window in the living room.

"Normally I would, but I have to run lines with a guy who goes cold as ice when he acts."

"Hm. Well, you can't let him ruin this chance for you, so what about if you spend the time together *in character*? He won't be able to help but let down his guard and fall into sync."

She heard the smile and challenge in Fiona's voice. "You know what? You're right. This is *my* shot. I can't let him ruin my mojo."

"Exactly, and think of how much stronger your acting will be for it. You've never had this opportunity with a co-star before. You have ten whole days to hone your skills and perfect the nuances of your chemistry."

"Um...*That's* part of the problem. I'm having a lot of trouble finding a balance between the fantasy of who I thought Boone was and reality."

Fiona laughed. "Well, duh."

"What's that supposed to mean?"

"We both know you're a kick-ass actress, but you forget that I know you better than anyone else in the entire world. You can tell me he's the biggest ass you've ever met, but I can still read between the lines. You're totally hot for him despite his assholishness."

"I am not." She totally was, but she was fighting it, and planned to fight it until the movie was over, when she could put enough space between them to get over her crush.

"Okay, we'll pretend you're not. But since when do you take anything another actor—especially a newbie actor—says to heart?" Fiona asked. "Usually you roll your eyes and carry on."

"Fine! I'll admit that when we're not acting, the sexual tension is white-hot, but when we act, it's like he turns it off. Not exactly an ego boost for me, or good for my acting."

"But you're totally *not* hot for him," Fiona teased. "Just in case you change your mind, you could always duct tape his mouth shut to keep him from saying something gruff and ruining your fantasy."

Trish laughed. "He'd rip it off."

"Then bind his hands," Fiona suggested. "To the *bed.*"

The image of Boone tethered to the bed, naked and blindfolded, brought goose bumps. *Definitely blindfolded*, because those soulful eyes of his made her forget her own name.

"Not helping, Fi."

"Oh, I think you're wrong. I can hear the gears in your mind churning."

"I'm hanging up now. Love you."

She ended the call, thinking about what Fiona had suggested about staying in character, and trying *not* to think about Boone tied to her bed. Staying in character was a perfect idea. It would be impossible for Boone to avoid doing the same.

Poor drug-addict girlfriend, here I come.

As she approached the house, a familiar melody filled the air. Boone was playing a song he'd written called "Beyond the Dust," one of her favorites. He wasn't singing, just strumming the tumultuous tune, but in her head she heard his raspy singing voice.

Strangers pass
Eyes full of stars
Full of themselves, full of pain
Full of dreams, full of shit
Over the bridge, on the road
They see the sky, passersby
But they don't see
They don't see
They don't see beyond the dust

Boone came into view on the back porch, silencing his voice in Trish's head. He sat on the top step with one leg stretched down the stairs, the other bent at the knee, as he played his guitar, gazing out at acres of barren land. She wondered what he was thinking about, or if he was thinking at all. When she acted, she fell into a zone where the only thing that existed was the moment she was creating. Was playing his guitar like that for him? Did he see the clouds rolling in, casting shadows that moved with the wind? Or was he lost in each pluck of the strings, in each word he did or didn't sing?

Her cell phone rang and he turned. Their eyes caught and held. Her pulse quickened and her brain registered a flash of all-consuming heat. Her phone rang again and she shifted her eyes away as she hurried inside and answered the call from Joel, Chuck's assistant. Her heart hammered against her ribs as she climbed the steps to her bedroom and dug out her script while answering Joel's questions. She assured him they had what they needed and were already running lines. It was a fib, but they would be running them soon enough, assuming she could get her crazy hormones under control.

**

BOONE HEARD THE screen door open and Trish's footsteps approaching. He'd wanted to apologize to her earlier, but she'd clammed up like a vise. And the next thing he knew, she'd stormed out of the house in

46

those sexy little shorts, her long legs carrying her fast and furious across the field, until she was so far away she'd faded into the trees. He'd told himself she wasn't his problem, as he did with almost every other woman he knew, and he'd gone about getting himself and the kitty settled. After feeding the kitten, he'd come outside to try to get his mind off of Trish and waited to hear from Harvey. When Harvey had called earlier he said he'd gone to Jude's place and Jude wasn't there. He'd put calls out and was trying to track him down. Boone had tried to call Jude a few times since they'd arrived, but all his calls had gone to voicemail. The incident with Trish hadn't helped his mood, and he knew the crap going on with Jude had driven his poor reaction to Trish.

Trish sat down beside him and reached into his guitar case to pet the sleeping kitty. He'd put a few of his T-shirts in the case for the kitten to sleep on. He didn't want to leave him alone in the house. There were too many places for him to get into trouble.

"You set up a bed for him."

The sweetness of Trish's tone drew his attention, and she smiled. Either this chick was batshit crazy or she'd smoked some wicked weed in the fields, because there wasn't a hint of the angry, intense woman who had stormed away from the house earlier. He had enough batshit crazy in his life to gag on, and if she was a toker or a tweaker he wanted no part of these next ten days *or* this movie.

He ran an assessing gaze over her face. Her eyes were clear and bright, but she was definitely acting different, giving off a lackadaisical vibe.

"I didn't see a pet bed at the store, and I wanted to keep an eye on him."

"That was sweet of you. What're you goin' to call him?"

Her dialect caught him by surprise. Trish was well spoken and he'd talked with her enough on the trip there to know she didn't say things like *goin'*. He rested his guitar on his thigh, trying to figure out what kind of game she was playing. "I haven't thought about it."

"Well, I'm sure you'll figure it out."

She gazed into his eyes with a trusting expression that made his gut knot up.

"All these years of listenin' to you play," she said. "I don't want to think about the day you'll no longer be here."

Ice ran down his spine at the softness and slow cadence of her words.

She ran a finger down his arm. "Come on, Ricky. Don't pretend anymore. We both know this time next month you'll be off becoming a star."

Ricky. Holy hell, she was acting, and she was so damn good at it she'd already knocked him off-balance. He closed his eyes for a second, trying to find his bearings. On the set he wasn't prepared for the unearthing of the past the scenes inevitably brought, but here, in the middle of nowhere, when he'd been ready to apologize and the script was far from his mind, he felt ambushed.

"Trish."

"*Delia*, honey." She smiled and tilted her head in an innocent pose that made his throat thicken.

She was good. *Too good.* She was the reason his walls came up when they were on set. He'd never anticipated that doing this movie would dredge up a part of his life he'd thought he'd moved past. How was he supposed to act in a movie when everything Trish did reminded him of one of the toughest moments of his life?

"Trish," he warned. "Whatever it is you're doing. Stop."

She reached behind her and dropped a copy of the *No Strings* script on his lap with a smirk. "This is what we're here for. Remember?"

He pushed to his feet. She was right, but that didn't change the fact that when she fell into the role of Delia he saw Destiny. And every time they got to the scenes where she was drugged out, a rush of anger and sadness wound around him until he felt like he was ready to explode.

"Of course I remember, but—"

"But nothing." She stepped closer. Her face filled with determination, contrasting sharply with the soft-spoken woman she'd portrayed only moments ago. "We have ten days to get this right, and even if I have to tie you down to get you to learn your lines, we're making this movie."

And just like that, she became the defiant, smart, talented actress, so different from the needy women he was used to, and she pushed all of his buttons. He hadn't had those buttons pushed in a very long time, and instead of fighting it, he went with it. The perfect distraction from a reality he didn't want to face.

"Honey, I'm not into being tied up, but I might make an exception for you."

Her smile turned sinful. "You have a very short memory." Her eyes roved over his face and down his chest, sending heat blazing south. When she met his gaze again, all that heat whooshed away, replaced with a cold, hard stare.

"I'm *not* a groupie. I'm a serious actress, and sleeping with you is last on my very long list of things I want to accomplish." The heat between them belied her tone.

"But I *am* on your list," he said, hoping to circle her back to the tying-up threat. He liked that image a hell of a lot more than the other emotions their scenes were dredging up.

She opened her mouth, then snapped it shut. Her eyes darkened, giving rise to gold flecks around her pupils. He remained silent, taking pleasure in the flush rising on her skin as he stepped closer.

"You have the most beautiful eyes." The shock of the unexpected compliment registered in her widening eyes at the same time it registered in his own head, but she made no move to step away.

"This isn't a game to me, Boone."

"It's not a game to me either. This movie really *is* important to me. Otherwise I wouldn't have taken it on. I'm not that kind of person. I take my commitments very seriously."

Her eyes narrowed, like she was once again trying

to decide if she could trust anything he said. "But you'd rather deflect, or run away, than figure out how to play the part of Rick Champion."

"I don't run away," he assured her. "I'm sorry I tried to distract you from rehearsing. It was a shitty thing to do, but it's not easy for me to get into character. I don't pretend well." *And apparently I have no control over what I say around you, either, because why the hell am I telling you all of this?*

"Obviously," she said, a little shaky.

His eyes dropped to her mouth, and she nervously licked her lips. His whole body filled with the need to feel her in his arms. When their eyes met, she was peering at him longingly, desire swimming in her eyes. Despite the warning bells going off in his head alerting him to the complications this would bring, he leaned down at the same time she tilted her face up toward him.

"Boone." Her breath whispered over his lips.

His life had become a plethora of commitments and expectations. There were so few things that gave him real pleasure, and it had been too long since he'd truly *wanted* to kiss someone. He savored the heat pulsing between them. He was in no hurry as he carefully slid one arm around her waist, tugging her body against his, reveling in her sharp gasp and the feel of her arms circling his neck. He brushed his lips over hers and she closed her eyes, just as Honor's ringtone sounded from his pocket.

Trish's eyes flew open and he instinctively tightened his grip around her even though he had to answer the call in case Honor had heard from Jude. Trish must have read the urgency in his expression, because as the ringtone sounded again, she pushed from his arms.

"I'm sorry," he said, digging his phone out of his pocket.

She waved a dismissive hand, avoiding his gaze.

"Damn it," he grumbled under his breath as she picked up the kitten. He answered Honor's call as Trish headed into the house. "Hey, babe, what's up?"

Chapter Five

AFTER BOONE HUNG up the phone he'd made another call and paced the fields while he talked. Trish, on the other hand, had a long, one-sided discussion with the kitten about how stupid she'd been to almost kiss Boone. Her hope of staying in character had gone out the window the minute she'd almost kissed him, and it had gone all the way down the road when she'd heard him call the person on the phone *babe*. What was she thinking? She was not about to become one of his groupies, and what kind of woman was she to kiss a guy who clearly had at least one gorgeous blond girlfriend? She hated herself for being such a fool.

She was sitting at the kitchen table watching the kitty bat a stuffed mouse across the floor when Boone came through the door. His eyes swept over the wooden cabinets and old-fashioned stove, following the stovepipe up to the ceiling. Trish's chest tightened. He was obviously trying to avoid looking at her, but he could have walked right through the kitchen to the living room, and he didn't. He stood a few feet from the table, his eyes dropped to the kitten, and a small smile lifted his lips.

"Guess he likes the toys you got him." He pulled out the chair beside Trish, spun it around, and straddled it, crossing his arms over the vinyl orange back, and finally met her gaze. "I'm sorry for—"

She held up her hand. "Don't. Let's not do this."

His brows knitted above his apologetic eyes. "But—"

"This is already complicated enough. We've got ten days to make this work, and I'm sorry for whatever I did to lead you on, but I have no intention of becoming one of your groupies." She pushed to her feet and he followed.

"My *groupies*?" he scoffed, his eyes filled with disbelief.

"Look, Boone. I've been around enough to hear all of the excuses and lines. We can write off that almost kiss to a momentary lack of judgment."

The muscles in his jaw jumped as he stepped closer. What was it about him and personal space? His presence was formidable enough from a few feet away, but every time he got close to her he brought a heat wave that Trish swore had hands that pinned her in place.

"Lack of judgment?" he challenged. "In other words, you'd never kiss a guy like me."

He was breathing heavily, making it hard to keep from dropping her eyes to his chest as it rose and fell mere inches from her face. She held her ground despite her hammering heart.

"If you mean a guy who hasn't prepared for a role because he's too busy playing the field, then yeah. That's what I mean."

His eyes narrowed even further. There was something deeply entrancing in the way he was looking at her, and she was powerless to look away.

"You know nothing about me."

"All I need to know is that you're willing to do what it takes to get this movie made."

"Is that so?" He closed the remaining gap between them. His earthy, masculine smell sent her senses reeling.

"Mm-hm," she managed.

He reached up and cupped her cheek, and her stupid legs wobbled.

"Fine. Then let's do this," he said sharply. He scooped up the kitty and headed out the door.

That was hours ago, and the sexual tension between them was still thick enough to slice up and serve for dinner. The sun had set long ago, but each time she mentioned taking a break, Boone nixed it. *We haven't done enough yet. Why waste time? Not until we do it right.* His vehemence had surprised her, but she went with it. What else was there to do? Sit around and stare at each other, thinking about their almost kiss?

She'd tried to get into character, but the tension was messing with her mojo, and she'd finally given up. They could work on the emotional delivery of the lines tomorrow. For now her goal was to at least have him learn what he needed to say.

"This isn't acting." Boone tossed his script on the porch. "All we're doing is reading lines, and they feel wrong."

"You have to *know* the lines before you can act them out, and it doesn't matter if they feel wrong or right. Don't *ever* improvise or Chuck will literally throw you off the set. He takes it as a personal affront, because he chose to direct the film as it's written."

"I'm not going to improvise. Hell, Trish, I can hardly get the words out. But if all you want to do is read the lines, then why were you in character earlier?" He had the kitty tucked against his chest, where it had been snuggling for the last few scenes. When the kitty had woken up and climbed out of the guitar case, Trish had suggested they go inside, but Boone had scooped him up and said it was too confining, too stifling, too dark inside. Too many *too*s to remember.

Seeing his heavily muscled, tattooed arm around the tiny kitten made him maddeningly irresistible.

"Because I thought it was worth a try. You know, to jolt you into character. But you're not exactly a natural actor."

"Is that so?" He lifted the kitten and looked into his eyes. "What do you think? Do I suck?"

"I didn't say you sucked." Trish rose from where she'd been sitting against the house and brushed the dust from her shorts. "I said you weren't a *natural actor*. You said as much yourself. I just don't get it. You should totally connect with Rick's character."

He headed for the door without responding, and she followed him into the kitchen. He set the kitten down by his food and filled a glass with water for himself, drinking it with his back to Trish.

"Maybe we should talk about what throws you off, or why it's hard for you to pretend, because you've got the whole badass rock star down pat, so..."

"You're right," he said without turning around. "I'm not a natural actor, but you're pretty judgy for a person who knows nothing about me."

"Well, that's not going to change by refusing to talk to me about why you're not connecting with the character. You need to let me in." She moved beside him and craned her neck so her face was in front of his. She'd hoped to at least make him crack a smile, but his scowl was firmly planted in his chiseled features.

"Now you want to get to know me?" He cocked a brow, and his luscious lips curved up.

Flutter, flutter.

"Not *that* way."

He folded his arms over his chest and turned to face her. "You think you've got me all figured out, don't you? You assume I meant that you wanted to sleep with me. I'm just a badass rock star out to get laid. Forget morals and ethics; they must have gone out the window ages ago."

"That's not what I said." But she knew it was what she'd implied, and having been judged her whole career, she felt bad for putting him in that position. "I'm sorry. I didn't mean to sound like I was judging you."

"Sorry to point this out, beautiful, but you were about to kiss me, too. What does that tell me about you?"

Her lips moved, but no words came. *Beautiful?* She clamped her mouth shut and turned away, leaning her rear end against the counter. She didn't really want to hear what he had to say, because it was probably harsh. *And true.*

"I'll tell you what it told me." He moved in front of her and curled a finger beneath her chin, lifting it so she had no choice but to look into his eyes.

His gaze was warm and steady, not angry or judgmental, which made her feel like a total bitch. She opened her mouth to apologize again and he pressed his finger to her lips. The gentle touch, his nearness, and the intensity of his gaze made her body pulse with desire.

"Let me speak." His voice was low and calm, which made her acutely aware that she was anything but calm. "You like to be in control, but when we're close like this, your body goes hot and your heart races. I see it in the pulse at the base of your neck."

She reached up and touched her neck.

"You can't cover it. It's in your eyes, in your voice, in the way you move. It scares you, but you don't want to admit the fear, so you force yourself to stand up a little taller, to pretend you're in control." His lips curved up in a genuine smile. "And right now you're wondering how the hell an arrogant asshole like me can see through you."

She rolled her eyes to cover the fact that he'd read her perfectly.

"How'd I do?"

"Fair," she lied.

His brows knitted. "Really? Hm."

"Okay, fine. Better than fair."

"That's because I don't fake a damn thing, but your whole life is spent in some middle ground between fake and real."

"It is not." She'd felt that way occasionally, but she wasn't about to admit it.

"You keep believing that." He scooped up the kitten again. "Let's put him in the bathroom where he can't get hurt, and then let's head down to the Rum Hummer for karaoke. See how you do live onstage without any retakes."

"What?" Karaoke? Was he kidding?

"Before you can judge me, you need to see what it feels like to *be* me."

"What's that supposed to mean?"

"I write every word I sing. I get up onstage and I've got one shot to make it or break it in front of thousands of fans. You get fifty takes, with no audience, and you're not even saying your own words. You're saying what someone else has thought up. It's a whole different ball game." He nodded at the kitten's food and water bowls. "Grab those, will you, please?"

She carried the kitten's bowls and followed him toward the bathroom. "Just because I get to reshoot scenes doesn't mean it's not hard or it doesn't take skill."

"Obviously," he said. "I thought it would be easy, and admittedly, I suck at pretending. But I'm willing to give it my best shot even if I fall short, or have a hard time figuring out what *my best shot* is."

They set the kitten and his bowls in the bathroom, where Boone had already set up the litter box. "Now it's your turn to step into my shoes. You get one chance to get it right."

She knew how to sing, and she'd done karaoke dozens of times, but this wasn't just karaoke. This was a challenge, and because he'd issued the challenge, she was nervous. "How is that fair?"

"Who said anything about fair? You wanted to get to know me. I'm opening a door." He flashed a cocky grin. "Chicken?"

"Hardly." She stepped into the hall. "I grew up with five brothers. Nothing scares me."

He closed the door behind them, openly studying her.

Except maybe the way you're looking at me right now.

Holding her gaze, he brushed the back of his fingers down her cheek, and her stomach quivered.

He winked. The smug, sexy bastard. "Then you should do just fine."

**

THE RUM HUMMER was dark, loud, and full of beer-drinking rednecks having a good time. Barrels stood on end, supporting round wooden tabletops, surrounded by backless wooden stools. Rough-looking men and women milled around two pool tables in the middle of the bar. Sounds of cue balls crashing mingled with off-key karaoke singers and the *clip-clop* of boots on the dance floor. Boone had noticed several men eyeing Trish from the moment they'd arrived, but one particular guy, who could easily pass for Scott Eastwood and looked like he chopped down trees with his bare hands for a living, hadn't stopped ogling her all night. He half expected Trish to turn around and walk out, but she hadn't blinked an eye at the intrusive leers or the scent of manual labor, fried foods, and alcohol that hung in the air. His protective urges had kicked into gear, and he'd slid an arm around her waist. She'd looked at him like he was nuts, but his comment, *Just trying to get into character,* had seemed to placate her.

He was glad no one had recognized them. Then again, he doubted the Podunk town even had a movie theater, and based on the karaoke choices—country, country, or more country—he was fairly certain this crowd didn't listen to his music.

"You need to eat something if you're going to drink." Boone pushed the plate of chicken wings he'd ordered across the table toward Trish. They'd been at the Rum Hummer for more than an hour and she still had yet to eat anything.

"I told you I can't eat those." Trish sipped her beer and pushed the plate away. "I starved myself for six weeks to get down to this size for the part. I'm not about to ruin it for greasy chicken wings. I shouldn't have beer, either, but tonight I need it."

"Yeah, about this whole not eating thing. It can't be healthy to live on a few carrots." Trish was already on her second drink. "How about if I have them bake a piece of chicken or make you a salad?"

"I eat more than carrots." She took another drink. "Besides, I think your choices here are limited to fried or barbecued, which normally I'd be all over."

"Really? I thought all actresses grazed on grass or seaweed," he said to try to lighten the mood.

"Ha-ha. Maybe most do, but I love to eat. I'm lucky. I have a great metabolism, but I also exercise so I can eat more. I just can't indulge right now."

I'd like to indulge, but not on food.

So much for hoping tonight would be a good distraction from the heat sizzling between them. The more time he spent with Trish, the more he wanted to know about her. Hopefully the Rum Hummer would at least take his mind off of Jude for a few hours. When Honor had called, she'd said one of their friends had seen Jude in their hometown, but they'd lost track of him again. Boone was debating leaving to try to find him, but he couldn't let Trish down like that.

Being *okay* with that thought was another issue altogether. He felt like he was letting Jude down, choosing Trish over him.

"We can cook up something healthy when we get back to the house," he suggested.

"I'm fine, really."

"You don't mind starving?"

She shrugged. "It was hard at first, but it's been so

long that I'm used to not eating. If I start to eat I'll realize I'm hungry, and then all hell will break loose."

"All hell, huh?" He laughed. "Well, we can't have that, now, can we?"

She shook her head and smiled. Man, her smile got to him every damn time.

"You about ready to sing?" He nodded toward the stage.

"Not really." She finished her beer and held up the empty bottle, waving it at the waitress, who held up a finger indicating she'd bring one right over.

"Whoa, maybe you should slow down."

"I think I know my limit."

The waitress set Trish's beer on the table, placed a hand on her hip, and ran an appreciative gaze over Boone. "What can I get you, big boy?"

He had no interest in the chunky blonde who showed too much cleavage and too little class.

Trish leaned across the table and patted his hand. "Yeah, *big boy*. What can she get you?"

He paid for Trish's drink. "I'm doing just fine, thank you."

Unless Trish was offering herself up, he wasn't interested.

"A'righty, then," the waitress said. "You let me know if you need, or *want*, anything at all."

As the waitress walked away, Trish said, "You just ruined her whole night."

"You're right." He went after the waitress and asked her to put Trish's name in for karaoke. Unfortunately, she recognized him and asked him for his autograph, then thrust her chest out and pointed to her shirt just above her left breast. He autographed her shirt as quickly as he could, hoping no one else noticed. He didn't want to deal with that kind of attention tonight.

When he returned to the table, Trish rolled her eyes.

"Seriously? *Her?* Did you really just autograph her boobs? What's next? Meeting her in the bathroom for a quickie?"

He let the comment roll off his back. She reached for her drink and Boone grabbed her hand.

She glared at him. "I told you I know my limit."

"I don't doubt that. But do you know your limit when you're existing on fumes rather than food?" She tried to pull her hand from his, but he held on tight. Tugging her closer, he lowered his voice. "I thought you weren't afraid of singing."

"I'm not." Her eyes never left his.

"If you're not afraid of singing, then why are you trying to get hammered?"

"Well, now, that would be none of your business." She grabbed the beer and sucked down half of it. With a haughty look, she jumped off her stool, strutted over to a group of guys standing by the pool table, and grabbed the hand of the Scott Eastwood lookalike. "Come on, *big guy*. Let's see if you can dance."

Are you shitting me? Boone's chest constricted as they headed to the dance floor. Trish spun into the guy's arms with a wide smile. Boone didn't think there was a man alive who could see her incredible smile and not smile himself, but the dumbass she was dancing with actually turned away and shot a greedy look to his buddies by the pool table, who held up their beers as if to say, *Go for it.*

Go for it, my ass.

Boone's hands fisted. Trish wasn't *his*, and she got on his last nerve—and under his skin in the sexiest of ways—but every muscle in his body flexed with possessiveness.

The woman onstage sang Miranda Lambert's "Mama's Broken Heart." Trish danced out of the man's arms, moving like she owned the dance floor as she pounded out some kind of country step dance. The other couples fanned out around her, clapping and tapping their booted feet. Trish sang every word, making hand gestures that indicated she was nobody's fool, tossing flirtatious smiles and winks like confetti, and acting out the lyrics as she moved her sweet little body with the grace and fluidity of a professional dancer. An incredibly sexy professional dancer.

The guys around the pool table headed for the dance floor, and Boone pushed to his feet like a lion protecting his pride. Trish wasn't shitting him. The woman was fearless, singing to the mesmerized crowd like she was the one onstage, swinging her hair like she was in a music video, and turning on every red-blooded male in the place.

Boone stood beside the guy she'd dragged to the dance floor, who was practically rubbing his hands together and drooling as she swayed her hips and shoulders to the beat.

"She's mine tonight," the guy said to one of his buddies. "One more dance and I'm taking that doll out back and..." He did several hip thrusts.

Not a chance in hell. He didn't care if Trish wanted to be with that guy or not. She was *not* leaving that bar with anyone but him, and if she thought he'd let some other guy put his hands on her, she was dead wrong.

When the song ended, everyone clapped, and Trish took a dramatic bow.

"Thank you." She flashed a dazzling smile, and her eyes landed on Boone with a look of smug satisfaction. Behind her, a guy with a scraggly beard took the stage and began singing.

Eastwood reached for Trish, and Boone stepped between them, sliding one arm around her waist and leveling the dude with a dark stare. He'd grown up fighting the good fight with druggies, assholes, and guys who were too stupid to know when they were uncaging a beast they had no business tangling with. He'd never lost a fight, and there wasn't a man on earth he was afraid to take on.

"Sorry, man. She's with me," Boone said, ignoring the angry glare Trish had locked on him.

The guy looked at Trish, and she impressively morphed her anger to a mask of sweet apology, driving it home with several flirtatious blinks of her long lashes.

"I'm sorry. He's right. I am."

"Fucking tease," the guy mumbled, and turned away.

Boone grabbed his arm and spun him around.

"Unless you want your buddies scraping your pretty-boy face off of the floor, I suggest you apologize to my girl."

"Boone!" Trish said with a harsh whisper.

The guy didn't respond, and Boone closed the gap between them, staring into his glassy eyes. "What's it going to be?"

"Sorry," the guy growled, then turned and walked away.

Boone wrapped his arms around Trish's waist, ignoring her efforts to pull free.

"You had no right," she seethed.

"You're right. But the way I see it, this was going to end one of two ways. Either you'd walk out the door with that scumbag and you'd whine for the rest of the week about how you're really not an easy lay, or I could close that door before you had a chance to walk out."

Her eyes widened in disbelief. "You thought I was going to have sex with him?"

"Doesn't matter what I thought. What matters is what he thought."

"You can't possibly know what he thought. I'm an attractive woman. What makes you think he didn't want to dance and get to know me, or ask me out like a normal person?"

"Because you *are* an insanely hot woman, and while you were shaking your sexy ass out there, he was telling his buddies how he was going to take you out back and fuck you."

Her jaw gaped. He guided her arms around his

67

neck. "We're on the dance floor, so at least pretend to dance. You can thank me later."

She was rigid in his arms.

"Come on, beautiful. Take it as a compliment."

He felt the tension in her body slip away, and disappointment rose in her expression, arousing those protective urges again. *My strong actress is sensitive after all.* He stumbled over *my*, but one look in her eyes and he knew that even if it was just because they were co-stars, just for tonight, she was his to protect.

"Did you really hear him say that?"

"What did you expect? I have to hand it to you, though. You weren't lying. You aren't afraid of anything."

Her lips curved up with a gratified smile. "Oh, I have fears. I told you singing isn't one of them, but I didn't expect the guy to think *that*."

"He's a guy. He wasn't *thinking*. A savvy woman with five brothers should know that." They both laughed with the tease.

"I could have handled myself, you know."

"Yeah, I'm sure you could have."

She ran her fingertips up the back of his neck, her eyes alit with mischief. "There's a rule in acting you might not be aware of. Never, ever fall for your co-star."

"Considering I've never *fallen* for a woman in my life, I think we're in the clear." When the song ended, he splayed his hand on her back, holding her tighter.

"Stay," he whispered.

A curious look washed over her face.

Another singer took the stage and began singing Blake Shelton's "Sangria."

Trish gazed into his eyes, singing the lyrics as if she meant every word just for him. She was an incredible actress, and though he couldn't tell if she was acting or not, he ate up every word out of her luscious mouth. Gone was her snarky facade and tough-girl demeanor, replaced with a soft, sexy woman who moved like the music was coming from somewhere deep inside her, which was exactly where he wanted to be.

Chapter Six

MAYBE THREE BEERS on an empty stomach wasn't such a good idea after all. Sometime during Trish's last four dances with Boone she'd gone from clearheaded to pleasantly buzzed. It felt wonderful to be out from under the weight of her thoughts, but she wasn't used to feeling so uninhibited. Seeing Boone guide that skanky waitress away to talk privately had bugged the heck out of her. And then he'd tried to tell her how much she could drink, like she'd needed a babysitter. She was pissed when he'd come between her and the guy she'd asked to dance, but something in Boone's eyes told her that he was telling the truth about what he'd overheard. Trish wasn't proud of how she'd acted, or that seeing him demand an apology from that other guy had totally turned her on. Knowing he cared enough to stand up for her regardless of how she'd acted endeared him to her, just as every minute they danced together was doing.

He came across as a hard-ass with walls so thick no one could penetrate them. That probably sent most people—other than groupies—running for the hills, but it made her want to get inside those walls and see what made him tick.

He held her tight as they danced, even to the fast songs. Every inch of his deliciously hard body pressed against her from thigh to shoulder. His arms enveloped her in a way that felt possessive and intimate, confusing and exciting her at once. She felt safe with him, which was a strange feeling, given that he was about as warm and open as a rock. But there was no denying that right this second, nestled in his arms, with her cheek resting against the sure and steady beat of his heart, she felt safe. She felt special. And, she realized with a little shock, she really liked Boone. He intrigued her, and he was willing to put time into rehearsing and had even made her put more time in than she'd intended. And when he was with the kitten—gosh, that sight gave her the highest high.

His hand slid beneath her hair, sending shivers of heat down her spine. His thumb brushed the nape of her neck to the rhythm of the music.

You dance like you speak, a little gruff and controlling, with an alluring challenge of seduction. Okay, that last part might be from the alcohol.

The song ended, and someone called her name through the microphone.

"Come on, beautiful. We're up." With an arm around her waist, he guided her up to the stage.

"*Beautiful?*" It took her fuzzy brain a second to

remember she'd promised to sing karaoke.

Boone ignored her question and handed her a mic. "Focus. You've got about ten seconds before you need to *wow* the crowd."

She looked out at the expectant crowd and back at Boone, who was also holding a mic. Her stomach tumbled. "You're singing with me?"

"You think I'd leave you hanging after you got strapped with me for ten days?" He mouthed, *You've got this.*

Don't I wish.

The music to Gloriana's "(Kissed You) Good Night" came on, and her heart did a little happy dance. It was one of her favorite songs. Boone sauntered across the stage and gazed into her eyes like she was the only person in the bar as he sang about how he should have kissed her. She was so caught up in the depth of emotions swimming in his eyes, and his raspy voice, she almost missed her lines. But years of training kicked in, and she hit every note. In those few seconds, singing about how he should have kissed her, her emotions rose to the surface, and everything else faded away. There was only her and Boone, and her mind reeled back to the porch, his mouth brushing against hers—she'd been ready to fall into that kiss.

His face came into focus, bringing her back to the moment. He stood inches away. Heat sizzled in the space between them, drawing them closer, until they were standing so close she could barely breathe—but she could sing like she was born to do it. She drew deeper into him, into their connection, the last note sailing from her lips like a prayer. The crowd went wild, and without thinking, she grabbed his shirt and went up on her toes as he leaned down. Their mouths came together hungrily. The kiss was deep and wet, and she greedily took and took and took, pressing into his hard, hot frame, fisting her hands in his chest. Her legs felt like rubber, but she didn't care, because *the kiss*...It was the type of kiss girls dreamed about their whole lives. The kiss of all kisses, deep and consuming. He wasn't just kissing her; he was *possessing* her, body and soul. They were becoming one being. He stroked every dip and recess of her mouth, her tongue, her teeth—and Lord help her, she wanted him to. His hand slid down her back and he cupped her ass, and she was so lost in him she moaned.

Oh God! She moaned! Onstage!

She pushed from his arms, her mouth burning for more. He had a soulful, tortured look in his eyes that completely knocked her off-balance. Literally. She stumbled sideways—and it had nothing to do with her buzz. Everyone was clapping and cheering, and she hadn't even heard them when they were kissing! She was such a fool! He was just doing what he did. He was putting on a show, and she was like a swooning groupie. She'd fallen right under his spell.

She was wrong—all of this had to be from the alcohol.

The kiss. The feeling of walking on a cloud. Her inability to hear!

She tried to force a smile and walk calmly off the stage, but she had no idea how her legs were functioning at all, because she was numb with embarrassment and couldn't feel them. Boone's arm circled her waist. His body was like an inferno searing through her clothes as he led her out the door and to the car. The night air stung her cheeks, helping to bring her mind back into focus.

"What was *that?*" She threw her hands up and paced beside the car. The gravel parking lot was dark, save for the illuminated RUM HUMMER sign over the door. Trucks and motorcycles filled the parking lot. Their shiny silver Lexus sparkled like a crystal among rocks in a riverbed.

"A hell of a kiss," he said casually, unlocking the passenger door. "You nailed the song, by the way."

"I nailed the song?" She stomped toward him. "That's all you have to say? I nailed the song? What about the kiss? I can't kiss you. You have a girlfriend, and groupies, and—" She clenched her fists and groaned.

"Trish, it was just a kiss."

"Yes! And I am not a groupie. You sucked me right in with your amazing stage presence and the way you were looking at me." She crossed her arms and leaned back against the car. "I can't believe I kissed you!"

He shoved the keys in his pocket and walked over to her. His eyes narrowed, and his plump, *very* kissable lips—the lips she now knew tasted like heaven and sweet, sinful pleasure—curved into a wicked grin. He pulled her from the car and wrapped her arms around his neck, as he'd done on the dance floor, and her heart went wild. It was presumptive and arrogant and she *did not* want to pull away even though she should, but she fought against that stupid-girl part of her brain.

"What do you think you're doing?"

"You said you can't believe you kissed me, but that kiss wasn't the kiss of someone who didn't want to kiss me." He pressed his hands flat against her lower back, keeping their bodies flush.

She felt every inch of his hard body, and he was hard. *Everywhere.* She was sure he could feel the effect he was having on her because her nipples were poking into his chest and her legs were trembling. Her senses whirled and she tried and tried to force them to a halt, but it was like trying to slow wild horses.

"Don't even try to kiss me."

"Don't worry, beautiful. I'm not who you think I am."

"Stop calling me 'beautiful.' For a guy who says he doesn't know how to pretend, you're doing a damn good job of it." She pressed her lips together, but he smelled so good, and his body—*God, his body.* She wanted to drag him into the car and feel the weight of him on top of her as they made out like teenagers.

"You still think you've got me figured out." He shook his head, and she wanted to slap that smug smile off his face, but his eyes were confusing her with their mix of adorable puppy pleas and you-know-you-want-me arrogance.

"If you're not going to try to kiss me, then what are you doing?" *And why don't you want to kiss me?*

"Just giving you a chance to decide if you really did

or didn't want to kiss me."

"Oh, I know I didn't." She looked away, just in case her nose grew with the lie.

He tightened his grip. "Okay. Sixty seconds."

"Huh?"

"We'll just stand here for sixty seconds. If after sixty seconds you still don't want to kiss me, we'll chalk this up to getting caught up in the moment."

"Fine!"

His hand moved over her, slow and firm, blazing a path up her back. He curled his fingers over her shoulder and gave it a gentle squeeze, holding her so tight she was sure he felt the frantic beat of her heart. His other arm circled her waist, and his fingers curled around her hip. His whiskey eyes smoldered, as dark and mysterious as the night sky.

Despite herself, all the air *whooshed* from her lungs and she arched against him, aching for his touch. Her lips tingled with anticipation, but somewhere in the back of her mind an image shook free of him walking with his arm around the blonde, and the groupies around his trailer. And she managed, "You have a girlfriend."

"Wrong."

"The blonde?" Guys lied. She knew that. She'd seen him with his arm around the woman, and the scene had been *very* cozy.

"Honor West. She's one of my best friends. Like a sister."

A sister? "Usually people don't sleep with their sisters."

"Oh, so now I've slept with Honor?" An amused smile lifted his lips. "Very judgy of you."

"I'm sure you have a hundred other women going through your revolving bedroom door, and I don't intend to be one of them."

That wiped the amusement off his face and replaced it with a look she wanted to run from. His eyes bored into her, silently sending a message of disbelief and honesty she was afraid to trust. Because guys *lied*.

He tightened his grip again.

A needy whimper escaped, and she clamped her mouth shut. Despite her hesitation, she wanted to kiss him so badly she could taste him, could feel his tongue sliding over hers and the press of those full, soft lips. This was crazy, standing so close to him, but she didn't want to walk away. She couldn't remember a time when she'd been as acutely aware of every point where her body touched a man, or every breath another person took. He wasn't running. He wasn't deflecting. He was fully present, and she found that so compelling it frightened her.

He reached up and touched her cheek, still holding her tight with one arm.

"What are you afraid of?"

He asked it in such a gentle, caring voice, had she not seen him speak, she wouldn't have believed it came from him. Her answer came without thought.

"You."

BOONE DIDN'T KNOW what he'd expected to hear, but *that* wasn't it. He had no idea what Trish meant or how to take it, but the truth was, she scared him, too. He was used to people bending to his will, covering his tracks, taking his word as gold. She challenged him at every turn, and it irritated and intrigued him at once.

Forcing his feet to move, he took a step away. "Okay, beautiful. Let's go." *Beautiful.* Where was that coming from? He'd never used the endearment toward any woman before. But hell, she was beautiful.

She shook her head as if she were confused. "What? Just like that?"

"You said you're afraid of me. What did you expect?" He walked around the car to the driver's side to put some space between them, because being near her made him want to reach out and touch her. And it bugged the heck out of him that he scared her.

"I don't know!" She glared at him over the roof of the car. "Maybe something like, 'Don't be afraid. I'm not going to hurt you.'"

"Seriously? I don't even think you know what you're afraid of." He climbed into the car, leaned across the console, and called to her through the open door, "You getting in or what?"

She climbed into the car and crossed her arms, staring straight ahead at the shacklike bar.

He turned on the radio to fill the silence and drove out of the parking lot.

"Wait," she said urgently. "Are you okay to drive?"

"I'm pretty sure you can't get drunk on club soda."

He glanced at her out of the corner of his eyes. "You can wipe that shocked look off your face."

He felt her assessing him as they drove away from the bar. Clouds hid the moon from the night sky, making the narrow tree-lined roads pitch-black, save for the headlights beaming in the foggy air. The oppressive sky fit the tension in the car. Why did he care that he scared her? Or that she was judging him? He'd been judged his whole life and had always let it roll off of him like water on a waxed surface, but when it came to Trish, he was having trouble finding his *disengage* switch.

He mulled that over as he turned onto the road that ran parallel to the creek.

"I'm sorry," she said quietly. "I thought you were drinking."

"You also thought I had a girlfriend and a revolving bedroom door. You're pretty sure of all the things you *don't know*."

"Oh, please. Your reputation speaks for itself."

He bristled at her comment. "That it does."

His reputation did speak for itself. It was another layer of protection between his real life and his public life, and he'd always been okay with that. Until now. He drove up the long driveway trying to figure out how to handle the torrent of emotions jetting through him. When they'd first arrived at the farmhouse, he'd been surprised at its state of disrepair, but after spending the afternoon reading through the script, he could see the old house was the perfect setting for the fictional rock star's rough beginning.

He cut the engine and turned to Trish. Even in the darkness of the car he could see the mix of emotions welling in her eyes. "Look, Trish. I don't know what you want to hear, but I told you I don't pretend well and I'm not a liar, so all I can do is tell it like it is."

He weighed his next thought, because the need to explain himself was another thing reserved for the few people he considered family. But one look in Trish's beautiful eyes and he had to say it.

"I'm just going to throw this out there because I need you to hear it. I'm not sorry we kissed. It was a hell of a kiss, and we both know there's something between us. But I've got enough people picking apart my life, and I have no interest in going through that with you. So, are we cool? Can we move on?"

She looked at him for an interminable, silent moment. His gut twisted as she pushed open her door.

With one foot on the gravel, she said, "Fine. Let's try to move on."

He had a feeling no matter how hard he tried, moving on from that kiss was going to be impossible.

Chapter Seven

TRISH STRUGGLED TO open the wood-framed bedroom window. The paint cracked and flaked beneath her fingers, falling like fairy dust into the sill. If only there were magical fairies that could help her wade through her whirling thoughts. The cool evening breeze carried the scent of arid earth vying for rain. A soulful melody sailed in with the breeze. Boone must have gone directly to the back porch to play his guitar. The smell of meat grilling hit her, and her stomach growled. She realized he'd never eaten the wings they'd ordered, which was her fault. Their conversation had been tumbling through her mind like the clouds that had rolled in, dark and stormy. She'd assured him that they could *move on*, which she knew meant he didn't want to talk about the kiss anymore, but it was all she could think about.

Her image reflected back at her in the thick glass, and she didn't like what she saw. She'd wanted that kiss as badly as he'd seemed to, and she'd made him feel like he'd done something wrong. That wasn't who she was. In fact, most of the way she'd acted tonight wasn't her typical behavior. She grabbed a zip-up sweatshirt from the closet and pushed her arms into the sleeves as she descended the steps and headed for the back porch.

Boone sat on the porch steps with his back to Trish. Spirals of gray smoke danced from the grill up toward the sky a few feet from the porch. He was singing softly, and she closed her eyes and leaned against the doorframe, soaking in the husky roughness of every word. She'd been drawn to the deep emotions in his voice from the very first time she'd heard his song "Under Me" on the radio. With the night air washing over her skin through the screen door and his voice tugging the knot in her stomach free, she had the urge to sink down to the floor unnoticed and revel in the moment like a thief in the night. But she'd been selfish enough.

Boone didn't miss a beat as she sank down to the step beside him. He turned and smiled, still singing. Her chest *and* stomach fluttered. She didn't think she deserved that smile, but she sure liked seeing it. Beside him, the top of the guitar case was propped up against the railing, blocking the wind from the sleeping kitten curled up in Boone's bed of shirts.

"*This* is where you shine," she said quietly. He stopped singing. "You have the most incredible voice, and when you sing, you really do become one with the music. It's fascinating, and impressive, and it made it easy for me to get lost in you when we were singing at the bar. You're *so* good."

He opened his mouth, and she pressed her finger over his lips, as he'd done to her. "I wanted to kiss you, regardless of whether I was lost in the moment or not."

He sighed, nodded.

"I'm sorry for being such a bitch. I'm really not a bitchy person, although I know I haven't done anything but proven to be one since we met."

"I never said, or felt, that you were acting bitchy." He set his guitar on the porch beside him.

"You didn't have to." She drew in a deep breath and pulled her sweatshirt across her chest against the chilly air—a barrier against the harsh reality she was exposing. "The truth is, you do scare me, but not in the way you probably think. I don't know what to make of you, and yes, there's something between us that is so strong *it* scares me, too."

He leaned his forearms on his thighs, clasped his hands together, and gazed out at the darkness.

"I am not a saint by any stretch of the imagination," she admitted. "And I don't claim to be better, or more important, than anyone, but I am careful with my heart."

He cocked his head to the side with a serious look in his eyes.

"Not that I think we...or you..." *Oh God, where am I going with this?* "I'm not a prude. I've had my share of flings, or whatever you call them, but I'm in this strange place right now. I'm almost thirty, and I've got this crush on you that makes me feel twenty. It's silly and childish, and honestly, it's hard to ignore."

He laughed softly and pushed to his feet. "A crush."

"Don't judge me, okay? This isn't easy to admit." She watched him flip something on the grill. Then he sat back down beside her and held up his hands.

"Hey, I'm not judging. But you know you don't really come across as a crush type of girl. You're ornery and abrasive, and—"

"I guess I deserve that." Her stomach sank.

"You didn't let me finish. Those are the things that make you strong and successful. We both know that being a celebrity changes a person."

"Maybe, but the truth is I was ornery and abrasive before I started acting." She shrugged, glad that he smiled again. "When you grow up in a house where testosterone practically flows through the faucets, you learn to keep up so you're not left behind. Not that my brothers would ever dream about leaving me anywhere. They practically have a leash on me at all times."

"That's what family does. I've got younger siblings, and I'm sure they feel the same way about me. I'm an overprotective pain in the ass. I think you should consider yourself lucky. It sounds like your brothers care about you."

The tone of his voice warmed when he talked about his family, and his understanding caught her by surprise. "I am lucky. I adore them, but growing up as a tomboy has never helped me in the dating world. I am pushy and stubborn. And I don't take crap from people very well. Not to mention that I'm hardly a delicate female, which doesn't help."

"Maybe you're dating the wrong guys." He turned on the step, giving her his full attention. "You might be all of those things, but you're sweet and sexy and beautiful, and I don't buy that you're not delicate. Not for a second."

She rolled her eyes. "You're not going to get lucky by lying."

"I already got lucky with that kiss."

He said it so seriously, her thoughts stuttered.

"The way I see it," he said, "you work pretty hard to keep up a strong front. You say you're not delicate, but what does delicate mean? Maybe you think it means weak? I think it means a lot of things, and where you're concerned, I think it means sensitive and feminine. At the bar, I obviously said or did something that sent you storming off to the dance floor with that guy. And when I said the world didn't revolve around you or the film, I saw the hurt in your eyes. I'm sorry for both of those things, but those moments were proof that you're sensitive and fragile, like most people are."

"Or maybe jealous is a better word."

His eyes lit up at that. "Jealous? Huh. I hadn't gone there."

She covered her face with her hands and shook her head, feeling like an idiot. When she lowered them, she groaned at his smirk. "It's the crush thing again. I thought you were arranging something with the waitress and…" She shrugged.

He reached for her hand, his thumb moving in slow circles over her wrist. "See? Delicate."

"Try stupid and childish," she argued, and although she loved the feel of his hand, she withdrew from his grasp. "Whatever it was, I'm seriously not interested in becoming one of the women to pass through your bedroom door. Maybe a few years ago, but I'm looking for more. So I'm going to take my ridiculous crush and put it away." She made a motion with her hands like she was tossing it into the wind.

"Just like that, huh?"

She nodded. "I have to. I'm serious about my career, and I'm serious about protecting my heart. Before I read the script for *No Strings* I was ready to take a hiatus and try to have a normal life. Maybe meet a guy who had nothing to do with the industry and see what happens. But this role spoke to me. It's my chance to really prove myself, and I know you get that."

"And getting involved with a guy like me could screw that up." His tone was cold, and his eyes narrowed with the accusation.

Trish held her breath for a beat, knowing what she had to say might send them reeling back into the uncomfortable place they'd been in earlier, but she'd come this far. She might as well lay it all out on the line.

"When I heard you took the role, I jumped at the chance to work with you. And I know you can pull this role off, but you didn't even show up for the preproduction meeting. And you showed up late for filming without a care for anyone else's time. I think we're just two very different people."

**

BOONE PUSHED TO his feet again, grinding his teeth against the urge to tell her the truth, but anger and something more burned like acid in his gut. He took the chicken off the grill, set it on the plate he'd brought out earlier, and placed it beside Trish.

"Nothing but protein." He pulled a fork and knife from his back pocket and set it on the plate.

"You made this for me?"

He shrugged. So he worried about her, that didn't mean anything. Did it? She was his co-star. If she got sick, the movie would be put on hold and that would only piss off the director even more. At least that's what he told himself.

"Thank you. That was really nice." She picked up the fork and knife. "Aren't you going to eat?"

He shook his head, and she set down the silverware.

"Christ, Trish. Really?"

She crossed her arms. "I hate eating alone."

"Fine, I'll eat. You are one stubborn woman."

She grinned with a triumphant look in her eyes. He pointed at the plate and she cut the chicken in half and pushed half to his side of the plate.

He'd kept his personal life locked far away from prying eyes for his entire career, but it pissed him off to hear her lumping him in with people who had no regard for anyone else. But the urge to confess the truth was driven by something stronger than being pissed off. He was a lousy liar, even to himself. The smoke and mirrors he put up to the public was one thing. He wasn't actually speaking to the press. His *people* did that for him. But being here with Trish, gazing into her eyes, knowing she'd just revealed something that couldn't have been easy for her? This was different.

"Maybe the reason you aren't finding the right kind of guys has more to do with your assumptions than anything else."

"I'm sorry I made you mad, but that's not an assumption. I was at the meeting. I know you didn't show up." She stuffed a piece of chicken in her mouth, her eyes locked on him as she chewed.

Why did she have to look so cute when she was angry?

"You know I missed a meeting, but do you know *why*? Have you bothered to ask me?" He stopped pacing and crossed his arms, holding her steady stare.

"I don't have to. It was in all the papers. You were at a party in Beverly Hills with a harem of models."

He pointed to the plate again, and she rolled her eyes, then ate a sliver of chicken.

"And rag magazines are reliable sources."

Her eyes narrowed. "What are you getting at?"

He paced again, feeling like his skin was too tight. "It shouldn't matter to me what you think. Hell, I spend my life not giving a shit about what anyone but those closest to me think, and half the time, if they don't like something, they can kiss my ass. But for whatever reason, you've gotten under my skin with your pushiness and smirky attitude."

"I'm pretty sure we've just figured out why you don't have a girlfriend." She grinned and shoved another piece of chicken in her mouth, which he was glad to see.

"The last thing I need is a woman telling me I'm doing everything in my life wrong."

She waved her fork like she was leading an orchestra. "Deflect, deflect, deflect."

He couldn't help but laugh.

She patted the seat beside her. "You're making me nervous moving like you're going to either blow up or take off."

He sat beside her. "Pushy."

"Arrogant," she retorted. Her eyes rolled over his face. "You look like you're ready to burst."

"A certain waifish actress has that effect on me."

She leaned closer and whispered, "I had a very *different* effect on you earlier."

He flashed back to their dance, and their kiss, stoking the fire that had been simmering ever since. She sat up straighter, her cheeks flushed with heat.

Guess you feel it, too.

She shifted her eyes over his shoulder and breathed deeply. "Why did you miss the preproduction meeting?"

"Look at me and maybe I'll tell you."

She met his gaze, and an electric current hummed

between them.

"My mother was admitted into the hospital an hour before the meeting. I thought I'd have time to call, but I got caught up in making sure she was okay and that my sister and brothers weren't going to fall apart." He shrugged.

Her lips parted and her eyes filled with empathy. "I'm sorry. Is she okay?"

He nodded, swallowing hard with the memory. "They thought it was a heart attack, but it was just stress."

"So, she's out of danger?"

"She worries about my youngest brother, which stresses her out. I'm working on him. It's been hard on her since we lost—" He turned away, his chest tight with the shock of his near confession. "For a long time."

"Oh, Boone. I'm so sorry. Not that I disbelieve you, but why did the press have pictures of you at the party?"

"They used old pictures. If you look hard enough, you'll see this was missing." He held out his left arm and pointed to the tattoo around his wrist. "My agent's got connections that owe him favors for years to come, and he has Tripp, my PR guy, feed them stories to keep them off my trail. You're an actress. You should know there isn't anything money can't buy."

"I feel like an idiot." She dropped her eyes.

He lifted her chin and smiled. "You're not an idiot. Everyone believed the press. That was the whole point."

"Yeah, but I should know about everything in the press not being true. My sister-in-law, Siena, is a model, and she was forced to date a football player when she first met my brother. She needed to scuff up her reputation and he needed to fix his. So I could have at least asked. But why didn't you tell me when I first mentioned it?"

He shrugged. "Because I don't talk about my family."

"But I pissed you off enough to tell me." She turned away. "See? Not exactly delicate."

"Or you could look at it like I care what you think and take that as a compliment. And I was wrong a moment ago. There's one thing money can't buy."

She gave him a curious look.

"You."

She laughed and shook her head like he was joking, though he wasn't. She stabbed a piece of chicken and held it up for him to eat. He narrowed his eyes, and she arched a brow, poking his lips with the fork.

"Pushy," he teased.

She shoved the food into his mouth, and he grabbed her hand. He wanted to tug her in and devour her whole. He swallowed the meat and set the fork down on the plate with his other hand.

"What is it about you, Trish Ryder?" Their faces were so close he could hear her breathing. "You said I scare you, but I think you're scared of who you *think* I am. And honestly, you scare the hell out of me, because you make me feel things I've never felt."

She trapped her lower lip between her teeth. He couldn't take his eyes off of that trapped lip. He had a burning desire to kiss it free, but it was trapped because of him, so he forced himself to lift his eyes to hers and work it free with the truth instead.

"I haven't slept with groupies in almost a decade."

Her eyes widened, then narrowed again. Her sexy mouth still held that luscious lip captive.

"I don't blame you for not believing me." He searched her eyes, but this time it wasn't her eyes giving away her desires. It was the way she leaned forward and wrapped her hand around his forearm. Her whole body seemed to be waiting for his next sentence.

Her lip sprang free, and she slicked her tongue over it. "It's not that I don't believe you. It's just so different from everything I've ever read about you."

He shrugged again. "It comes with the territory. You've heard my music. It's not exactly pure or wholesome. An image has to match the brand."

"I guess, but what are you saying? That it's all a farce?"

"Depends on your definition of a farce. I party with my friends. I make appearances at the after-parties when I'm on tour, but that's not my life. I've got too many other things on my plate to get tangled up in groupies and their games, or to waste brain cells on getting stoned or drunk."

"So you don't drink? Like at all?"

"Sure. I have a drink now and again if I'm at home with my buddies. But having a drink isn't the same as *drinking."*

She traced his tattoos with her finger. "Is there a reason? I mean, do you, have you, had a problem?"

She was being careful, and he knew that must be hard for her, given her propensity for being pushy, and he was even more attracted to her because of it. He took her hand in his. The sounds of the trees rustling in the breeze filled the silence as he wrestled with his answer.

"Some people might call it a problem. But I think it's just common sense."

Her brows knitted with confusion. He didn't want to get lost in his painful past, but he wanted her to know the truth.

"We lost my father to a drunk driver when I was twelve." He was surprised at how easily the words came. "I don't have the same passion for drinking that other people do."

She squeezed his hand. "Oh, Boone. I'm so sorry. And there I was sucking down beer like water tonight."

"Hey, everyone has their vices."

"But I'm not like that." She lowered her eyes, then raised them again. "I'm saying that an awful lot lately, aren't I? I did drink as a vice tonight, because I feel so much when I'm with you, it's hard to handle. But I don't usually drink like that, and I didn't realize it would affect me so strongly."

"I'm not judging you, and if there's ever a good excuse for drinking, I think you've just found it."

"You aren't judging, but you did try to warn me.

You pointed out that I might not know my limit, living on fumes."

"Sorry. It wasn't my place to try to stop you."

"Would you try to stop one of those groupies at your trailer the other night?"

"I'm really not in the mood to play this game." He rose to his feet and she came up beside him and touched his arm.

"I'm not playing a game. I really want to know."

"No, okay? And they aren't *my* groupies. I let my buddy stay with me and he left them behind." He didn't mean to raise his voice, but it was hard for him to admit what he had, and he was edgy and tense, made worse by the oil and water effect they had on each other. Adrenaline and heat pumped through his veins, and when she stepped closer he fisted his hands to keep from taking her in his arms.

She gazed silently up at him, her hazel eyes darkening seductively as they moved over his face. He wanted to dive in and never come up for air.

"Would you have warned Honor?"

"Of course. Or my brothers, or sister, or—"

She pressed her hands to his chest and whispered his name. He raised his brows, afraid if he exerted any more effort he wouldn't be able to resist taking the kiss he'd been craving since they left the bar.

"Why did you pick that karaoke song tonight?" The challenge in her eyes told him she already knew the answer.

"Why do you think?"

She moved *his* arms around her waist, just as he'd

moved hers around his neck earlier, and he grabbed hold. Forget restraint. Forget how they clashed and sparked at every turn. All that existed right at that moment was the flush on her skin, the passion in her voice, and her sweet, glistening lips. And when she pressed her soft body against his, he was barely able to bite back a greedy groan.

"For the same reason you warned me about not drinking too much and the reason you made me dinner. I might be stubborn and thick-headed and overly careful, but I'm not stupid."

He slid his hand to the nape of her neck. "Don't forget pushy."

She slicked her tongue over her lips. "Boone?"

He tangled his hand in her hair, and she sucked in a sharp breath. His other hand slid to her ass, pressing her against his hard length. "Yes, beautiful?"

She smiled. "I know it's been longer than sixty seconds, but I definitely want to kiss you."

He pressed his lips to the corner of her mouth, tasting her sweetness. "You do, do you?" He traced her lower lip with his tongue. "I've been wanting to do this since you held this lip hostage." He sucked her lower lip into his mouth, and her whole body shuddered.

"Oh God," she whispered.

He kissed the swell of her upper lip, teasing her as much as he was torturing himself. She tried to capture his mouth, but he tightened his grip on her hair, holding her in place, and she moaned. It was a pleading, heady sound, and he wanted to hear more of them.

He took her in a series of slow, drugging kisses. She tasted like fear and risk and wicked, savage desire aching to be set free. She moaned again, and it vibrated through him. Her body arched against him, trying to get closer, clawing at his skin, but he was in no hurry to end this feast.

"Boone," she pleaded as he trailed kisses over her jaw, nipping as he went.

"Shh. Now it's my turn."

Chapter Eight

COLD AIR SWEPT over Trish's legs and face, but it was no match for the heat consuming her. Boone's kisses were divine. Soft and tender, then rough and hungry. Lust pulsed through her limbs, between her legs, and radiated through her chest with every touch of his lips. He teased and taunted until she was ready to explode. His hand ran up her bare thigh, leaving a trail of heat, and slid beneath her shorts. She rocked against him, urging him on. His fingertips grazed her panties, and her sex pulsed in anticipation. Thoughts raced through her mind, but the only one that stuck was more, more, *more!*

His mouth—*God, your glorious mouth*—was an inferno, hot and wet and strong. Every kiss was more incredible than the last. He wasn't just kissing her. He was devouring her, killing her brain cells with every stroke of his talented tongue. He took the kiss deeper, harder, rougher. She pushed her hands into his hair and held him to her, opening her mouth—and her legs—wider. He groaned, and it was the sexiest sound she'd ever heard. Their bodies ground together, his hard shaft pressing into her belly. His hand moved from between her legs around to her ass, slipping beneath her shorts again and searing a five-finger burn through her panties. Her needy pleas were garbled and lost in their kisses. He tugged her head back and sealed his mouth over her neck, sucking and licking and driving her out of her mind. He pushed his hand under her shirt and, *good Lord*, she lost herself in the feel of his rough hand moving over her heated flesh. His thumb grazed the underside of her breast.

Yes. Please, more.

Her nipples were on fire, and when he palmed her breast she moaned again. Her plea sailed into the air. She wanted him to shred her clothes and take her right there in the grass, beneath the clouds and the starless night sky. To feel all of his strength and torment, to *finally* feel him letting her in.

Boone tore his mouth from hers, his eyes blazing, his lips red from their toe-curling kisses, so tempting she had to have them again. She grabbed his head and tugged him in for another scorching kiss. Her hands traveled over his back, down his flanks, to his firm ass, memorizing the feel of every inch to draw upon later, because as much as she wanted to feel him sinking into her and hear him groan out her name in the throes of passion, she needed to slow this runaway train. She wanted—needed—to know more about him, what he'd gone through, where his head was, before they went any further.

He kissed her jaw, her neck, and—*oh God, yes*—he slicked his tongue along the shell of her ear, and her whole body shivered.

"Trish," he whispered in a rough voice. He drew back, both of them breathless, and cradled her face between his hands. He pressed his lips to hers in a tender, delicious kiss, and when he drew back again, the hunger in his gaze softened and somehow became even more penetrating.

Neither of them moved. A handful of silent messages passed between them. *Holy hell, that was amazing. What now? I want you. You scare me.* The strongest message of all—*This is only the tip of the iceberg*—lingered loud and clear.

The breeze picked up, kicking her brain back to life. Feeling self-conscious, she smoothed her shirt and tugged at the hem of her shorts. He kept one hand on her cheek and reached for her hand with the other. His brows slanted, and his jaw suddenly tightened.

"Don't."

She stilled at the command.

He stepped closer, their bodies smoldering like molten lava. She was trembling, not from the cool air whisking over her skin but from the sheer, unadulterated lust thrumming through her. She'd just finished telling him she wasn't interested in a fling, and then she'd practically attacked him. Had she lost her mind?

He laced their fingers and touched his lips to hers again in another surprisingly tender kiss, and her only thought was if this was insanity, she was moving to Crazytown, USA.

"Don't let the awkwardness steal any part of what we just felt. Of what we *feel*."

Was this really the man she'd been arguing with for the past week? His lips curved up in a confused and hopeful smile that softened some of his hard edges. Her lips burned with abrasions from their rough kisses, and her heart pined for more. Warmth and affection washed over his features, followed by a wave of ice, and a second later his expression relaxed into an unnameable middle ground, as heated and confused as her thoughts. It was all she could do to nod.

She turned toward the porch, having absolutely no idea how long their make-out session had lasted. Had they been kissing for hours, or was it only a few all-consuming minutes? She was suddenly too exhausted to try to figure it out. All she wanted was more of him. She wanted to curl up in his arms and talk and kiss and touch and feel, which made no logical sense. Boone wasn't a touchy-feely guy, and *he* was telling her not to let the awkwardness steal any part of what they'd felt? She thought he'd be the one scoffing and playing it off like it hadn't meant a darn thing. But he was still holding her hand as they walked up the porch steps.

"Trish?"

She turned to face him, and in the dim light coming through the screen door she recalled his torturous expression as he'd told her about losing his father and about his mother's health. He'd said only a few sentences, but his confession felt monumental. She didn't know what to make of this side of him, or of her overwhelming emotions, but she felt herself getting caught up in him again and wondered if this was what people meant when they said the heart wanted what the heart wanted. It must be, she deduced, because she wanted him to take her in his arms and kiss her again, to carry her upstairs and—

He gathered her in his arms and gazed into her eyes, bringing her back from her fantasy.

"Six months," he said with a serious tone that made her wonder if she'd missed something he'd said.

"I'm sorry. What?"

"It's been six months since I've kissed a woman."

Holy cow. Six months? "I...I didn't ask."

"No, but you assume a lot of things about me, and I wanted you to know so you wouldn't stay up all night thinking you'd just added your name to another one of the fictional lists you think I have."

She fed off of each secret he shared, like a mouse following a trail of the most delicious cheese. "You don't have to prove anything to me. I *wanted* to kiss you."

"Yeah, I know. And what I want to do goes so far beyond kissing that I wanted you to know the truth." He knelt to pick up the plate and silverware they'd left on the porch.

Her mind reeled at his confession.

He looked up at her with an unexpected smile. "I've got this."

She glanced at the sleeping kitten.

"I've got him, too. You should go get some sleep. We have a lot of lines to go over tomorrow."

Lines? She was still stuck on going beyond kissing. *She* wanted to go beyond kissing, despite the red flags waving in her head. She wasn't ready to walk inside. She moved to pick up the kitten sleeping soundly in the guitar case, and Boone touched her arm.

"Really, go get some sleep. I'm holding on to my control by a thread. If I touch you again, I'm not going to stop."

She debated that for a minute. She wanted to step forward and be consumed by him.

As if he'd read her thoughts, he said, "You're not sure about me, and I've got so much shit going on in my life. I can't make any promises." He paused long enough for that to settle in. "Whatever this is between us, I have a feeling you could break me into a million little pieces, and I have too many people counting on me to let myself go there."

**

AFTER TOO FEW hours of sleep, Boone awoke to the kitten's tiny paws batting at his hair. He lay there thinking about the incredible kisses he and Trish had shared and reliving every touch. He'd told her things he'd never told anyone, and the strangest part of it all was that long after she'd gone to sleep, he wished she hadn't, and not just so they could have sex. He wanted to get to know her better. To talk about her family and see what was really going on in her pretty little head. When he'd finally gone inside and up to his bedroom, he'd lain in bed for hours thinking about Trish. As usual, his thoughts had moved down his list of responsibilities: Jude, Lucky, his mother, and the movie he was supposed to be focusing on. He'd tried calling Jude again, and when his call went to voicemail he left another message. Now he was restless, and there were only three remedies to this sort of restlessness—music, sex, and cooking. He'd sworn off meaningless sex—and he knew if he landed in bed with Trish it would be far from meaningless, which meant it was still on the list. *Forbidden fruit.* All that was left was music and cooking.

Trish's door was still closed after he'd showered and dressed, with no signs of life coming from the other side, so music wasn't an option. He headed down to the kitchen with the nameless kitten tucked under his arm and went to work scrambling out his frustrations.

A while later, after eating breakfast and washing the dishes, he gazed out the window over the sink, watching storm clouds roll in and thinking about Trish. He tried to convince himself that what he felt for her was nothing more than lust. Lust was something he could understand and deal with. He knew how to turn lust off. Hell, he'd become a master at it, because turning it off was easier than dealing with the self-loathing that came after having sex with women he didn't give a shit about.

"You cooked."

His heart did a weird thumping dance at the sound of Trish's voice. He turned as she padded across the kitchen floor wearing a T-shirt that barely covered her ass. Every ounce of his body came to life. She leaned over the table eyeing the feast he'd prepared, and the hem of her shirt lifted, exposing the curve of her ass and the creamy expanse of her upper thighs. Even with his cock's full salute, his heart was what had Boone's mind spinning unfamiliar webs.

He cleared his throat and tried to pull himself together. "I made you an egg-white omelet. No fat. Help yourself to the fruit."

"You thought about me?" She tucked her right foot behind the left, her knee slightly bent, and trapped her lower lip between her teeth, looking impossibly sexy and sweet.

"All night long," he mumbled, and handed her a plate from the cabinet. "So, we're going to actually try to act today instead of just reading lines?" That was dangerous territory for him, almost as dangerous as standing beside her wondering if she was wearing a thong or going commando under her shirt.

"If you think you can handle it," she said with a seductive shake of her shoulders and a sinful smile.

"There's not much I can't handle."

"Hm?" She arched a brow and closed her eyes as she bit into a strawberry. "Mm. This is *so* delicious."

Chalk him up to being a caveman, because as she licked her fingers his mind saw them wrapped around his cock while she licked him like a lollipop.

He headed back upstairs to take a cold shower. A

very cold shower.
Or two.

Chapter Nine

TRISH AND BOONE had been rehearsing for hours. Boone had been running hot from the moment they'd begun practicing, and he'd only gotten hotter since. Every time they were near, he got this look in his eyes like he was fighting his desire to kiss her, and she was no better. Her stomach fluttered and her nipples pebbled with every brush of his skin. Because of that, and the fact that Boone seemed to detach from his character during intimate scenes, she'd been careful to choose scenes that didn't require close proximity. If she were being honest with herself, she'd admit the real reason she'd chosen those safer, distant scenes was that this primal dance they were executing was too exciting to chance ruining it.

Since they weren't rehearsing scenes that caused Boone to detach from his character, she had the added bonus of watching him come into his own in the role of Rick Champion. He was not only taking the rehearsal seriously, but he'd also asked for advice on several key lines, and he'd practiced them over and over until he'd gotten them right. He was owning the role instead of just acting it out.

Trish held her breath as he wrapped a scene where his character was getting ready to play his first big gig after arriving in Hollywood. His emotions were spot-on, fear and excitement as real and palpable as the damp prestorm summer air whipping around them.

"Let's show this town who's boss." Boone pretended to high-five a band member and strutted off the porch.

"That was amazing!" Trish followed him down the steps and into the grass.

"I wouldn't go that far."

He turned and their arms brushed. It was simple skin-to-skin contact, but her entire body tingled with awareness. *Sweet heavens. If this slow burn ignites, we'll set the fields ablaze.*

She was about ready to pounce, but she forced herself to focus.

As the afternoon turned to early evening, fast-moving clouds rolled in, and the wind picked up.

Boone looked up at the ominous gray sky. "Do you want me to grab you a sweatshirt?"

He'd been overly attentive all day, asking if she wanted a drink, practically demanding she eat something because *existing on fumes isn't healthy*, and when she'd gotten a call from Fiona and screamed with delight at the news of Jake's new movie, he was quick to land by her side to make sure she was okay. He was suddenly treating her as he had the kitten, like she was his to take care of. And she was surprised by how much she liked it.

"No, thanks, but maybe we should move inside."

He shook his head. "Too confining. I think we have a little more time before the rain reaches us."

"You wouldn't practice inside yesterday either." She crossed her arms and stared him down. "In fact, other than cooking, sleeping, and showering, you haven't been inside at all. What's going on?"

"I don't like to feel boxed in."

"Okay. I get that. But what are you going to do when we have to do the bedroom scene?"

He waggled his brows. He'd made a few playful gestures this afternoon, and she loved seeing that side of him, although she had a feeling it was an avoidance tactic.

"I'm serious, Boone. We have to rehearse them at some point, and the more time we put into the scenes that you're uncomfortable with, the easier they'll be when the crew arrives."

"Who says I'm uncomfortable with the bedroom scene?" He stepped closer, bringing a full-on heat wave with him.

"No one," she managed. "I meant because you hate rehearsing inside. It's the warehouse scenes and the other scenes where you're confronted with Delia's addiction that seem to make you the most uncomfortable. But I wondered about the bedroom scene because you really don't want to rehearse inside."

Slowly, and seductively, his gaze slid down her body. "Baby, if you want to take me to bed, all you have to do is ask."

"Yes, please." She slapped her hand over her mouth. "I didn't mean that." She was seriously losing it, and he was seriously deflecting. And now he had the sexiest grin on his lips. She. Needed. To. Focus.

"I'm going to table that offer for a little while." *Little while* came out as a whisper, or maybe a whimper.

"You? On the table?" An illicit grin formed on his lips. "I'm liking the sound of this."

She held her palm out to keep him from coming any closer. "And you're the master of deflection." He shifted his eyes away, and she knew she'd hit the nail on the head. "Boone, if you have an issue with acting out the scenes that deal with Delia's addiction, you need to clue me in."

He hiked his thumb over his shoulder toward the house. "Bedroom scene. Let's do that."

"Boone."

He wrapped his arms around her and leaned down like he was going to kiss her. As badly as she wanted him to, her concern over his reluctance to talk about whatever was holding him back from those scenes won out.

"Sounds like *you're* afraid of the bedroom scene. I promise to be gentle. At least at first," he said coaxingly.

She pushed from his arms. "First of all, I wouldn't

want you to be gentle." She waved a hand in the air, trying to slow her racing heart and get the image of being in bed with Boone out of her mind. "Just throwing that out there."

His lips curved up in a devilish grin. "Thought you weren't into meaningless sex."

"I'm not, and stop distracting me. What's going on with you and the druggie scenes?"

"Nothing."

"Bullshit."

He walked away through the knee-high grass, and she followed.

"Boone, you can talk to me."

"I am talking to you."

"Then let's do the warehouse scene." The wind kicked up and she crossed her arms to ward off the chill. "We can do it on the porch. It's only a couple of lines."

He gritted his teeth, making no move to follow her to the porch.

"I thought there wasn't a problem." She set her best speak-up-or-else stare on him.

He shifted his eyes away. "There's not."

"Then come on before the storm hits. God only knows how hard it'll be to get you to practice once we're trapped inside." She dragged him toward the porch.

"There's always the bedroom scene."

"Aren't you so kind to remind me?" She lay down on the porch, as if it were the warehouse floor, and smiled up at him. "I'll remind you, when they're in the bedroom, Delia is higher than a kite, and you seem to have issues when she's like that."

He stood over her, watching her intently. "Aren't you supposed to be totally out of it and *silent*?"

She sat up and pointed at him. "I know you can do this scene, so whatever's going on in that crazy head of yours, turn it off. You can do this. I know you can."

His gaze softened. "Why do you have so much faith in me?"

She grabbed his hand and pulled him down on one knee. "I've heard you sing. I fell under your spell last night and kissed you in front of the whole frigging town. I've watched you rehearse all day and you have been brilliant. Passion lives inside you, Boone. Even when you try to hide it, it's lying in wait. All you have to do is set it free."

Without any cognitive thought, she leaned up and pressed her lips to his, and in the next breath, he took control, sliding his tongue along the seam of her lips. She opened for him, soaking in every delicious second of their long-awaited first kiss of the day. His lips were soft, though the kiss was hard. He lowered himself down to both knees and cradled her in his arms, deepening the kiss. Thunder rumbled in the distance, competing with the pounding of her heart.

"See?" she said as their mouths parted. "It's right there. Passion."

**

THE PASSION BOONE felt when he was with Trish was

unequivocally more powerful than anything he'd ever experienced. He'd been trying to ignore it all day, but she was like a force of nature, believing in him, pushing him like no one else had the guts to.

"That hasn't been there for a very long time," he admitted. "That's all you, beautiful."

She smiled up at him, looking so feminine and happy, he wanted this moment to stretch on forever. Her hair tumbled over her shoulders, her eyes were like grass and honey, with amber flames burning just for him. She touched his cheek, and he closed his eyes, reveling in her softness, the intimacy he hadn't realized he'd been longing for.

"Then we should be able to nail this scene," she said sweetly.

The scene. His eyes came open. *Delia, overdosed and unconscious on the warehouse floor.* In his mind he saw Destiny strung out. Destiny promising she'd get clean. Destiny in her coffin. His chest constricted, and he rose abruptly, trying to breathe past the ice coursing through his veins.

"Boone? What just happened?"

He paced the length of the porch, but she was on his heels, peppering him with questions.

"What's wrong? Why won't you look at me?" She followed his every step. "Talk to me, please. Was it the kiss?"

Every word echoed in his head, pinging between the painful memories.

"Boone?" Trish touched his shoulder and he spun around. Their eyes connected, and as if his gaze had

115

burned her, her hand flew to her chest. "Good Lord, Boone. What's wrong?"

He stormed around her and off the porch, but she was relentless, and she followed him across the field in the dimming light and the cold wind.

"Trish, go back to the house," he shouted against the looming storm.

"No!" She grabbed his arm, but he kept walking, trying to outrun the memories. "Talk to me."

"I've got nothing to say." Thunder boomed in the distance. He stopped walking and stared at the trees bending to the wind. "Go back, Trish. Please. I'll be inside in a few minutes. I just need some space."

"No." She looped her arm though his and gripped his forearm.

The worry in her eyes crushed him. He wanted to take her in his arms and kiss her as he had last night. Kiss her until the pain went away and all that was left was the fire between them, but that wouldn't be fair. She didn't need to deal with his crap. He'd barely been able to pull away last night. He didn't trust himself to pull away now.

"It's starting to rain. Please go back."

She shook her head.

"Damn it, Trish. You're too stubborn. This has nothing to do with you."

"But it has to do with you." She gazed into his eyes, and in a softer voice she said, "Let me in, Boone. Talk to me. *Please.*"

"Ever since I took this role, my life has imploded." The wind picked up, howling between the trees. "You don't need this in your life."

"How do you know what I need or don't need? That's presumptive."

She smiled with the tease, and he closed his eyes against the rush of emotions bubbling up inside him. How could he tell her about Destiny and those awful years when reliving them was the last thing he wanted to do?

"Boone, can you really look me in the eyes and tell me you *want* me to walk away?"

He cupped her face in his hands, desperate to let her in, to soak in her comfort, and afraid to hurt her— afraid to hurt himself. "Why? Why do you want to be closer to me of all people? Can't you see I've got shit going on in my head that's not normal?"

"Normal? What the hell is normal? Was it normal that I stayed up all night thinking about how I wished we hadn't stopped kissing last night after I'd just told you I didn't want to be a groupie?" She smiled, and his heart squeezed.

"I told you I don't have groupies!"

"No shit. You're so stubborn that's *all* you heard, just like I'm so stubborn I don't care if this isn't about me, or if you don't want to deal with me because you would rather keep your feelings all bottled up until you explode."

He paced as raindrops wet his cheeks. "Go back, Trish."

"What happened back there?" she pushed. "Why did you detach like that?"

He ground his teeth against the truth.

"Boone, I won't judge you. If you can't do the movie, that's okay, but at least tell me why. Whatever happened back there, whatever is happening now, it's not good for you."

He took a step back, but she stepped forward with a determined look in her eyes.

"Tell me." She took another step closer. "Tell me what you're running from."

"I've lived it, okay?" He pushed away and paced, the rain and wind picking up speed. "We lost Honor's sister to an overdose, and I thought I'd dealt with it, but apparently I didn't, because those scenes that you claim I'm avoiding? They're fucking killing me. Dragging me back to a place I don't want to be."

He pushed his hands into his hair and clenched his eyes shut, turning his face up toward the rain, wishing it could wash away the memories—and at the same time, wishing it wouldn't. Because he didn't want to forget Destiny; he just didn't want to feel the pain of losing her—especially to something so meaningless as drugs.

He felt Trish's hand on his shoulder and shook his head. Her arms wound around his neck and he drew in a jagged breath.

"Trish," he warned, anger and hurt cutting like knives through his skin, his heart, his guts.

"Shut up. Ryders don't run from the hard stuff. So you might as well give in, because even if you do want me to fuck off, you've gotten under my skin. You're pretty much stuck with me."

"I don't want to feel it," he said through gritted

teeth. "Don't you see that?"

"Yes."

"Then please, go back to the house before you get soaked." He twisted out of her grip and turned away.

She stalked around him and crossed her arms, chin held high. Her hair was wet, matting against her face. Her shirt and shorts clung to her body like a second skin, and she was trembling with cold, but the look she gave him was a thousand degrees of compassion.

"You think acting is pretending, and I get that, because that's exactly what it looks like, but it's not. Do you know *why* I'm an A-list actress? Because I climb into the heads of my characters and *feel* what they feel. The story might be pretend, but the gut-wrenching sadness, the pain, the glory, and the joy?" She pointed at him as she spoke. "That's as real as the day is long. So when you say you don't want to feel the pain of losing someone you loved, I get it. When I'm acting, the lights, the crew, and the cameras? They all fail to exist. When I'm in Delia's head, I *am* Delia. I'm feeling the agony of being controlled by a drug I can't get out from under. Of losing the man I love day by day because of that drug. Of knowing that I alone have the power to set him free from the fucking nightmare that I've created for him by needing to be taken care of and worried about."

He didn't want to hear it, and at the same time, he was mesmerized by her. She totally understood what he was feeling—and that scared the living hell out of him. "Stop! It's too much. It's too fucking much." He stormed off again, rounding his shoulders against the rain.

"Don't you see?" she said as she caught up to him. "Feeling that pain is the *only* thing that can ever set you free from being wrecked by it the next time something dredges it up, or the time after that, or the time after that. You said you were having trouble writing songs, and who knows. Maybe that's all tangled up in this, too." She grabbed his arm and yanked him to a stop.

"Damn it, Boone! What are you afraid of? You already pour your heart and soul into your music. Feel your pain and earn yourself an Oscar. Or don't. I don't care about the movie. But all that stuff you're too afraid to feel is what's missing—and maybe not *just* in the movie. Was she your first love? Are you afraid hurting makes you weak? Talk to me!"

"What am I afraid of? Feeling like I'm dying inside. She and Honor went through hell because of their fucking parents, and me and my brother Cage and the rest of us *ghetto dwellers* protected them. We snuck them into our homes, trying to protect them from their drunken, drug-addicted parents." He stalked toward Trish, driven by anger he couldn't control. "I loved her like a sister, and *none* of us could save her. We were kids trying to save a drug-addicted fifteen-year-old."

He stood in the pouring rain staring at the woman who had dredged up his demons, and he was unable to stop the rest from coming out. "And then there's you, giving everything you've got to this role. Studying all

120

night, starving yourself. You're on set for ten, fifteen grueling hours a day, not only kicking ass with your role, but when they're sick and tired of me messing up, you're telling them you believe in me every damn day, when *I* don't even know if I believe in myself. And day after day I'm watching you, wanting you, and trying to hold back because no matter what I know in my head when we're acting out those vile scenes"—he tapped angrily on the side of his head—"*you* become *her.*"

Chapter Ten

TRISH'S MIND SPUN as she tried to grasp *all* of what Boone had said. Selfishly, she wanted to address his feelings for her, but Boone was hurting and angry, and he'd laid more important parts of himself out between them.

She reached for his hand as thunder rolled through the sky and the clouds sobbed overhead. "You said this movie was important to you, and now I understand why. But what I don't understand is why you would willingly put yourself through this if you didn't want to feel the effects of it."

He scrubbed a hand down his tension-ridden face. "The movie resonates with me for a million reasons. It's important that the world knows people struggle with demons bigger than they could ever imagine and how those struggles affect others. But I had no idea it would be this intense, or that your acting would be so real."

He pulled her closer, and she willingly went to him. He pressed his hands to her cheeks. Rain streamed down their faces, hanging from his lashes like teardrops above his stormy eyes.

"I didn't realize I'd feel anything for you, or that your acting would affect me this much." He touched his forehead to hers and closed his eyes.

She expected him to say he was pulling out of the movie and ending whatever this was between them. She waited for an interminable moment, shivering against the frigid rain and wind and trying to contain her mounting panic. She wasn't ready for him to walk away. The hell with the movie. She'd never, *ever*, felt so drawn to a person, and the more she learned about him, the more connected she felt. She wondered, briefly, if she was caught up in Rick and Delia, but she'd always been good about keeping a clear line between reality and make-believe, and never in all her years of acting had she felt like this. Never in her *life* had she felt like this.

When she could no longer battle her own thoughts, she covered his hands with hers, and he opened his eyes, revealing so much raw emotion, she knew this was real—and she wasn't alone in what she felt.

"What do you want, Boone?"

"What I want isn't fair."

Her heart swelled with his painful honestly. If she felt this tortured, how must he feel? "Maybe you aren't the one who should make that decision."

He searched her eyes, and she knew by the firm

press of his hands against her skin, and the warring emotions trampling his features like a battlefield, that he was fighting against himself.

A hot ache grew in her throat, and she fisted her hands in his shirt, dragging him closer. "*Feel*, Boone. Let yourself *feel*."

Passion flared in his eyes, and his response came in the hard press of his fingers curling around the base of her skull, holding her captive to a punishingly intense and beautiful kiss. She went up on her toes, accepting everything he was willing to give, wanting to feel the pain and anger of the past so he wasn't alone in experiencing them.

"You," he said between kisses. "I want you."

"Take me, Boone."

They groped and kissed, as hot and frantic as the raging storm. His mouth was everywhere at once, on her lips, her jaw, her neck. His greedy hands clutched her ass, groped her breasts, her hips, her face. Their bodies bumped and ground, and there in the field, among the howling wind and treacherous rain, they tore at each other's clothes, falling to the wet grass in a frantic tangle of lust and nakedness.

She bowed off the ground. "More. I need more."

Grasping at his shoulders, her hands slid off his rain-soaked skin. He moved down her body, pressing hot kisses to her chilled flesh, and captured her breast in his mouth. She cried out at the scintillating pleasure as he worked his magic. His hand moved between her legs, and holy mother of orgasms, within seconds she was writhing and moaning and the world careened around her as she surrendered to their passion.

He came down over her, his hard length perched against her center, and their eyes locked.

"Condom," they said in unison.

His head dropped between his shoulders.

"Don't you have one? In your wallet or something?"

He shook his head. "Contrary to my reputation, I don't sleep around."

She closed her eyes and whimpered. "I never thought I'd *ever* say this, but why the hell not?"

He slid his hands beneath her head, cradling it as he smiled down at her.

"Because I always hoped one day I'd meet someone like you, and I didn't want a string of senseless mistakes hanging around my neck."

"Boone," she whispered, feeling him slip into her heart as raindrops slid between their bodies. "That's the sweetest thing I've ever heard."

"Come on, beautiful." He rose to his feet in all his naked glory and helped her up.

"Where?" she asked as they gathered their clothes.

"We need to make a run to the store."

They hurried toward the house hand in hand.

"Um." Trish tucked herself against his side, wondering if he was going to think less of her for what she said next. "No, we don't."

He looked down at her with a quizzical expression as they climbed the porch steps. She nibbled at her lower lip, and he tugged her against him with a hearty laugh.

"You little minx!"

"*Ugh!*" She laughed as he crashed his mouth over hers, and they stumbled into the kitchen. "I don't sleep around," she insisted between kisses.

They kissed and stumbled through the living room, tumbling down to the couch and laughing as they made out with reckless abandon.

"Upstairs," Boone managed, and lifted her into his arms, carrying her toward the stairs. "So you have condoms because..."

She buried her face in his chest. "I could lie and say it has to do with working with the man I've had a crush on for too many years to admit without outing myself as a ridiculous girl, or I can tell you the truth."

"That's an excellent lie," he said as he carried her into his bedroom and found the kitten sleeping soundly on his pillow.

"My room," she whispered.

He leaned in for another kiss and headed down the hall. "Does the truth have to do with some other guy?"

"Actually, no," she said as he set her down beside her bed. "I haven't done this in so long, I'm not sure I'll remember how. The truth is, my father was in search and rescue. My brother Jake followed in his footsteps, and my brother Cash is a fireman." She went to her closet and pulled out an enormous first-aid kit. "My family has a thing about being prepared. I have about six of these kits at home, although I have to admit, I never thought I'd actually have a need to use anything but a bandage."

He arched a brow as she dug through the plastic box and tossed two condoms on the bedside table. The window was open, and a cool breeze brought goose bumps to her damp skin.

"They came with the kit. Four of them."

"Remind me to thank your overprotective brothers."

**

TRISH LAUGHED AS they tumbled to the bed. "If you value your life, you might not want to mention this to them."

"I don't think you're supposed to laugh during sex." Boone nipped at her chin, earning another sweet giggle from the sexy woman who was making his heart turn over in his chest.

Trish reached up and stroked his cheek. "Then maybe you should kiss me instead of teasing me with that mouth I've been dreaming of forever."

"Oh, you like my mouth, do you?" He kissed her deeply, loving the quickening of her breath, the feel of her writhing beneath him. He moved from her lips to her cheek, to the sensitive skin just below her ear.

"Yeah," she whispered. "I like your mouth a lot."

He chuckled against her neck, kissing and sucking his way down her damp flesh to the swell of her breast, dragging his tongue over one, then the other. His hands traveled up her ribs, and she gasped as he pushed her breasts together and moved his tongue over her taut, dusky nipples, then blew on them. He rolled one between finger and thumb, lowering his mouth over the other and sucking hard. She arched beneath him, her fingernails digging into his skin.

"Oh God, that feels so good."

He sucked and licked until she was trembling. Then he lavished her other breast with the same attention. She grasped his head, holding him to her, but Boone didn't want to just pleasure her. He wanted to drive her out of her ever-loving mind. He took her hands and moved them above her head, curling her fingers around the decorative iron bars on the headboard.

"Hold tight, beautiful."

She blinked up at him, and he brushed his lips over hers. She reached for him, and he drew her hand back to the bars.

"Hold tight. I promise I won't disappoint you." He sealed his vow with another passionate kiss. "Okay?"

She nodded and trapped her lower lip between her teeth. He slicked his tongue over it, and her lips parted.

"If you don't like anything I do, tell me." He ran his tongue around her nipple and sucked it into his mouth, holding her gaze. "I can't wait to be buried deep inside you." He held her ribs as he kissed her sides, her stomach, and the dip beside each hip, loving the way her breathing hitched and her body arched and writhed as he moved lower. His fingers trailed lightly over her thighs, spreading them gently, revealing her glistening sex.

She closed her eyes, and he knew she was

embarrassed, but he loved her eyes and he wanted to see them.

"Watch me," he coaxed.

Her eyes came open and a flush rose on her skin. He held her gaze as he kissed the sensitive flesh just beside her cleanly waxed sex. The scent of her desire filled his senses. He slicked his tongue up her inner thigh, and her eyes fluttered closed again.

"You're so beautiful, baby. Open your eyes. Trust me to take care of you." He brought his mouth to her other thigh, laving his tongue in slow circles as he lifted her knees and spread her legs wider.

She was openly watching him now, breathing harder as he ran his tongue along the crease between her thighs and her sex. Seeing her hands above her head, her hungry eyes on him, so full of lust he could feel it rolling off of her, was almost too much to take.

"I've been dying to taste you." He dragged his tongue between her wet lips, and she moaned. Her eyes closed again. He did it again, and her hips rose off the mattress.

He pressed his hands to her inner thighs, holding her down as he sealed his mouth over her wet heat and took his fill. She rocked against his strength, whimpering and gasping as he loved her with his mouth. When he released her thighs and slid his hands beneath her, she rose to meet his efforts. He angled her hips so he could take more of her, and take he did, with his tongue, his fingers, his teeth. Her legs went rigid, and he lowered her hips to the mattress and trapped her thighs again, holding them apart. She lifted her head from the mattress, and her eyes blazed a path to his, watching as he flicked her most sensitive nerves with his tongue and slid two fingers into her, curling them upward and stroking the spot that sent his name streaming from her lips in desperate cries of pleasure.

When the last quake rumbled through her, she fell to the mattress panting for air. Her hands went to her chest, and Boone's mouth went to the tender spot behind her knees, seeking Trish's undiscovered pleasures. She nearly leaped off the bed with the first slick of his tongue.

"Holy cow." She leaned up on her elbows. "*What was that?*"

He slithered up her body, kissing her belly, which sent her hips off the bed again. Damn, he loved the way she moved. When he reached her mouth, he cupped her jaw possessively and poured all the emotions he'd been holding back into their kiss.

"*That,*" he said, kissing her softly, "was me discovering you."

"You're like a treasure hunter. A very talented treasure hunter."

"And you're so cute and sexy you're going to make me crazy." He guided her trembling hands back up to the iron bars at the head of the bed. "Trust me?"

She nodded, and he kissed her again.

"When you look at me like that, I want to skip the foreplay and get right to the main event."

"Look at you how?" she asked with wide, innocent eyes. "Because I'm loving this foreplay, and I want to be sure not to look at you that way."

They both laughed as he brought his tongue to the crook of her elbow. "Every way," he whispered against her skin.

"Uh-oh. I'm closing my eyes." She didn't close them.

He shook his head, then laughed when she rolled her eyes.

As he discovered the spots that made her quiver and beg—the base of her neck, the soft flesh beside her breast, the dip at the base of her spine, and his favorite, the crease where her gorgeous ass joined her thighs—she filled the room with sensual pleas, each one hitting Boone right in the heart.

She lay beneath him, her damp hair spread over the pillow, her body flushed and trembling. Her arms had long ago left the iron spokes, and as he came down over her, his hard length sheathed and eager against her center, she reached for him.

Emotions swamped him. "Trish, this is..."

"I know," she whispered. "I feel it, too."

"Every ounce of me craves you, from my heart, to my hands, to..."

She smiled up at him, her cheeks flushing anew. "Is that bad? Because you've just gotten to know me *very* intimately, so if you're going to run, please do it now instead of later."

"I told you I don't run." He kissed her softly, struck by the intensity of their connection. "Being with you is like playing with fire. You push me like no one else ever has. I should run, but I can't imagine going a single day without seeing you."

She touched his cheek the way she'd done so many times over the last few hours that he'd come to expect it and revel in it. "Then don't."

"My life is crazy, Trish. You might not want to get mixed up with me."

"I like crazy, and in case you haven't noticed, I'm already mixed up with you."

"Baby," he whispered. "You make me feel like I can get through anything."

He pressed his lips to hers again, and as their bodies joined together, the pleasure was pure and explosive. They didn't gaze into each other's eyes. There was no slow build. This was a *strap yourself in and get ready for the ride of your life* connection, and Boone's world spun on its axis. Trish moved with him, arching into his hands, lifting and angling her hips to take him deeper and touching him in ways he'd never been touched—with as much care as passion. She sank her teeth into his skin, cried out his name, and took him to heights he never imagined possible. They played, made love, and *fucked* for hours, using the two condoms she'd set aside, then going back to the first-aid kit for another. When she insisted on discovering *his* pleasure points, he thought he'd died and gone to heaven.

Long after Trish dozed off, nestled safely within his arms, Boone lay awake. He'd been bound by his own restraints for so many years, he had a hard time accepting his quiet mind. Guilt tried to work its way in, reminding him of the list of people he needed to check up on and the worries that followed him like a shadow.

As the storm faded into the distance, he pressed his lips to Trish's forehead and allowed himself to enjoy the sense of peace coming over him. The kitten climbed up the blanket and snuggled against his other side, and Boone closed his eyes, mentally adding Trish and the kitten to his lists. It was time to give that little guy a name.

Chapter Eleven

THE SUN STREAMED in through the open window across the empty side of the bed. Trish didn't have much morning-after experience to draw upon, but she was pretty sure waking up alone after the night she and Boone had shared wasn't a good sign. She listened for Boone and heard footsteps downstairs. She thought they'd turned a corner from friends to something much more meaningful, but now she wondered if that feeling was one-sided. She thought back to the things they'd said and winced with the memory of how hard she'd pushed him to talk to her. Was last night's incredible sex nothing more than post-argument passion run amuck? What if it was? She didn't do meaningless sex.

Well, if that's where his head is, then I just did.

She snagged her phone from the bedside table and called Fiona.

Fiona answered on the first ring. "How's the hottie

rocker and not-interested-actress thing going?"

"I think I made a mistake," she said quietly and rushed. "Only it doesn't feel like a mistake. But it probably is. And I don't want it to be, but—"

"Stop right there. This is what I heard. *I slept with Boone and I'm freaking out.*"

"God, I love you for making this easy." Trish lowered her voice. "We went out to a bar and I *might* have gotten jealous and dragged a guy to the dance floor." She told Fiona all about their rocky, and amazing, evening. "So?"

"I'm still hung up on the doing-it-for-hours part."

"Fi! Focus. I have to face him, but I don't know how to act. I'm not good at this."

"And you think *I* am? I've got less experience than you do. Maybe we should consult one of my sisters-in-law or Shea. I bet Shea would know what to do."

"No! You are not going to tell *anyone* about this." Fiona's sister, Shea, was Trish's public relations rep and she would definitely know how to handle this because she dealt with her clients' sticky situations all the time, as would Fiona's sisters-in-law, because they were just all-around cool like that. But Trish didn't need all of Weston, Colorado, and New York City talking about her night of unbelievable sex.

"Well, if it were me, I'd go downstairs and act like you didn't do anything," Fiona suggested. "Then watch his reaction. If he's cold or acts disinterested, then I think you can write it off as a hookup."

Even though she had pretty much convinced herself that Boone would only escape the bedroom if he wasn't interested in taking their relationship further, she couldn't stop thinking about the things he'd said. *I can't imagine going a single day without seeing you.*

"I hope he doesn't act that way, because it would mean I'm a terrible judge of character. He told me things last night about his past that were really personal." She stopped short of sharing those things with Fiona, because Boone trusted her and they weren't her stories to tell.

"Then you probably have nothing to worry about. Just go downstairs and act natural."

Trish lay in bed after their call, listening to the sounds of dishes clanking and Boone's voice drifting up from the kitchen. She couldn't tell if he was on the phone or talking to himself. Or the kitten, which he did a lot. She forced herself to her feet, pulled a T-shirt over her head, and looked around the room, like maybe she'd find the answers to her worries there. The first-aid kit sat open on the floor.

Proof of our frantic search for a third condom.

Not the answer she was looking for. She pulled on a pair of underwear and shorts, then stood for a moment reconsidering the shorts. If he *was* into her, then wouldn't it be sexier to go downstairs without anything on under her shirt?

Yes, but if he's not...

She rolled her eyes. She was thinking too much, and that always led her to feel even more self-conscious, which wouldn't bode well for either direction. She washed her face and brushed her teeth, then headed downstairs to figure out where she stood.

She followed a heavenly aroma to the kitchen and heard Boone talking.

"You're sure?" He paused, and so did Trish, by the entrance to the kitchen. "Tell Lucky I said to get his ass to work this week. All right. Love you, too, Mom."

Mom. Their conversation about his parents came back to her, and her chest constricted. She walked into the kitchen just as Boone turned. He was looking down at his phone with a serious expression and holding the kitten in his other hand. The table was set for two, with plates of French toast, eggs, and fruit. He shoved his phone in his pocket, and when his eyes landed on Trish, he smiled.

"Hey, beautiful." He sounded a little hesitant.

She approached cautiously, although her heart was doing a happy dance at the way he was smiling at her.

"Are you okay?" He reached for her hand.

"Uh-huh." *I'm not sure.* "Are you?"

He leaned in for a kiss. "I'm better now. My phone went off at around five and I didn't want to wake you." He searched her face, and his expression turned serious again. "Are you sure you're okay?"

"I don't know," she finally admitted. "I don't have much experience with morning afters. You seem fine, but that could just be because the sex was good and you want more." *Jesus. Open mouth, insert foot.*

He set the kitten on the floor and pulled her into his arms. "You're wondering if last night was a mistake?"

"No. Not for me. But...*yes*." He didn't need to say a thing. The way he was holding her, tight yet gently, and the caring, seductive look in his eyes were definitely not the actions of a guy who was only after sex.

"Part of me wishes I could chalk this up to my favorite mistake," he said softly. "But carnal desire is *not* the winner here."

"I should probably hold on to the good parts of what you just said and tuck away the rest, but—"

"You can't, because Ryders don't run from the hard stuff."

"You heard that, huh?" She was glad he had, because she could no sooner pretend to not care about what was left unsaid than she could pretend that being in his arms wasn't warming her up in all the best places.

"You didn't really give me a choice." He kissed her again, a quick, tender press of his lips. "Do you want coffee?"

"Sure, thanks." She followed him to the table. "This smells delicious."

"I cook when I'm edgy." He handed her a mug of coffee and motioned for her to sit down, then took the seat beside her.

She took a hearty sip of coffee. "Well, Mr. Edgy, let me have it. Why do you wish you could chalk this up to a mistake? And don't sugarcoat your answer, because I'll probably see right through it."

He shifted in his chair, bringing her legs between his. "Okay, no sugarcoating. All that shit you dragged out of me last night? I don't talk about it. As in *ever.*"

This didn't sound like it was leading up to anything warm and fuzzy.

"And when we were together?" He shook his head. "Trish, there are no words for what I feel when I'm with you. I thought I got a rush performing onstage, but being with you?" He shook his head again, and she hoped that was a good sign.

"But…?" She set her coffee cup on the table.

"Being with you is beyond incredible. But I need you to know that I've got a long list of people relying on me. People I care about, and I can't afford to let any one of them down."

And there it was. She thought she could handle it if he said last night was a one-time thing, but a mass of confused thoughts and hurt feelings assailed her. How could she have felt so much in one night? Had it just been so long since she'd been with a man that she was making a connection where there was none? She couldn't believe it. Didn't want to believe it. How could the aftermath of a single night and a handful of days make her ache?

He took her hand in his, and she couldn't meet his eyes. She should get up and walk way, even if just to save face, but she couldn't muster the energy to do that.

"You're pushy and demanding and so damn sexy it's hard to focus when I'm near you," he said with such sincerity it gave her goose bumps. However, the word *but* still lingered in his voice. "And you care *so much* when I say I don't want to feel something. You *make* me feel it."

She wrenched her hand from his and forced herself to her feet. "Okay, you can stop now. I get it. I am aggressive. We've already established that. I don't really need to hear it again."

Boone rose in front of her, his face a mask of concern. "Are you mad?"

She crossed her arms. "Not *mad*, per se." The lie tasted bitter. She was mad, but more at herself than at him. *Heartbroken? A little. Embarrassed for feeling so much for you when you felt so little? Yes.* He was watching her expectantly, and she felt like she was either going to cry or scream.

She threw her arms up in the air and turned away, hoping he wouldn't see how much she hurt. "I thought we connected last night."

"We did," he said vehemently.

"Obviously not in the way I thought. It's fine." She took a step away, and he grabbed her arm.

"Whoa there, beautiful. Ryders don't run away, remember?" His eyes narrowed. "I obviously suck at this, which doesn't surprise me and shouldn't surprise you."

"I don't know what you mean. You blew me off just fine."

"No, I didn't. Or if I did, I didn't mean to."

He spoke so softly the knot in her stomach loosened.

"The last thing I want to do is blow you off. Last night you forced me to feel things that scare the hell out of me, both good and bad. I'm not trying to blow you off. I'm trying to say that I care. That I want you. I want *this*. I wish I could write us off as a mistake because that's the easy way out. I've been shutting myself off for years. It's what I know, what I do best. But you—" He drew her into his arms and cradled her face in his hands. "You force me to be a better person."

She brushed her fingers over his chest, buying herself a second to try to calm her racing heart. "But what about your list? I don't want to come between you and anyone you care about."

He smiled, then laughed softly. It was the kind of laugh that said, *Only you would push for more details,* and he was probably right.

"You're on the top of that list now, beautiful. Last night, for the first time ever, I felt like I was exactly where I should be. Where I wanted to be."

She swallowed past her mounting relief and burgeoning emotions. "Boone, that's exactly how I felt. How I feel."

"I need you to be sure about being with me, Trish. I've already opened up to you so much it feels like I'm hanging on the edge of a cliff, and this probably makes me look weak, but I really do believe you've got the power to shatter me into a million little pieces. You make me feel vulnerable, and as you've seen, I'm not an easy person to get close to."

She pressed her lips to his chest and breathed in his musky scent. "Then it's a good thing *I'm* easy, because two difficult people is a recipe for disaster."

BOONE WAS ASTOUNDED at how badly he'd screwed this up and how easily they were coming back from his mistake. Trish was there for him, saving him from himself *again*. He hated himself for causing her to worry, but at the same time, she was getting a good, honest dose of his weaknesses. And she was still there.

"I'm not kidding, beautiful." He brushed his thumb over her jaw, feeling the tension ease with his touch. "I think we crossed into new territory last night, at least for me. I don't know how to do this, and I'm worried that this misunderstanding is just the beginning."

"To do what exactly?" She smiled up at him, but it didn't quite erase the lingering concern in her eyes.

"To be in a relationship, and I want that with you. But I'm going to screw up."

"I want that with you, too." Her brows knitted, and she pressed her lips together for a few seconds, as if she were working out a puzzle. "But screw up how? I won't forgive you being with another woman, so if that's what you mean, you've got the wrong girl."

He let out a long, frustrated breath. "Before you, I hadn't even kissed a woman for months. I am not going to suddenly start sleeping around. That's not what I mean, and it's not who I am."

"Then tell me what you mean, please, and end this torture, because it really hurt to wake up to an empty bed and then to feel like I had misread everything. I know that's my fault, but let's get past it."

"I'm sorry. I didn't want to wake you when I

answered the call." He couldn't help smiling at her vehemence. "I do like how feisty you are."

"Boone." She laughed.

"Sorry, but I do. All I meant was that I probably won't always say the right thing. And if last night was any indication, then if a guy hits on you, I might turn into a jealous asshole."

"That's it?" She pressed her hands to his chest.

He shrugged. "Probably not, but I've never had a real girlfriend, so who knows what other things you'll uncover."

"Never? As in, not ever?" She looked skeptical.

He shook his head.

"Then what was that line about hoping one day to meet someone like me and not wanting a string of senseless mistakes hanging around your neck?"

"You don't miss a thing, do you?" He sat down and pulled her onto his lap. "That was the truth. My parents got married when they were seventeen, and when we were growing up, we had nothing. We lived in this little rented house in a bad neighborhood, where you could hear the neighbors arguing all night and police sirens going off at all hours. We didn't have bikes or video games or *things*, but we had love. My parents were there for us, and they were there for each other. My father loved my mother so deeply, you could see it in his eyes. And my mother? She refuses to move from that crappy little house because her memories, her life with my father, are there."

"Oh, Boone. You and your family must miss him so much."

"We do. I do, every damn day. My parents showed us what mattered in life. It wasn't the things we had; it was the sense of family. They taught us how to love and showed us what caring about another person looks like." He brushed her hair from her shoulder and curled his hand around the nape of her neck. "You should know that I was the guy who slept around the first year I was in the business. I was careful, never had unprotected sex, never did drugs, but I had my fair share of hookups in that year."

She traced one of his tattoos along his arm. "Maybe we don't need to share *all* the details."

"I want you to know. I think I had to go through that to realize it's not what I wanted. About that same time, I figured out why so many people were throwing themselves at me. I had made it, and they wanted a piece of what I had."

"Oh, trust me. Any woman who was with you wanted you, too."

"Maybe, maybe not. All I know is I didn't feel anything for any of them. And one weekend I went home to visit my mother, and I knew I was done with that lifestyle." He gazed into her eyes and saw a million questions lying in wait. "Why don't we eat and you can ask me whatever you want to know."

"You made enough food for an army." She looked at the table, then back at him. "But I really do have to be careful about what I eat. You can eat if you haven't yet."

"Oh, I plan on eating, but what I want isn't on the table." He picked up a strawberry and ran it over her

145

lips, then followed it with his tongue. "I worry about you not eating. Take a bite. For me."

She opened her mouth, and he dragged the tip of the strawberry over her tongue. She moaned as she bit into the juicy fruit.

"Sweet *and* sexy. The perfect woman."

He lowered his mouth to hers. Cool sweetness burst over their tongues, and they deepened the kiss. Her fingers trailed down his bare chest, and he snatched them up and kissed the tips of them.

"I love your mouth," she whispered.

They shared a series of slow, shivery kisses, and she arched her neck. He nibbled and sucked all the way up her neck to her ear and trapped her lobe between his teeth. She squirmed and shifted, straddling him, and took the kiss deeper. He ached to be inside her. He grabbed her hips, grinding his shaft against her.

"I thought we were done," she said in a heated breath.

"Never." He couldn't think, could only feel as she pushed her hands into his hair and sealed her mouth over his neck. Her mouth was so hot, so wet, every stroke of her tongue fed the inferno burning inside him. And when she cranked up the heat and sucked, he felt it between his legs.

He tugged on her shorts. "These have to go."

Lifting her off his lap, he tore open the button, and she wiggled out of them, her eyes trained on him.

"Beautiful girl, I could watch you strip all day long."

He guided her so she stood between his legs and lifted her shirt above her breasts. "You're gorgeous." He took one nipple in his mouth, squeezing the other between his finger and thumb.

"Ohmygod. Boone that feels too good."

He sucked harder, loving the whimpering sounds she made and the way she clawed at his head, holding his mouth to her breast. She tasted like morning dew in the land of temptation, and he wanted to stake a tent and stay there forever. She made an appreciative sound in the back of her throat, which vibrated through her. He rose to his feet and crashed his mouth over hers.

"Need more of you," he said, unzipping his pants as they ate at each other's mouths. He tore her shirt over her head and tossed it to the floor, lifted her in his arms, and her legs wound around his hips. Like magnet to metal, his fingers sought the damp heat between her legs.

She grabbed his head and kissed him like she'd been waiting her whole life to do it. His mind spun and his heart swelled. When he looked into her eyes, he knew he was driven by something bigger than lust, more powerful than the promise of sex.

"Condom," she said in a rush.

Holding her with one arm, he reached for the box of condoms beside the fridge, and her smile turned sinful.

She grabbed the box from him and tore it open. "The condom fairies came while we were sleeping?"

He laughed and took her in another kiss. "Another

reason I was up at five."

She waved a condom with a tease in her eyes and dropped the box on the counter. "I think you're *very* good at this boyfriend thing."

With one arm he swept the kitchen table clean. Dishes crashed to the floor, sending the poor kitten scampering into the living room. As Boone lowered Trish to the table, she visually feasted on every inch of him. Heat seared through him with every sweep of her eyes. He fisted his cock and gave it a few tight strokes.

"Oh," she whispered. "I like seeing you do that."

He made a mental note of that secret pleasure, splayed his hands over her thighs, and pushed her legs apart. "I seem to remember you like this, too."

He lowered his mouth to her, and she squirmed and moaned, filling the kitchen with a stream of sexy sounds. Her arousal coated his mouth, his tongue, his lips. When he slid his fingers into her tight heat and teased her most sensitive nerves with his mouth, she cried out his name, and he fucking loved it. When the last of her orgasm pulsed through her, he slicked his tongue between her wet lips and then rose up and claimed her in another demanding kiss.

"Got to have you." He grabbed the condom and tore it open with his teeth.

She took it from his hands and held it over her head. Heat flared in her eyes. "Not yet. Let me see you touch yourself again."

Holy hell. This woman was a naughty, sweet dream come true. "I see your bossiness isn't limited to outside the bedroom." She blushed, and he guided her hand between her legs. "Fair's fair."

"But..."

He held his hand in front of her mouth and said, "Lick." She dragged her tongue up his palm, sending white-hot sparks shooting through him. He fisted his shaft and stepped closer, bringing their mouths a whisper apart. "You wanna play?"

Her eyes narrowed with challenge. He lifted her hand to his mouth and swirled his tongue around her fingers. Her eyes fluttered closed. When he guided her hand between her legs, she opened her eyes. He stroked his shaft with one hand and used his other to guide hers, then slid his fingers into her slick heat.

"Tease your clit," he commanded. "That's it, baby."

Her eyes were locked on his hand as he worked his shaft and he stroked the magic spot inside her that made her eyes slam shut.

"Eyes open," he said, fighting the urge to drive into her.

She obeyed, and it became a test of wills as her climax gripped her. Her sex swelled and pulsed around his fingers as she came in a wild symphony of pleas. Watching her come was like seeing the most impassioned songs come to life, taking him up, up, up to a place where only they existed. He squeezed the base of his shaft, willing himself not to come. He sheathed his throbbing erection and moved her to the edge of the table. She moved her fingers from between her legs, and he guided them back, holding them there.

"For me." He gripped her hips and drove into her. Hot spikes of pleasure shot through him.

"Ohmy*god*." She clung to his arm with one hand, working herself with the other. Her head tipped back as he pounded into her tight heat, and her hand stilled as a stream of pleas sailed from her lungs.

"Harder. So good. Oh God, more."

He kissed the corners of her mouth, soft and tender as he took her rough and wild.

"Harder. Kiss me harder," she begged.

He crushed her to him, greedily feasting on her mouth. He felt her entire body flex, and he quickened his pace, wanting to come *with* her. Heat seared down his spine, and just as she gave in to her own release, she sank her teeth into his shoulder, and the world exploded in a fiery storm of white-hot sensations.

Chapter Twelve

IT TURNED OUT that sending dishes and food into the air took a lot longer to clean up than it did to actually have sex. Trish and Boone spent two hours getting food out from under cabinets, off walls, countertops, and even the ledge of drawer panels. They made good use of the time, kissing and teasing and getting to know more about each other. Trish told Boone about her love for geology and how she'd gone to college to appease her parents so she'd have an education to fall back on in case acting didn't work out. She'd seen a flicker of something in his eyes, and when he pointed out that they came from completely different worlds, she didn't try to deny it. He seemed to appreciate that she didn't say otherwise, and she appreciated that he didn't have a chip on his shoulder because of it. He asked about her friends, and she told him all about Fiona and how they'd been roommates in college and had remained as close as sisters. She'd even admitted to calling Fiona and complaining about him, which he got a kick out of and swore to remedy by making her *very, very happy.*

By the time they'd tracked down the kitten— snuggled on Boone's pillow—showered, and finally ate real food, it was after noon. A few clouds lingered in the sky, but it was a nice, breezy day. The grass and trees seemed brighter and livelier in the wake of the storm. Trish was surprised to see that Boone had hung their clothes from last night over the porch railing to dry.

Trish watched him pacing the yard as he talked on the phone. They'd been rehearsing for a few hours, and the change in Boone was like night and day. He was far more relaxed, although they hadn't attempted the pivotal warehouse scene yet. Knowing the depth of painful emotions it stirred in him, she was nervous about bringing it up, but she knew she had to. If they didn't get every scene right, the movie could be canceled, and that wouldn't be good for either of them.

Boone ran a hand through his hair and smiled as he headed toward the porch in a pair of low-slung jeans. The sun shone brightly behind him, outlining his broad shoulders and slim waist. His colorful tattoos snaked out from beneath his shirtsleeves. He hadn't shaved, and his scruff came in patchy and rough, adding to his badass image. But even with all that delicious eye candy, Trish no longer saw only the hard-ass rocker. She saw the man who had held her in his arms, opened his heart, and had a world of turmoil riding just beneath the surface. She really, really liked the man she was getting to know, faults and all. He was more real, more honest than any man she'd ever dated.

"Sorry." He sat down beside her on the porch step and leaned his elbows on his thighs. "That was my brother Cage. He just wanted to touch base and tell me about his next fight."

"Cage? Is that his real name?"

Boone smiled. "No. He's a fighter. That's his stage name, but he's pretty much become Cage to everyone. His real name is Carl, and if you're wondering about my name, it's always been Boone. We call our youngest brother, Lucas, *Lucky*. He's eighteen and has the best luck of anyone I've ever known. When he was a kid, he'd lose his homework and someone would find it and turn it in. He's *that* kind of lucky. Always just barely on the right side of the law. I'm forever trying to get him to straighten up. He's wicked smart, but he's *eighteen*." He shrugged like he totally got his teenage brother, and the love in his expression was palpable.

"We also have a sister, Maggie. She's older than Lucky, younger than Cage. She's a caterer, and my mom works with her part-time. And since I know you always want more, I'll give up my last name so you don't have to ask." He smiled and she laughed. "Our last name is Rekyrts. Turn it around and you get Stryker."

"That's clever."

"Yeah, we got some of my brother's luck with that one."

"Do you mind if I ask how you got your start? The

articles I've read said you were discovered on YouTube, but the only videos I can find of you performing are after Harvey Bauer started repping you."

He turned and leaned his back against the railing, like he was settling in for a long story. "You can ask me anything."

He reached for her hand, and she realized how calm he seemed. He'd been vibrating with tension since the day they'd met, and now he seemed much more content.

"My mom worked as a janitor at the Epson School of the Arts, and when we were little she didn't want to leave us, so she took us with her. We spent hours in that old brick building. I can still remember her wearing one of those baby carriers with Lucky on her chest while she cleaned."

"How did she get anything done with four kids running around?"

His lips quirked up. "When we got to be too much, she'd say, 'Maybe I should leave you guys with Mrs. Carther.' Mrs. Carther was about eighty years old with whiskers coming out of her chin and a big hump on her back. Poor thing. She wasn't actually all that bad, but she got a bad rap because she'd come out on her porch and wave a broom around, yelling at the kids who trampled through her yard. That threat was enough for us to fall back into line."

"I think I like your mother already."

"You can't help but like her. She's amazing. She's smart and funny, and Lord knows how she put up with us and remained sane, but she's supported our endeavors and given us hell when we needed it. She never finished high school, because she had me, but she's never held that over my head."

"She's your mother. She shouldn't hold it over your head."

He lifted her hand to his lips and kissed it, nodding in agreement. "When you've seen the things I have, you realize that what should or shouldn't happen doesn't always matter."

"I'm sorry about your dad, and about your friends and how hard they had it."

"Anyway," he said, clearly wanting to change the subject. "Cage, Mags, and I hung around the school so much, we got to know the teachers and students, and over the years they showed us a few things. I fell in love with the sounds of guitars: acoustic, electric, twelve-string, six-string, steel, bass. I loved them all. Still do. I had an ear for music, and I learned to listen to songs and emulate them without reading music. One day there was a guy sitting outside playing guitar and we started talking. His name was Charley Evers. He manages Bailey Bray's band now, but back then he was just this cool guy helping a kid discover music."

"I know Bailey. Her sister Leanna lives on Cape Cod. She's friends with my brother Blue."

"How can you raise questions about Cage's name when your brother's name is Blue?"

"Stop changing the subject," she teased. "Tell me more. We can talk about my brothers later."

He whispered, "Pushy," then leaned in for a quick

kiss. "Over the course of a few weeks he taught me to read music and play the guitar. He and his buddies made a video and put it up on YouTube. Lucky for me, they sucked at editing, and the first few minutes was them talking about the song they were going to play and me standing in the background playing a song I'd made up. I had no idea I was even on the video until Harvey Bauer sought me out."

"That's crazy. Your life really does mirror Rick Champion's."

He shook his head. "That part of my life might, getting discovered on YouTube, but the rest doesn't. Although Destiny was never my girlfriend, Rick's strung-out girlfriend gets clean at the end of the movie. He works hard to get *out* of the area he grew up and never looks back. I'm making the movie to show the struggle, but I've never wanted to get away from the place where I grew up."

"Because your mom is still there?" she asked.

"Partly. But it's more than that. I have difficult memories, but they're *my* memories. Who I am is the guy from the Bronx, not the rock star. Being a rock star is my job, like Cage is a fighter and Mags is a caterer and you're an actress. There's a lot of bad stuff that went on, as I've told you, but all the things that come with fame? The money, the parties, the *groupies*? They don't come close to the value of lifelong friends or the lessons I learned growing up in those conditions. If I lost all my fame tomorrow, I'd be okay. I had my run."

"You wouldn't miss it?"

"Sure. I'd miss the rush of being onstage, but the

other reason I took the role was to challenge myself. To see what else I could do. I've had a hell of a time coming up with songs lately." He leaned forward and slid his hand to the back of her neck. "I'm so glad I sucked at it."

"Mm." Feeling their bond strengthen with every word, she pressed her lips to his. "Know what I think?"

"That we should rehearse more kissing and fewer lines?"

"That and..." She kissed him again. "I think that while the physical worlds we come from may differ, the things that matter most—morals and values, family, friends—aren't so different after all."

**

LATER THAT EVENING, after several frustrating attempts at rehearsing the dreaded warehouse scene, they gave up and had dinner—salad for Trish, steak for Boone.

"Tell me what I can do to help you get through this." Trish sat on the porch petting the kitten, who was curled up in her lap. She'd been relentless in her pursuit of him taking one last stab at the scene for the day, and he'd reluctantly given in.

"If I knew, I'd tell you." He paced, feeling his chest constrict before they even began.

"Yesterday you said when you see me lying there, I become Destiny, and that's when you detach from the character."

He stopped pacing and crouched beside her. "I'm

sorry. I know this makes it harder, and I hope that wasn't a callous thing to say."

She smiled up at him. "Callous? Not at all. It was real, and real is good. Real is what we want."

"The things you make me feel are about as real as it gets." He petted the kitten. "I think I've come up with a name for him."

"I see the Great Deflector is back." Trish put her hand over his. "But he does need a name."

"Sparky."

"Sparky? It's cute." She smiled "Why Sparky?"

"Because every time you're near me, sparks fly. And we found him on the way here, the place where we've come together."

"I love that." She leaned forward and kissed him. "I think you have a bit of a romantic heart behind all those walls."

He took that compliment to heart. His father had been a true romantic, and to Boone, being like his father was the biggest compliment of all. "Maybe so, but only you could push your way in to find out."

"Lucky me!" Her tone softened. "If you're up to it, I have an idea that might work for the scene. It's something one of my acting coaches taught me, but it'll be hard, and if you'd rather not try it, I understand."

"Let me hear it. I want to get past this."

She picked up the kitten and set him inside the kitchen door. "I think it might help if we pretend I'm Destiny and try to work through the emotions you're feeling."

He shot to his feet and paced. His gut reaction was

to tell her absolutely not. No way. Just the thought of purposely going through that scene and imagining Destiny made him nauseous.

"I know it sounds crazy," Trish said empathetically. "But if you think about it, it makes sense to work through your real feelings to clear the way to acting."

They stood at opposite ends of the porch, like they were getting ready to duel, only they were on the same team. Compassion emanated from her so strongly, that as she closed the distance between them he could feel it wrapping around him like an embrace.

"I want to try it for *you*," he admitted. "But I honestly don't know if I'm capable of that."

She reached for his hand. "How about if you don't do it for me or even for the movie, but you do it for you? Because this movie will go on, or it won't. And I told you Ryders don't run from the hard things in life, so if you can't deal with it now, I'm still not going anywhere. I'll be here to help you, if you want my help, when you're ready."

He took her in his arms and touched his forehead to hers. "How did I get so lucky to suck at acting and be sent to this Podunk town with you?"

She went up on her toes and kissed him. He loved that for all his standoffishness, she was open with her affection. Every touch, every kiss, every tender gaze from her beautiful eyes made it easier for him to try to step outside his walls—and even easier to create a crack to let her in.

"I think it was all part of your evil plan to get into

my pants."

"Unfortunately, I'm not that manipulative." He realized he'd been so distracted with rehearsing and their new relationship, he still hadn't told her about Jude. Chasing the realization, his protective urges surged, only this time they were aimed at protecting Jude, not Trish. But as she suggested trying to work through the scene without her lying down, guilt began gnawing away at him. He had never been a good liar, and any way he looked at it, when it came to talking with someone he cared about, a lie of omission was still a lie.

"Trish," he interrupted. "I need to tell you something else that probably plays into my reluctance to deal with the scene, even if I don't want to believe it does."

With serious intent, she turned his hands over and inspected the crook of his arms.

"I'm not a user."

She grinned up at him, and he knew she was teasing. "I can handle anything else, so go ahead. Get it all out in the open."

They sat on the steps again.

"I feel like our whole relationship is unfolding on these rickety old steps."

She leaned in to his shoulder. "Funny. They don't feel rickety or old to me. They feel romantic and private."

He draped an arm over her shoulder. "That's because you have a unique way of seeing things." *Like the way you see all of me, not just what I want everyone else to see.*

"I was brought up not to judge anything by what it looks like. Houses, books, *people.*" She traced a tattoo down his forearm and turned her alluring eyes toward him. "Sometimes we have to look beyond the camouflage to get to the heart of things."

Boy, if that isn't the truth. He told her about Jude, how he'd already been in rehab twice and that they were trying to track him down to get him into rehab again.

"He was spotted in our old neighborhood. But no one's been able to find him since."

"I assume he's on that long list of people relying on you? The one you said I'm at the top of?"

He nodded. "Along with my family, bandmates, Harvey and his wife, and a handful of friends I grew up with. That day you got pissed when I showed up late to the set?"

"Yes."

"I was on the phone with Jude. I almost had him convinced to go, but right before we hung up, he backed out."

She laced their fingers together. "I'm not sure if I should yell at you or hug you."

"Why do I deserve either? I mean, I'll take the hug, but..."

"Boone, this is the second time that I know of that you took the heat to protect someone else, and you let everyone think you were unreliable. First when you missed the preproduction meeting and your mom was in the hospital, and then showing up late on set."

161

"So?"

Her expression softened. "And you take it all in stride."

"They're family," he said vehemently.

"I know. I get it. I meant it with awe, not exasperation."

He let out a breath he hadn't realized he was holding.

"You do have a lot of people counting on you," she said sweetly. "So for now, I want you to put me down a notch on that list of yours. At least below Jude."

When he opened his mouth to respond, she silenced him with a kiss.

"Don't even try to argue with me. Some people need more worry than others. We could go look for him if you want. Right now, we can drive to your old neighborhood, ask around."

His throat thickened with emotion at her generosity and understanding. "Trish." He framed her face with his hands and kissed her. "How many women would offer to drive for hours and spend the night searching the bad parts of town for a drug addict?"

She shrugged. "He's important to you."

"Baby," he whispered. "Do you have any idea how special you are?"

"I'm not special. I care about you, and when you care about someone, what they want or need or care about becomes important to you."

"Thank you. You can't imagine how much it means to me to hear you say that and that you're willing to put our work aside to help Jude, but I've got people looking for him. And I don't want to let you down either. At some point they'll track him down and I'll need to take off, but until then, let's try to work through this project."

"Okay, but just so you know, you're on *my* list now, too."

"What does that mean?" He couldn't suppress his smile. "I've never been on someone else's list before."

"It means that now you have someone looking after you, too." She squeezed his hand, and he wondered if she could see how deeply she'd touched him. "And don't fool yourself into thinking you're not on anyone else's list. I'd imagine all those people on your list have you on their lists, too. But you're the protector, so you're very low-maintenance."

"Low-maintenance? That's one thing I've never been called." He pulled her into his lap. "Now you know all my dirty secrets and you're still here. I guess that means I owe it to you to try to deal with the warehouse scene."

"You don't owe me anything, but I think you owe it to yourself."

Chapter Thirteen

TRISH WASN'T SURE if she was doing the right thing or not by pushing Boone to deal with what he felt when they tried to get through the warehouse scene, but she hoped this exercise might work. They stayed out on the porch even though the sun had set, because he was far more comfortable outside, and she wanted him to be as comfortable as possible. Especially since neither one of them knew what to expect. She lay down on the porch, listening to the sound of him pacing. He made it halfway across the porch to where she lay, then turned back several times.

Trish sat up and pulled her knees to her chest, watching him move like a caged lion. His shoulders rode just below his ears, his fingers flexed repeatedly, and his eyes were downcast and brooding.

"Hey," she said softly, and patted the space beside her.

The fact that he didn't step off the porch and head

to the field did not go unnoticed. He actually managed a smile as he sank down to the porch beside her.

"Why don't we just talk about it?" Trish suggested. "That might be better."

He nodded and reached for her hand. She wondered if he was going to be able to share anything at all, or if this was going to prove to be too difficult.

"What do you feel right now?"

"Feel?" He shook his head. "I don't know how to describe it. It's not anger, but I feel like a monster is clawing its way out of my chest."

"Okay." *That's not good.* Or maybe it was. "What if we coax him out?"

He arched a brow, like that was a crazy idea.

"I know it sounds like we're inviting trouble, but I think we're inviting trouble by not getting it out in the open."

"But how can I let out what I'm not sure of? I wasn't there when she overdosed, and it's not like it was my fault, or anyone else's. Except maybe her parents'." His eyes filled with anger.

"Maybe that's it," Trish said urgently. "Could it be that your feelings have more to do with her parents? Not to diminish the pain of losing your friend. I'm sure that's overwhelming. But something flashed in your eyes when you mentioned her parents."

"Because I'd like to beat the hell out of them." His free hand fisted.

"Did you ever talk with them? Confront them?"

He shook his head. "You don't confront deadbeat parents who lost their daughter."

"Good point. Sorry." They sat in silence for a few minutes, lost in their own thoughts. Trish wanted to get him talking about his feelings, because even the little bit she'd just learned seemed important. "I have a crazy idea."

"You mean *another* crazy idea." He bumped her shoulder.

"It's still part of the first idea. Pretend I'm her parents and just get it out there. Tell me what you want to say to them."

"I don't know."

"Why not? I'm an actress. I've been through the ringer with different roles. Just get it out and see how you feel." Her pulse quickened with the idea. "I think this might help. Look how much more relaxed you've been since you first told me about Destiny. You were able to nail the other lines perfectly. It's just the ones around the really heart-wrenching scene that you're having trouble with. Where you find her on the brink of death."

Boone drew in a deep breath. The muscles in his jaw jumped repeatedly. He released her hand and stared out into the darkness for so long she worried he was going to give up altogether.

He finally turned to face her, his dark eyes filled with warmth and torture. She hated asking him to delve into that torture, but knowing it was gnawing away at him from the inside out pained her.

"I can't look at you and say the things I want to say," he finally admitted.

"Pretend I'm not me."

"Not possible." He kissed her softly. "No one else comes close to the person you are."

She sighed. "You are *so* not the guy I thought you were."

"I'm going to take that as a good sign," he said. "When I said you became her when we rehearsed, what I meant wasn't that I actually saw her. I ached at the prospect of you *becoming* her, getting lost in drugs. I was too into you even back at the set in LA to separate the two."

"You were into me back then?" She waved her hand. "Wait. I can't get sidetracked, but I love knowing that. Luckily you won't have to worry about me and drugs. I can promise you that's something I've never done or will ever do. But now that I know about Jude and Destiny, your reluctance makes sense to me."

"Thanks for understanding. It's a helpless feeling. They say you can lead a horse to water and all that, and it's true. Jude has it all. He's got fame and money, friends and family, and he still can't resist doing drugs."

"But you know you can't control that, right? You can help him get into rehab and be there for him, but only he can actually make the change."

He nodded again. "Like I said. Helpless."

"But you *are* helping by being supportive, even if you feel helpless. I don't know what happened with Destiny, but you said you helped Jude get into rehab twice, and you've got people looking for him now."

"It's a cycle, Trish. A cycle that doesn't seem to have an end, and it's frustrating as hell." He pushed to his feet and paced again. "When I see you lying there, acting like you're drugged out, I want to scream. I want to beg you not to fall into that darkness. It's fucked up. I get that."

Trish rose, watching in silence as Boone fisted his hands and his face twisted in anger. *Thank God. You're feeling. You're getting it out.*

"And then my head races back to when I heard about Destiny, and I went to her parents' house ready to kill them. But you can't kill people for being fuckups. Cage and Jude and my other buddies dragged me away, which was good, because who knows what I might have said. I was a stupid kid."

"*You* do," she said softly. "You know what you might have said."

His nostrils flared, and he whipped around, staring into the field again. "She was their *daughter.* When you're a parent, your selfish needs have to go. All of them. You take on the responsibility of a child, and that child depends on you."

He leaned on the railing, and his head dropped between his shoulders. His fingers curled tightly around the aged wood, and Trish's heart ached for him. She wanted desperately to go to him, but she sensed that this was exactly what he needed. Even if he didn't realize it, he was probably letting out what he'd been holding in all these years.

"My parents were only seventeen when they had me. Even as kids they knew how to put us first. They knew how to love us and teach us to do the right things—even if Lucky skirts that line, he doesn't cross it. He knows. My mother and all of us taught him that much." He cocked his head, and his arm blocked all but his tormented eyes.

"The thing is, I know if I'd said anything to Destiny's parents, it wouldn't have mattered. How could it? They were users. They knew she was doing drugs and they didn't change or try to help her."

She went to him then, unable to stay away for a second longer, and wrapped one arm around his waist. "It sounds like they were helpless, too," she said softly. "They were addicts, and you know from dealing with Jude, who has much more than it sounds like they ever did, that addictions aren't tied to intelligence, age, or social status. Addictions are powerful, and once they take hold, it's a wonder anyone can break free from them. They were as helpless as you were, just in a different way. It doesn't mean they had an excuse. It just means that maybe they weren't equipped to do anything differently."

She ducked beneath his arms and slid between him and the railing so she could put her arms around him. "I don't have all the answers, and I'm saying *maybe* a lot, but have you considered forgiving her parents? It's really hard to carry around all that anger. You said you feel like a monster is trying to claw its way out of you, and I think you're probably right. But you're chasing the wrong demon."

Chapter Fourteen

"I THINK WE deserve a break." Boone shifted the groceries they'd just bought and unlocked the passenger door for Trish. It had been three days since they'd talked about Destiny and her parents and what they had come to call *the scene*. Although Boone didn't think he had the scene down pat yet, he had come a long way. Their talk had given him perspective, and that allowed him enough distance to approach the scene differently.

"Isn't that what we're doing?" Trish climbed into the car while Boone put the groceries in the backseat.

"Getting groceries is not a break. It's a necessity, despite how little you're eating." He sat in the driver's seat and leaned across the console to kiss her. She grabbed his shirt, and heat spread through him like wildfire with the possessive move. He loved the way they were so in sync. Whether they were in the bedroom, rehearsing, or taking a walk around the yard, they'd begun to sense each other's moods.

"You *have* done an incredible job of pouring your emotions into the scene lately." She touched her cheek to his and whispered, "Didn't we take a sex break this morning?"

"And last night." He nibbled on her neck, and she tipped her head back with a sweet sound of appreciation.

"God, what are you doing to me? You've turned me into a binge nymph." She laughed. "It's like a binge eater, but the only cure is more Boone Stryker."

"I like the sound of that." He kissed her just below her ear and inhaled her sweet feminine scent. "You smell good enough to eat. Maybe we should go find a back road to park on and make out like a couple of teenagers."

She nipped at his earlobe. "Oh, you are a naughty boy."

"Only with you, beautiful." He kissed her again. "Or we can go to the country music festival at the creek and make out later. Or make out while we're there." He waggled his brows, pulled a flyer from his back pocket, and handed it to Trish. "There was a stack of flyers by the register."

She scanned the flyer. "Sounds like fun. The festival, *and* the making out part. Oh! I have a great idea!"

"Last time you had a great idea you tricked me into telling you things I didn't realize I felt." He tugged her in for another kiss. "God, I love your kisses." Pushing his hands into her hair, he took the kiss deeper.

"Forget my idea," she murmured. "This is better."

She clung to his neck and rose off the seat, arching her whole body into his. It took all of his restraint not to climb over the seat and take her right there. She moaned, loud and needy, into the kiss.

"You're killing me," he growled against her lips.

She tugged him harder, pulling him halfway out of his seat. "Don't stop kissing me. We don't need to go further, but *kiss* me," she said breathlessly.

He glanced out the window, glad they'd parked at the far end of the lot. He reached across her lap to hit the recline button. They kissed as he climbed over the console. His knee hit the door and his foot got stuck between the dash and the console, causing Trish to burst into giggles.

"We should have rented a mobile home," she teased as he came down over her.

They managed to push the seat back, giving him more leg room. She scooted up, and they both groaned when their bodies aligned perfectly. They kissed and ground their bodies together until he was out of his mind with desire. He pushed a hand beneath her shirt and teased her nipple through her lacy bra.

"Oh God, I love that." She arched into his hand. "Use your mouth."

"You are sinful."

He peeked out the car window, noting that they were still alone on their side of the parking lot, and lifted her shirt. He pulled the lace down and sealed his mouth over her breast. She wiggled and squirmed, and he sucked harder.

"Oh, oh, *oh!*"

Hearing her so lost in him she couldn't form words spurred him on. He ground his hips harder, reveling in the mind-numbing friction, and stilled when she began her own momentum, allowing her to ride him through their clothes. The car filled with her needy moans and whimpers.

"That's it, baby. Come for me. Come good and hard."

She grabbed his ass and held him firmly where she needed him most, and he continued devouring her mouth and breast. Seeing her on edge, hearing her heady gasps, feeling her trembling *for him*, sent desire thrumming through him, pounding beneath his zipper, aching in his chest. When she cried out, bucking and shaking, he took her in another desperate kiss. They kissed until she was sighing with pleasure.

He smiled down at her. "You're amazing, beautiful girl." A rosy blush bloomed on her cheeks. "Hey, I mean it. You're smart and sexy and I adore you."

"I can't believe I just did that in the parking lot," she whispered, but her smile told him how much she enjoyed it.

"Are you kidding? That was so hot, *I* nearly came."

She rolled her eyes. "*Nearly* is not the same."

"Is that an offer? Because I'd happily bury myself deep inside you and make you come again before finding sweet redemption in my own release."

Her mouth gaped.

"Too much, huh? Sorry." He rose onto his palms,

and she snagged him by the collar. A spark of wickedness flared in her eyes.

"Do you have a condom?"

"I like where this is headed." He patted his wallet. "It just so happens I loaded up for my very feisty girlfriend." He peeked out the window.

"Is there anyone out there?"

"Not a person in sight."

She tugged him into a wet and wild kiss. They didn't even try to restrain themselves as they tore at each other's pants and wrestled them down to their ankles. In seconds he sheathed his eager length and buried himself to the root. Her inner muscles squeezed and he groaned.

"Do that," he commanded. "*A lot.*"

Their bodies and mouths crashed together. Sounds of flesh smacking, groans, and pleas—*Harder. More. So good. There!*—echoed off the windows. Sweat beaded their skin; raw passion burned through their tangled limbs. Trish bit into his shoulder, sending exquisite pain down his chest, and rivers of passion flooded his veins. He gripped her ass and lifted, taking her deeper, harder.

"Gonna come," she cried. "Oh God!"

He buried his head in her neck, groaning out her name as he surrendered to his own heart-pounding release.

He pushed up on his palms and gazed at the sensual, loving woman beneath him, unable to believe they'd found their way into each other's arms.

**

THEY STOPPED AT the farmhouse to put away the groceries and shower and then loved up Sparky. Boone left another message for Jude. He called his brother Lucky and asked him to see if he could find out where Jude was hiding out. Trish asked again if he wanted to go look for Jude, but Boone explained that it would be like looking for a needle in a haystack.

They followed the directions on the flyer to the creek where the music festival was taking place and parked in a small lot up the hill. They followed the sounds of music through the woods down to the water. The scent of damp earth and carefree summer days filled the air as they neared the creek. People gathered along the rocky edge of the creek, drinking beer from kegs and carrying red plastic cups. Two bands were set up at either end of a small clearing, taking turns playing covers and songs Trish hadn't heard before.

Thankfully, no one recognized them, and they were able to enjoy the afternoon. They danced and mingled and eyed each other flirtatiously from across the grass.

Trish noticed two busty girls wearing cutoff jeans shorts and cowgirl boots eyeing Boone. A wave of jealousy swam through her. If Fiona were there, she'd tease her about being jealous, because Trish was a gorgeous actress, but it didn't matter whether the women eyeing Boone were hotter than her or not. Girlfriend claws had a mind of their own, and though she'd never really liked anyone enough to feel jealous, her claws were out in full force over Boone. She was tempted to march over and claim him with a blatant PDA, which she knew he'd love. She'd noticed the way his eyes darkened when she asserted herself sexually, or to snuggle, or even hold his hand.

One of the pretty gawkers flipped her hair over her shoulder and blinked flirtatiously at Boone. Boone flashed a practiced, kind smile. A vastly different smile from the predatory, sensual smile that landed on Trish one second later. Her heart went a little crazy as he stalked toward her with long, purposeful strides. His eyes sent the clear message, *They can look, but you get to touch.* Every step made her ache to be in his arms. A shiver of warmth whispered down her spine.

"Hey there, beautiful," he said with a noticeable country twang, and slid an arm around her waist. "Come here often?"

"I haven't *come* here yet," she teased. "But I had a good time in a parking lot around the corner."

He pressed a kiss beside her ear and whispered, "You are a dirty, dirty girl."

She was impressed by his ability to dive into cowboy mode so seamlessly, which gave her another idea. Ever since their talk, Boone had been doing a much better job of getting into his character while they rehearsed his most difficult scenes. She had every confidence in his abilities, but she could tell he wasn't quite as convinced. She eyed him curiously, thinking about how they could take his acting to the next level and get him to own it.

"Your dirty, dirty girl has an idea." She grinned up at him, knowing he would hate the idea of rehearsing in front of an audience, but what better way to hone his craft than to dive in and sink or swim?

"If it's the kind of idea you had in the car, I'm all in." His gorgeous eyes sparked with heat.

She looked around, debating her idea. She could ask him about doing a few lines in character, but she knew he'd nix it, mostly because it would require her to look like a druggie. Her heartbeat sped up as she mulled over the idea of slipping to the ground in character and forcing him to step up to the plate.

He leaned closer. "What's that look in your eyes?"

I'm getting up the courage to suddenly become a drugged-out Delia. She smiled innocently. "What look?" Before he could answer, she said, "I'm sorry, but I'm Delia." She fell gracefully to the ground, feeling an icy chill coming from Boone.

"Christ, Trish," he said under his breath as she stared blankly toward the sky. He crouched beside her. "What am I supposed to do now?" he said in a hushed, annoyed tone, with a hint of embarrassment.

Staying in character, she didn't look at him. She waited with her heart in her throat, silently urging him on. He took her hand; his was shaking a little.

"How could you do this?" He cursed under his breath. "After everything we've been through, how far we've come?"

She wanted to cheer him on for nailing the emotions, but he was doing so well, she wanted to keep the ruse going. She lay limply as he scooped her into his arms. Her head lolled back, but not before she caught a glimpse of the tortured look on his face. Her chest swelled, and her heart ached at the depth of emotions she saw there. She was sure part of that torture was the mere fact that he'd been thrown into this without any warning, but it was working. People began to take notice, closing in on them as he gathered her closer, pressing her limp body against his chest.

"Goddamn it, baby. Don't you die on me. Don't you die!" He spoke through gritted teeth, every vehement word hitting her square in the center of her chest.

"Hey, dude. Should I call 911?" a guy asked.

She had a flash of panic about headlines—ACTRESS TRISH RYDER FAINTS AT CREEK PARTY—but she wasn't about to back out now. Not when he was doing such an amazing acting job.

Boone's hand went to the back of Trish's head. He pressed her face to his shoulder. "No. I've got her, thanks."

"Is she okay?" a woman asked. "Did she pass out?"

"She's...uh...yeah," he lied. "She passed out, but I've got her." He hurried up the hill. "Damn it, Delia, don't you fucking die." He spoke low enough for each word to hit Trish with the impact of thunder, but quiet enough for only her ears. "Don't you fucking die on me." His voice cracked with emotion as he picked up his pace, running toward the car.

Trish heard rapid footsteps following them. "Hey! Is she drunk? Sick?" a woman called after them. "I'm a nurse. Maybe I can help."

"Christ," he muttered.

Trish wrapped an arm around his neck, catching the dark frustration in Boone's gaze, and a second later, a frisson of amusement.

"I'm okay," Trish said in a woozy voice. "I haven't eaten since early this morning. Silly me." She batted her eyelashes at the worried stranger and ran a hand through Boone's hair. "My honey has been telling me all day to eat something, but you know, we're recently married, and I lose track of just about everything but him." She leaned up and kissed Boone's cheek.

"Are you sure, sweetie?" the woman asked.

"Oh yes, thank you. Plus"—she lowered her voice to a whisper—"I'm pregnant. We just found out this morning, which is why I was too excited to eat."

Boone's eyes sprang open wider.

"Right, honey?" Trish said in her sweetest voice.

"Sure," he mumbled, then louder. "Yes. Just found out. I'll get her right home. Thank you, but she's in good hands now." He turned away from the woman and moved quickly toward the car. "Pregnant?" he whispered.

"Okay, then, good luck!" The woman hurried toward the creek waving her hands. "She's pregnant!"

Trish burst into hysterics. "Don't kill me."

"Oh, I'm going to kill you, all right. Pregnant?" He set her on the hood of the car and kissed her hard. "Pregnant?"

Laughter burst from her mouth. "At least I said we were married instead of saying you were my brother or something."

"Brother?" He laughed. "You're insane, and pushy,

and you put me in a really difficult position. I should hate you, but..." His eyes heated. "Do you have any idea how much I like you?"

She scooted forward on the hood and locked her legs around his waist. "About nine inches worth."

"Hey! Ten, easy." He slid his hands into her hair, taking her in a long, languid kiss that went on forever and left them both breathless.

"Mm. You deserve an award."

"For the kiss?"

"For nailing that scene like a pro." She tugged him in close again. "Now kiss me again, you fake impregnator."

As their lips came together, Boone's phone rang. He pulled it from his pocket and his face blanched. "It's Jude."

Chapter Fifteen

BOONE STUFFED HIS clothes into a suitcase after calling Harvey and Honor to let them know he'd heard from Jude and he was on his way to their old neighborhood to meet up with him. He'd also called his mother. She had been a safe haven for his friends in their darkest hours, and if he knew Jude, now that he said he was ready to get help, he would probably end up at his mother's house before the night was over.

He zipped his bag, thinking about Destiny. If only she had turned to his mother all those years ago. But her distrust of adults had run deeper than her desire to get clean.

"I'm ready."

Boone spun around. Trish stood in the doorway holding her suitcase and carrying a big bag over her shoulder. His stomach knotted up. "For...?"

"To go with you, of course." She smiled brightly.

He'd been so wrapped up in the relief and worry that Jude's call had brought, he hadn't thought about Trish wanting to come along. He set his suitcase by the door and tugged her in close. "I'm sorry, beautiful, but you can't come with me."

"Can't, or you don't want me to?" Her eyes narrowed, and he had no doubt she already knew the answer.

"It's not that I don't want you with me," he explained. "This isn't going to be fun. Jude's high as a kite, holed up in some abandoned house with God knows who else. I don't know if he'll still be there when I get there, or who he'll be with. I don't want you around that."

"I had a feeling you might say that. But you didn't take into account that I don't want *you* going into that situation alone." She went up on her toes and pressed a firm kiss to his lips. "There's nothing I can't handle, and at the end of the day, after you do whatever you need to do with Jude, I want to be there for *you*. You're on my list, remember?"

How could he forget? It meant the world to him, and he wanted to stay on that list for as long as she'd let him. "This is different."

"No, it's not," she said adamantly. "Siamese twins, remember? Where you go, I go, and vice versa. We don't have long to get through the rest of the scenes so we can whip through filming when the crew gets here."

The movie. Was that what all of this was about? Was she playing up to him because of the damn movie? Had she been all along? His mind took that idea and ran with it, because why else would a movie star like Trish want to go rescue a junkie in the dregs of New York? Hell, why would she want to be locked away in a farmhouse for ten days? *I'm such an idiot.*

He picked up his suitcase and headed down the stairs with Trish on his heels.

"Coming with me is *not* going to get you an Oscar."

She dropped her suitcase at the bottom of the stairs with a *thunk*. "That was low, and cruel." The torment in her voice was nothing compared to the anguish in her eyes. "Running away isn't going to make your feelings for me go away."

Damn it. He was an idiot, all right. He dropped his suitcase and gathered her in his arms, astonished by her vehemence and his stupidity to even contemplate that her feelings had been an act. She tried to push away, but he held her tighter.

"I'm so sorry, baby. I wasn't thinking. Or I was overthinking. My head is totally messed up right now. My insides are going a million miles an hour because I want to get to Jude before he does something stupid or takes off again." He gazed into her eyes, and pain pierced his heart. "Remember when I told you I'd screw up?"

She cracked a small smile, though hurt lingered in her eyes. "You're a jerk, you know that? How can you think I'm worried about an Oscar after how close we've gotten?"

"Because I *am* an idiot." He pressed a kiss to her forehead and heard a *meow*. Sparky's head popped out of the bag hanging over her shoulder. "You packed Sparky?"

"Unlike you, I don't leave behind anyone I care about."

He hugged her and breathed deeply. "I care very much about you, and about him. I just don't want you around that nightmare."

"Trust me, Boone. What you don't want is to tell me what I can and can't do. I'm not very likable when I'm mad."

He took her hand in his. "I have a feeling nothing could make you unlikable. Are you sure you want to do this? I'm driving to New York, and if I can convince Jude to go to rehab, Harvey's going to take him. I'm too high profile, and Jude doesn't need that. But it could be a grueling night of searching and arguments and who knows what else."

She went up on her toes and kissed him. "That's why I wore my jeans and sneakers. So I can run and look tough and have your back."

He wasn't about to tell her that a beautiful waif like her, no matter how tough, would offer no protection where they were going. Or that if he had his way, he'd drop her off at his mother's house to keep her safe once they got there. As she looked at him with the confidence of a person three times her size and strength, he knew he was wrong. She offered him protection against himself—and his ability to push people away.

This was not going to be an easy trip, but having her with him would make it bearable. He just needed to figure out how to keep her safe.

Several hours later they drove down the dark, deserted streets where he'd grown up. Boone was used to the immediate and intense feelings of caution and unease that crept over his skin and hardened like armor whenever he visited his old stomping grounds. But tonight the feeling was even more profound, because tonight he had Trish to look after. She looked out the window at the old apartment buildings, each one in worse shape than the next, and pulled her shoulders in tight, covering Sparky protectively with her hands as he slept in her lap. Missing windows gaped like black eyes on weathered and worn brick faces. Graffiti defaced the desolate buildings. Battered and rancid furniture sat on cracked and dirty sidewalks. A group of thuglike teenagers huddled on a porch step.

"This is where you grew up?" Trish asked, without a hint of judgment.

"Nearby," he said. His phone rang, and his mother's image flashed on the screen. He answered it, watching Trish take in the streets he was sure were vastly different from where she'd grown up.

"Hi, sweetheart," his mother said. "Jude is here."

Worry and relief fought for dominance. "Are you okay? Is he okay?" He turned to Trish, said, "Hold on tight," and made a quick U-turn, speeding toward his mother's house.

"He's okay," his mother said. "Exhausted. He's lying down in Lucky's room. The poor boy, he needs help."

"Mom, where's Lucky? Are you okay? I should be there in less than ten minutes." He didn't like his mother alone with anyone who was on drugs, and even though he trusted Jude, he'd feel better if Lucky were there, too.

"Oh, sweetheart, you know Jude would never hurt me. I'm fine." She sighed. "And Lucky? I don't know. Work? Out with friends? You know, he's at that age."

Yeah, the self-centered, unreliable age Boone couldn't wait for him to outgrow. "Okay, let Jude be, Mom, just in case. I'll be there as fast as I can. Can you call Harvey and Honor and let them know he's with you and that I'll call them after I talk to Jude?"

"Of course."

"Thanks. Love you."

After he ended the call, he met Trish's curious gaze. "Jude's at my mom's house."

"That's good, right? At least he's safe."

He reached for her hand. "Yes, it's good. He trusts my mom, and this means he really does want help. Thank you for not tossing me to the curb for being inconsiderate earlier. I'm glad you're here with me."

"You're not annoyed that I was pushy?"

"No, beautiful. I'm annoyed with myself for thinking I had to keep you out of this part of my life."

**

IF TRISH THOUGHT she was nervous riding down the scary-looking streets a few minutes ago, she'd been sorely mistaken. The idea of meeting Boone's mother had spiders crawling along her nerves.

"Are you sure Sparky will be okay in the car? I can wait out here with him," she suggested as they rushed up the front steps of his mother's split-foyer home. He looked as nervous as she did, but she knew that was because he was worried about Jude.

"He'll be fine until we get Jude settled. Then we'll bring him in." He pushed open the door and flew inside. "Mom?"

Trish took in her cozy surroundings. Hardwood floors led from the foyer to the tidy living room. Red couches created a nook by a television set and two bookcases. A wooden rocking chair sat by one of two smallish windows. Colorful throw pillows complemented pretty floral curtains. There were pictures on every surface and hanging at different heights on the walls. Pictures of Boone and, she assumed, his brothers and sister, as well as pictures of a young couple who could only be Boone's parents. It was startling how much Boone looked like his father, with the same deep-set, emotive eyes, chiseled chin, and tall, broad frame.

"Shh. Jude's resting." A tall, slender woman hurried down the hall. Her bright brown eyes swept over Boone's face, and she threw her arms around his neck. "Sweetheart. I'm glad you're here."

"How is he?" Boone peered down the hall.

"He's a mess, but he wants to get help." His mother touched his cheek. "You look so much like your father with that scruffy face." She turned at the same time Boone reached for Trish's hand. His mother's brows knitted, and her eyes fell to their joined hands, turning her confusion to an eager smile.

"Trish, this is my mom, Raine Rekyrts. Mom, this is Trish Ryder, my girlfriend."

"It's nice to meet you," Trish said.

Raine covered her mouth, hiding her pretty smile, and whispered, "Girlfriend?" She glanced at Boone with delight and disbelief in her eyes and opened her arms to embrace Trish. "Forgive me for acting surprised. He's been rattling on and on about how talented you are since the day you started filming together and how excited he was to work with you, but I had no idea you two were dating."

Trish soaked in the unexpected compliment.

"I should have told you, but life's been crazy lately." Boone kissed Trish's cheek and pointed down the hall. "Will you two be okay if I go see Jude?"

"Of course. Go." Raine took Trish's arm as Boone disappeared down the hall. "The kitchen is this way. Chocolate, tea, and gossip are on tap. Okay?"

Trish laughed, instantly liking his mother's warm and open personality. "Sounds perfect to me. Do you think Jude's okay?"

"He is now that Boone's here." Raine set a teakettle on the stove. "Boone will know what to do."

He always seemed to know what to do when it came to everyone else. He was everyone else's anchor, and Trish was glad she was there to be his.

Candid family photos hung on the kitchen walls in bold, colorful frames. White cabinets lined two walls, and an old-fashioned wood-burning stove sat in the corner, beside which was a comfy-looking oversized chair for two and an ottoman.

"My reading nook," Raine said as she opened the refrigerator and took out a tray of delicious-looking chocolate truffles. "Boone put the stove in for me last winter, and Cage and Mags gave me the reading chair." She set the chocolates on a plate and put it in the middle of the round kitchen table. "See the scratch in the floor? That's how you know Lucky tried to help." She laughed, and even her laughter spoke of the love she had for her children. "He's so smart with computers and numbers, but I think Boone and Cage got all the talent in the working with their hands department."

"Every family has a Lucky. In my family it would probably be my brother Jake. He loves the outdoors, and when he was younger he'd bring home snakes, frogs, lizards." Trish rolled her eyes and sat at the table. "But he hates anything confining. Sort of like Boone, actually."

"My boys definitely have restless souls. Do you come from a big family?"

"Mm-hm. I have five brothers. I grew up just outside the city. My parents still live there." She knew she shouldn't eat chocolate and risk gaining weight this close to filming, but she couldn't resist. "These look delicious. Thank you for sharing them with me."

"I'm happy to." Raine pulled out a chair and picked up one of the mouthwatering treats. "Mm. These days I don't sample much of what I make, but who can resist chocolate? I love to cook. When I'm not working with

Maggie at her catering company or cleaning at Epson, this is what I do. Well, I either cook or read. Or both. Usually both, actually." She took a bite of the truffle.

"That explains Boone's love of cooking."

"I think it had less to do with me and more to do with his father. It was their thing, making weekend breakfast feasts. We never had much, but we always had big weekend breakfasts, and half the time Boone's friends would join us." She looked up at a picture of a young Boone and his father hanging near the light switch. "That's Boone and Jerry. Boone used to tag along with his father after work and help him fix things around the house."

"You must miss him very much."

"Not a day goes by that I don't miss him. But he's still here, in these walls, in my children." Her expression warmed. "Boone reminds me of him, protective and confident. Like he was made for taking care of people. That's how his father was, too. My everyday hero. He was helping our elderly neighbor, Mrs. Carther, across the street when he was hit by a drunk driver." Her eyes glazed over. "But I don't want to talk about that."

"I'm so sorry about your husband. And I love hearing about him, and Boone, and your family."

Raine folded her arms on the table and leaned closer to Trish. Her hair tumbled over her shoulders. "You must be a family girl yourself for Boone to have opened up to you. He guards his heart like he guards his friends." She pressed her hand to her chest and swallowed hard. "Sorry. I should know better than to eat chocolate this late at night. It gets me every time."

"You sure you're okay?"

She waved a hand. "Of course. It's my body's way of telling me to cut back on sweets. Tell me about your family."

"We're really close, but I'm also pushy, which would probably be the more accurate reason Boone opened up to me. I kind of didn't give him an option not to."

His mother laughed. "You are *exactly* what he needed."

Trish hoped that was true. Being with his mother, in the house where he grew up, Trish felt insulated from the scarier streets they'd driven by earlier. The sense of family and love here was as rich and alive as it was in her family's homes. No wonder Boone didn't want to forget where he came from, and no wonder his mother never wanted to leave.

"I want to know all about you two," Raine whispered, as if they were best friends. "He's never brought a girlfriend home. Not even as a teenager. When most boys were sneaking their girlfriends into their bedrooms, Boone was watching over Honor, or playing music with Jude, or making sure I was okay." She shook her head like she could hardly believe the way her son had spent his youth.

The front door opened and an older man with thick dark hair and kind dark eyes waved as he strode across the floor.

Raine rose to her feet. "That's Harvey Bauer, Boone's agent, and our family's godsend."

"Hi, Raine." Harvey hugged Raine. Then he offered a hand to Trish. "Trish, I'm Harvey Bauer. Boone called a little while ago and said you were here. It's nice to finally meet you. I hope he's not driving you crazy out at that farmhouse."

"He's making me crazy, but not in a bad way," she said with a smile. "He's actually doing an incredible job with the role. He's really turned a corner."

Harvey smiled. "No doubt that was all thanks to you. I know it's important to him to do a good job. He respects your acting abilities tremendously."

Another unexpected jewel for Trish to tuck away.

Harvey eyed the chocolates. "I see you've been busy."

"Go ahead, but don't tell Victory I saw you take them." Raine looked at Trish. "His wife is trying to keep his cholesterol down, but I know better than to come between Harvey Bauer and his chocolates."

Boone came into the kitchen a few minutes later and apologized for taking so long. He and Harvey embraced and spoke quietly about Jude. Then they collected Jude, and Boone helped Harvey get him in the car. When Boone returned to the house, he dropped the bag of Sparky's supplies on the kitchen table and carried him directly to Trish. Trish nuzzled the kitty and kissed his fuzzy little head.

"A kitten!" His mother rifled through the bag and put a dish of food and water on the floor, then snuck the kitty from Trish's arms like he was a tiny baby, leaving her arms free to hold Boone.

"I'm sorry that took so long, but at least he's ready

to get help." He leaned down and kissed her. "Are you okay?"

"I'm fine," she assured him. "We're here for Jude, so don't think twice about me. The real question is, are you okay?"

His lips curved up in a thoughtful smile. "Better than I've been in a very long time. Not just because Jude is getting help." He looked at his mother, then brought his warm whiskey eyes back to Trish. "Seeing you here..."

She pressed her hands to his chest. "I know. It's doing something to me, too. Being with your mom, seeing the pictures of your family, hearing about your father. Even meeting Harvey, the man who has done so much for you. I think it all made me fall a little harder for you."

The roar of a motorcycle broke through their intimate moment.

"Lucky might change your mind about that," Boone said, shaking his head.

The motorcycle sounded like it was coming toward the house. Then suddenly it silenced, the back door flew open, and a young, dark-haired guy ran through the kitchen, slamming the door behind him. "I've been here all night," he yelled, and came to a screeching halt beside his mother. He kissed her cheek and handed her a paperback novel from inside his leather jacket. "Got this for you, Ma. Cute kitty."

She shook her head, flashing a warm smile. "Sweetheart, you're so thoughtful."

He rushed past Boone and patted his shoulder.

"Hey, bro." He waggled his brows at Trish, flopped on the sofa in the living room, and kicked his booted feet up on the coffee table.

"What'd you do now?" Boone sat on the other couch and pulled Trish down beside him.

Three loud raps sounded on the front door. They all looked at the door. Boone mumbled a curse.

His mother came out of the kitchen with the plate of chocolates and glared at Lucky. "One day I won't be here to play nice for you, Lucas Rekyrts." She opened the door to an angry-faced police officer standing on the front porch.

Lucky snickered.

The officer's expression softened when he smiled at their mother. "Evening, Raine. I'm sorry to bother you so late. Just want to ask Lucky a few questions."

"No problem, Officer Payne. Won't you come in?" She waved a hand and held out the chocolates, as if he were an invited guest. "Truffle?"

"You know I can never turn down your chocolates." He lifted a truffle to his lips and took a bite. "Mm. Perfect, thank you. Raine, you've known me since we were kids. Can't you call me Patrick?"

"Not when you're here on official business," she said with a sweet smile that spoke of her admiration for the handsome man in uniform.

The officer nodded, as if he understood, and turned his attention to Boone. "I didn't know you were in town."

Boone's eyes were stone cold and aimed at his younger brother. Trish got the impression this wasn't the first time a scene like this had unfolded in this house.

Boone turned a softer gaze toward the policeman, though his eyes bounced between his mother and the officer. "Just in for a quick visit."

The officer nodded, then looked curiously at Trish. "Aren't you...?"

"Trish Ryder," Boone said. "Trish, this is Officer Payne. He's been patrolling this area since I was a teenager."

She stood and shook his hand. "It's nice to meet you."

"*Raiders of the Past.* That's what I know you from. Great movie," Officer Payne said. "I can't believe it. Wait until I tell the guys at the station."

Trish blushed. Boone cleared his throat. "She's with me."

Oh, how she loved that possessive side of him.

Officer Payne's face turned serious again. "Yeah, I got that by the death grip you have on her hand." He pointed to Lucky. "Son, want to step outside?"

"Not really," Lucky said.

Boone pushed Lucky's feet off the coffee table. "Show some respect."

Lucky sat up straighter. "You can say whatever you have to say in front of my family."

Officer Payne eyed Raine and ground his teeth for a minute. "I'm sorry, Raine, but Chastity is home from college for the weekend and I caught Lucky in her room."

"Not true," Lucky said casually.

"Lucky?" Raine raised her brows.

"Officer Payne, did you see my face?"

"No," the officer said sharply. "I caught your backside when you were jumping out of her bedroom window."

Lucky nodded. "So you never saw my face."

"I chased you on your motorcycle," the officer said.

"Did you?" Lucky challenged. "Where is that motorcycle?"

"Lucky—" Boone chided him.

"Okay," Lucky admitted. "I was there, but I was fully dressed. I was helping her with her homework."

"She's third-year premed," Officer Payne pointed out. "You're in and out of jobs and in and out of trouble. Just last month you hacked into the State Highway's computer system and made the roadway signs say 'Slow the Hell Down.'"

"That was never tied to me," Lucky mumbled. "I may not be in college, but I know a lot about the human body."

Officer Payne stepped forward and Lucky rose to his feet. Boone stood between them.

"Lucky, sit down," Boone commanded. "Officer Payne, I'll have a talk with him."

He looked around Boone at Lucky. "You're a smart kid, but you've been through every single woman in this neighborhood." He turned to Raine, whose expression was more amused than angry. "I'm sorry, Raine, but she's my little girl."

Raine turned her hands palm up. "She's also

twenty-one. Maybe you should let her decide who she shares her time with."

Officer Payne opened his mouth to respond, and before he could say a word, Raine handed him another chocolate. "It's okay. It's your job to be a dad, and it's my job to be a mom."

Boone gave Lucky a *we're-not-finished* glare and Trish gave Boone an *I'm-falling-hard-for-you-and-your-family* sigh. Confusion passed over Boone's face, and as his mother and Officer Payne headed for the front door, she drew her man into her arms and said, "He's young. He's having fun, not breaking the law."

"And that woman," Lucky said with a smile full of trouble, "is a keeper."

Chapter Sixteen

THE NEXT MORNING Boone woke up in his childhood bedroom with Sparky curled against his shoulder and Trish tucked against his side. His brother might have the moniker, but Boone had no doubt he was the luckiest guy around. He and Trish had stayed up late talking about Jude and about how much she liked Boone's family. She told him about her brothers, Duke, Cash, Gage, Blue, and Jake, and how close they all were. The worry on her face when she told him about her brother Gage and his unrequited love for his friend Sally was obvious. And when she told him that her brother Blue was building a gazebo for Duke's wedding, she got teary-eyed. It was easy to see how much she adored them, even when she complained about how overprotective they were.

He transferred the kitty to Trish's other side and slipped out of bed to shower and have a little time alone to talk some sense into Lucky before Trish and their mother woke up. Boone crept down the hall to wake him. There were morning people, and then there were night people. Lucky was the rare breed of *anytime person*, as was their sister, Maggie. Lucky woke up with a contagious smile and quick wit at the ready regardless of whether he'd slept for one or eight hours.

Mags and Cage showed up while they were making breakfast. Mags looked so much like their mother they could be sisters, with long wavy hair in so many shades of blond and brown it was as if they'd been kissed by the sun, the moon, and the stars. Cage was the quiet, brooding type, with serious eyes and hair tightly shorn. The four of them laughed and tossed barbs at one another as only siblings could do, and when their mother and Trish joined them, they chimed right in. Mags and Trish hit it off instantly. Cage watched the scene unfold with his typical quiet demeanor. When Boone got up to throw something away, Cage followed.

"It's serious, huh?" Cage asked quietly.

"Yeah, I think it is." Boone watched Lucky flirting with Trish. He shouldn't be jealous of his younger brother, but he couldn't deny the gnawing in his gut with each flirtatious smile Lucky flashed. Trish took it all in stride, and by her mischievous grin, he had a feeling she was locked and loaded for teasing him later.

Cage's expression turned thoughtful. "You've got that look Dad used to get when he looked at Mom. Do you remember?"

How could I forget? The silent message passed between them. Boone fought the rush of emotions crashing forward at the thought of Cage's comparison. "Thanks," he managed.

Mags and their mother were busy pumping Trish for details about what it was like to be an actress, among other things.

"What did you really think of Boone before you two got together?" Mags gave Boone a coy look.

He stood beside Trish's chair. "You don't have to answer that."

She reached up and covered his hand with hers. "I thought he was an incredibly hot jerk who didn't care about anything but himself." She brought his hand to her lips and kissed it before he could think too long about her answer and added, "But then I realized how very wrong I was."

He leaned down and kissed her. "Thank you, beautiful."

"You thought he was self-centered?" Cage laughed. "Boone couldn't figure out how to put himself above anyone else if you gave him a step-by-step guide."

"He'd be too busy watching over everyone else to read it," Lucky said as he rose to his feet to clear the table.

"Whatever." Boone shook his head.

"Did you hear from Harvey?" his mother asked as they all got up to help Lucky.

"Yes. Jude's all settled in at the rehab center. You know the drill—no visitors for a week, a long stretch of rehab, and then the hard part begins." Boone thought back to the depth of despair in Jude's eyes and the convoluted conversation they'd had. Dealing with an addict was like dealing with an apologetic child and an angry adult all wrapped up in one confused and volatile person. Boone had wanted to give him hell for his self-destructive behavior and for causing everyone to worry when he had so much in life to be thankful for. But he loved Jude like a brother, and no matter how many times his friend relapsed, Boone would be there to help him get back on his feet. Trish's words sailed through his mind. *Addictions are powerful, and once they take hold, it's a wonder anyone can break free from them. They were just as helpless as you were, just in a different way.*

They'd get to the giving him hell part after he was clean, when he was past the worst of it.

"Some people might call you an enabler," Lucky quipped.

"Ha!" Mags and Raine exchanged a headshake.

"Dude, you think I should have walked away and told Jude he was on his own?" Boone glared at Lucky. "If he's too weak to fight the addiction in the first place, how would making him do it alone be better?"

"I don't know, but how's he going to learn to deal with it if you're there picking him up when he falls?" Lucky shrugged and went back to washing the dishes.

"Isn't that the kettle calling the coffee black, or whatever that saying is, Lucas?" their mother asked.

"I don't do drugs," Lucky quipped.

"No, but Boone and I are forever cleaning up your messes." She winked at Boone.

Lucky turned around, cocky grin in place, his dark eyes full of the arrogance of an invincible eighteen-year-old. "How bored would you be without me in your lives?"

Trish laughed as she put a bottle of juice in the fridge.

"Why are you laughing?" Lucky asked.

"Because you're so full of yourself." Trish crossed her arms and met his stare.

Boone watched with amusement. His brother had no idea who he was dealing with.

Cage sidled up to him and said, "This ought to be good."

Mags leaned closer to Boone and whispered, "I love her!"

Yeah, I think I'm heading that way, too.

"You barged in here last night knowing you were going to wreak havoc with your mom's evening," Trish said to Lucky. "Why didn't you go hide someplace else?"

"Because this is my house." Lucky smirked.

"True. But it's also your mother's home. Don't you think you came here because you knew she'd have your back? Because this home, and your mom, are your safety net? I'm not trying to be a bitch," Trish said. "You're funny, and obviously smart, and from what I've seen, you're a caring person. But come on. You have to admit you came here because you knew your mom would have your back."

She turned to Raine. "No offense. I actually thought last night was awesome. That policeman should have taken that up with his daughter, not you guys, but I'm just trying to make a point."

"Have at it," Raine said with an amused—or maybe impressed—smile.

"Thank you," Trish said. "Lucky, if you think Boone's an enabler, then take another look. He's not *giving* Jude the drugs. He's giving up whatever's on his plate to *help* Jude *fight* the addiction. Jude's lucky to have him." She reached for Boone's hand. "Hopefully one day Jude will be strong enough to realize he doesn't need to keep falling back on drugs to fill whatever emptiness he's feeling."

Lucky stared at her for a long time, then glanced at Boone. "Man, why couldn't you go out with a mousy girl?"

They all laughed.

"You think she's tough on you?" Boone teased, drawing Trish in closer and feeling the warmth of his mother's approval.

"I'm sorry," Trish said. "I can be a little pushy, but I have a great deal of respect for Boone. There aren't many men like him around, and you could learn a thing or two from him."

"Thanks, baby. That means the world to me, because I learned from my father, and I'd like to think I'm doing him proud." Boone leaned in for another kiss.

"Boone," his mother said softly. The depth of emotions in her eyes, coupled with her sweet smile and reassuring nod, brought another wave of emotions.

He cleared his throat to speak past the emotions clogging it. "I think Jude's figuring it out. This time when he had the urge to go from snorting cocaine to freebasing, he called me instead of taking the hit. That's progress."

As he gazed into Trish's eyes, words floated through his mind. *Lyrics.* Adrenaline rushed through him as the words began stringing themselves together in his mind. Jude wasn't the only one making progress, and he knew he owed his to the woman in his arms.

He grabbed a napkin and pen and let the lyrics flow.

"What's that?" Trish asked.

"Song," he said cryptically, scribbling as fast as he could to keep up with his thoughts. "A song, baby. A real song."

A little while later, Mags and Trish exchanged phone numbers, and they gathered Sparky's things, said their goodbyes, and got on the road. Boone felt like he'd been home for a week. He'd missed seeing his family and was glad they'd gotten to meet Trish. Before leaving, Mags told him he was a fool if he messed things up. His mother told him not to worry about Lucky; she was sure he'd get his act together, and, she'd said, it was time for Boone to worry about himself. He wasn't very good at that. He reached across the console and squeezed Trish's hand. She was good at worrying about others *and* herself. It wasn't just Lucky who could learn a thing or two from someone else.

"Thanks for letting me come with you," Trish said

with a sweet smile.

"Beautiful girl, I'm powerless to say no to you and *mean* it."

"I'm definitely going to use that to my advantage in the bedroom."

"I can't wait."

"I'm sorry for being so pushy with Lucky. I really do like him. He reminds me of my brother Jake. He's cocky like that, and I could totally see him jumping out of a girl's window when he was younger."

"What about you?" Boone asked. "What were you like as a teenager?"

"I have five older brothers. What do you think I was like?"

He tugged her across the console for a quick kiss.

"The girl who waded through groupies to give me hell? I'd bet my best guitar you were sneaky as hell, and I wish I'd known you back then. You could have made my days a lot brighter."

"That's not what you're thinking." She ran her fingers up the nape of his neck. "You're thinking I would have made your nights a lot steamier. Your mom told me you never snuck girls into your bedroom, but I bet if we'd have known each other back then, you would have tried."

"And would you have let me?"

"Probably not. I like you too much, and my brothers would have killed you." She smirked and added, "I would have found someplace they'd never think to look."

BOONE AND TRISH'S private time ended three days later when the crew showed up bright and early and began prepping the property for filming. Production assistants, equipment specialists, set designers, makeup artists, and various other crew and extras traipsed through the property, sending poor Sparky scurrying up to Boone's bedroom to hide out in his guitar case. The natural light they'd enjoyed was replaced with overbearing movie lighting that heated up the small farmhouse like a greenhouse. The porch where they'd spent their evenings getting to know each other, where arguments turned to heartfelt confessions and first kisses turned to exquisite nights of passion, paving the way for Trish and Boone to open their hearts to each other, was suddenly overtaken by too many people, making it feel small and inadequate, when it had felt so heavenly before. Voices carried from one end of the yard to the other, from the front porch to the kitchen, vibrating off the walls like invisible interlopers.

Trish walked into the kitchen where the crew was rearranging the things she and Boone had on the counter. Last night Boone had picked a handful of flowers from the edge of the woods and arranged them in a glass. The glass now sat empty beside the sink, causing Trish a pang of sadness. They moved the table where she and Boone had made love so it was flush with the wall. It felt constricted—a feeling she knew Boone hated. She bit back the urge to tell them to back off. She felt as though their privacy had been invaded, despite the fact this wasn't hers and Boone's house. It *felt* as if it were. Their imprints were all over and around it: in the yard, where they'd first fallen into each other's arms; on the porch, where they'd argued and rehearsed and fallen a little more for each other with every passing minute; in the small space at the foot of the stairs, where they'd had the heated discussion before leaving for New York; on the couch in the living room, where they'd tumbled during the storm; upstairs, where they'd learned the dips and curves of each other's bodies. The only room free from their hands was Boone's bedroom, where they'd set up camp for Sparky.

Trish usually thrived off of the excitement of filming, but now everything felt different and wrong, and she wished she could join the kitten and hide away.

"How'd it go with the grumpy sex god slash rocker?" Zoe, one of the set assistants, asked as she walked by. "Did you guys make any progress, or was it mostly gnarly grunts and a lot of eye rolling?"

"He was great," Trish answered absently, wondering where Boone had gone. It was midafternoon and she hadn't seen him since earlier that morning, when he'd called Harvey to check on Jude and his mother to check on Lucky. They'd been pulled in a hundred different directions ever since, discussing scenes, reviewing minor script changes, and finally they'd met with Chuck and assured him they were ready to film.

"*Great*, as in you're going to kill Chuck for exiling you to ten days with a partying womanizer?" Zoe asked. "Or *great* as in you think Boone can pull his weight?"

She'd forgotten how far from prying eyes they'd been for the past week. Not only did no one beyond Boone's family and Fiona—she'd finally clued her in two days ago—know about their relationship, but no one here knew his reputation was a finely tuned concerto of lies and distractions constructed by Boone and his public relations team to enhance his rocker image and protect his family's privacy.

"Oh no." Zoe sighed, clearly making the wrong assumption based on Trish's silence. "Was he a total jerk?"

"He's not a jerk." Irritation crept up her spine. She wanted to hammer that point home, to let the crew know his rep was a farce. But she couldn't. It wasn't her place to shatter his carefully crafted reputation.

"I have to tell you," Zoe whispered conspiratorially, "some of us had bets he'd try to hook up with you and you'd set him straight."

Who makes bets on other people's love lives, anyway? Okay, so she and Fiona would. And Shea. *Shea!* She needed to clue in her public relations rep to her new relationship status, although she was pretty sure Fiona would have already taken care of that. They were sisters, after all. Not that Trish had any plans of formally announcing that she and Boone were dating, but now that she was thinking like an actress and not a love-struck girl, she knew she had to cover all her bases. With Boone's less-than-stellar reputation and her good-girl rep, who knew what kind of backlash the media would throw at them.

"I had your back, though," Zoe assured her. "Don't worry. I know you have high standards."

High standards? She wanted to tell her that Boone more than lived up to any standards she might have and that he was more loyal and caring than any man she'd ever met. But then she'd have to answer questions about his past—gossipers always wanted more, and she had no desire to spend the next week defending her relationship with Boone. Better to take the high road and say nothing at all. But her response burned just beneath her skin, clawing for release. She curled her fingers into her palm, focusing all of her frustrations there, instead of opening her mouth, because if she did, there would be no turning back. Every celebrity knew how the press could twist and misconstrue just about anything, which could lead to months of speculation and marring of reputations. Boone needed his rocker-image rep in place, and she'd respect that even if it killed her.

"Well," Zoe said, pausing as if she were waiting for Trish to fill the silence. "I better get out there before someone bellows."

Trish was too lost in her own thoughts to respond. She didn't have much time to stew before she was called into the makeup trailer to get ready for their first scene of the day.

The front yard had become a sea of trailers and canopies. It was amazing how quickly a peaceful setting could morph into a world all its own. Set designers stood before large easels with fat, colorful markers, talking through transitions. Director chairs and tables full of snacks and drinks were set up in a screened-in tent, where women and men talked into headsets between bites. She spotted Boone walking across the field with his phone pressed to his ear. Her pulse quickened and somehow her heartbeat slowed. Seeing him brought a thread of calm to the chaotic storm going on around them. His eyes were downcast. His face was a mask of tension and focus. He reached an arm up and rubbed the back of his neck, flashing his colorful tattoos. She took a long look at the man who had challenged her at every turn and had taken her by surprise with his kindness and dedication to his family and friends. The man who had completely captivated her heart. She remembered the night she'd seen him with Honor and realized how quickly and easily she'd misjudged him. How easy it was for others to take his reputation as the truth.

How was she going to navigate this new landscape of their lives? She'd always been so sure of herself. Confident that she could handle anything. But after what Zoe had said, she was no longer so sure. She wasn't used to having to bite her tongue, but when she gazed out at the man who had rooted himself into her very soul, she couldn't imagine doing anything that would jeopardize the safe bubble he'd created for himself and his family.

Boone Stryker might be her private calm within a storm, but to everyone besides his family and closest friends, he *was* the storm.

Chapter Seventeen

THE SUN SLID toward the horizon, bringing the temperature down with it. They'd been filming since late afternoon, and Chuck had them working at breakneck speed, trying to make up for the time they'd taken off so Boone could get his head out of his ass and learn to act. Boone accepted responsibility for the delays, but it did nothing to ease the frustration over feeling like vultures had swooped into his and Trish's cozy nest and torn it to shreds.

Because of the shorter timeline, people didn't walk or linger; they hurried, scurried, and ran, creating a buzz of tension and excitement in the air. It was as nerve-racking as it was stimulating, and Boone fed off of it like he fed off of the crowds at concerts. Every second seemed more intense than the last, every scene more critical. It was that rush, and the time and attention Trish had poured into helping him deal with his ghosts and open his heart, that allowed him to finally connect with his character. He could *feel* Rick Champion breathing inside him. The anger and excitement, the irritation and adrenaline rush was *Rick's*, and when he acted with Trish, Rick was right there with them. Boone no longer saw Trish; he saw Delia. It was all coming together, just as they'd hoped it would, and according to Chuck, his performance resonated beautifully on camera.

Trish had fallen right back into professional actress mode, and when she was acting in solo scenes, she was amazing. He watched in complete and utter awe of her transformation from the fun-loving woman who'd feigned a pregnancy at the creek to the broken and vulnerable Delia. Her intensity, and her love of her craft, were just a few of the things that had drawn Boone's attention when they'd first begun working together. He hadn't expected anything less than stellar performances from Trish. But something had changed. When they were acting in scenes together, their deep connection seemed to get lost—on her side. He felt locked out, like she was afraid to let the emotions she'd once portrayed as fluidly as a river be seen. It was almost as if their coming together had created a line she was afraid to cross in her acting, the complete opposite of what their coming together had done for him. It was as though the real world collided with how far they'd evolved as a couple and had stolen a piece of her. And that worried him to no end. Not just because of what it could mean for their relationship but for the way it was hindering her acting.

After the week they'd had, their chemistry *should*

have been off the charts, especially when they hadn't had a minute alone since the crew arrived. He was sure everyone could see the way he was watching her, waiting for his chance to be alone with her. She was edgy, and he was desperate to talk to her and figure out what he could do to help her move past whatever was holding her back. It didn't help that some of the crew were speculating about whether he and Trish had hooked up. He was adept at ignoring bullshit, but he wondered if Trish had heard the gossiping whispers and if that was part of the issue.

He drew in a deep breath, tired of biding his time until he could steal a moment alone with her. She was standing by the front porch talking with crew members Jared and Kate. Never before had he craved a single moment with anyone so fiercely. Except maybe his father, he realized unexpectedly. He'd give anything to have another moment with his father. To tell him how much he missed him and loved him. To hear his deep laugh and see his smiling eyes as he doled out life lessons or taught Boone to check the filter on the water heater or change the oil on his car. Damn, he missed him.

Glancing at Trish, he felt the same gut-wrenching longing. He was expected five minutes ago, but all he wanted was one minute with Trish. Just enough time to touch base, so she knew she wasn't alone in whatever she was going through. He headed back up the hill. He'd sworn he'd do everything right this time, show up on time, where he was expected, and give every scene his all, so he wouldn't undermine all of

Trish's hard work. But she needed *him* now, his support, his love, his attention. Makeup could wait.

Trish looked gorgeous in a wispy blue dress and a pair of cowgirl boots. He wanted to wrap her in his arms, to taste her sweet lips, feel her body melt against him with the strength and safety of their coupledom, knowing that no matter what was going on, they'd get through it together.

Jared's eyes narrowed curiously as Boone approached. Boone paid him no attention and placed a hand on the small of Trish's back.

She managed a troubled smile that slayed him and said, "Hey."

"Hi. Sorry to interrupt. Can we talk? I'm supposed to be in makeup. I'll be quick."

"Can you guys give us a sec?" Trish asked the others.

Jared and Kate exchanged a slightly disapproving look. Boone wasn't about to waste his time with whatever *that* meant. He guided Trish a few feet away so they could speak privately.

"What's up?" she asked, glancing back at Jared and Kate. "They're gearing up for my freak-out scene."

"That's one of your best scenes. You'll do great. I just wanted to touch base and make sure you're okay."

"You know how it is, getting back into the swing of things." She looked at the others again. "It's weird, working together now that we're close. Don't you think?"

And there it was, the elephant on the set. Her trouble was his fault.

"For me it's a million times better," he said honestly. "But I saw Chuck talking with you after the last scene. Is our being together causing you to have trouble connecting? Is it me?"

"It's not you. I don't know what it is. Maybe it's all in my head. Have you gotten any weird looks from the crew? I think they're gossiping about us, and I can't figure out why. We're not exactly holding hands on set."

"I don't give a shit about the crew. I just don't want to let you down. This is *your* movie, beautiful, and if I'm messing you up, tell me what I can do to make it better."

She sighed loudly, then smiled up at him. It was a troubled smile, but a smile nonetheless. Jared cleared his throat and checked his watch, clearly annoyed at the interruption.

"Nothing. It's not you. You're nailing all of your scenes." Trish took a nervous step away and hiked a thumb over her shoulder. "I'd better..."

"Okay. We'll catch up later." He leaned in for a quick kiss and headed toward the makeup trailer.

"What was *that*?" Jared's voice landed in Boone's ears like nails dragging down a chalkboard.

He shouldn't have kissed her. She'd taken a step back. Was that a hint not to kiss her? Had he messed that up, too? The thought pissed him off even more. He wasn't about to purposely hide their relationship, but surely Trish would never do that. All this tension must be messing with his head.

After spending half an hour in makeup and filming

two more intense solo scenes, he was back in the makeup trailer for what he hoped was the last time that evening. He needed a break from the odd looks and whispers he'd been trying to ignore since he'd given Trish that quick kiss. *They hooked up. Trish would never do that. Don't you read the rags? He sleeps with anyone. Who could turn him down? I saw them kiss.* He felt like he'd spent the last few hours in a high school girls' locker room.

"Are we done?" Boone tried to push from the chair where two makeup artists were messing with him.

"No," they said in unison.

He looked up at April, a petite blonde wielding a makeup brush with the intensity of Picasso. "So," she said with a coy smile. "You and Trish, huh?"

He wasn't about to feed the gossip pool. He tried to push to his feet again, and Ronnie, a tall guy with skin so shiny he looked polished, pursed his lips and waved a beard trimmer as he pushed Boone into the chair.

"Mr. Stryker," Ronnie said sharply. "We all want to call it a night. Do you mind?"

"Yeah, I do."

"Two minutes," April assured him. "Your fans expect you to look a certain way. We don't want to disappoint them."

"My fans love me without any makeup on my face *or* any manscaping." Boone exhaled loudly. He was too worried about Trish to sit still.

"You'll learn to love this." April tipped his head back, layering more makeup around his eyes as

Ronnie brought the trimmer to his jaw.

"No, I won't."

Ronnie chuckled. "Mr. Stryker will never enjoy this. He's too rough and tough for makeup."

Whatever.

He was sick of being messed with and about to lose his cool when Trish and Jared came through the door. Her tired eyes moved over their faces, bristling against their curious glances, but she held her chin up and smiled at Boone.

"Chuck changed the location and lighting of the next scene," Jared said with a note of urgency in his voice. "He wants to talk to April and Ronnie right away."

"One sec." April ran the makeup brush under Boone's chin, then stepped back, hands up. "Okay. Don't touch your face." She turned to Trish. "Hey, girlfriend. Take a seat. We'll be right back."

April and Ronnie followed Jared out of the trailer. Alone with Trish for the first time all day, Boone finally felt like he could breathe.

"Are you as ready for the crew to disappear as I am?" He leaned toward Trish and pulled her into a kiss. She went rigid in his arms. "What's wrong?"

"Everyone's talking about us." She exhaled a long breath. A clear indication of how much she'd been stewing over this.

Boone was equally tired of hearing comments and catching sideways stares, but he didn't understand how what anyone else said should stop her from kissing him. "So what? Let them talk. What does it matter?"

"I've never been in this position before." She spoke fast, in a hushed whisper. "You've got a reputation as a partying womanizer, and every time I hear a stupid comment about how someone can't believe I would be with you, I want to defend you—and myself. I know you're not that way, but I can't help it. I want to tell them they're wrong and tell them what you're really like. But I can't because you worked hard to create and maintain that rep for your career."

"Baby, I don't need defending, and I sure as hell don't care what anyone around here thinks, except for you and Chuck. We're only here for a few weeks. Less if Chuck keeps up this pace."

"But I don't know how to react. I've never had to battle rumors about bad reputations and co-star hookups before." She curled her fingers around the edge of the chair so tight her knuckles blanched.

He placed his hand over hers and softened his tone. "You don't need to battle them now. Let them roll off your back."

"I can't pretend!" she said loudly, then glanced at the trailer door and lowered her voice. "I've never had to deal with anything like this. I don't date co-stars, and I don't know *how* to do this. It's totally throwing me off."

His gut fisted at what he read between the lines. "What do you want to do? Not see each other? Have me make some kind of blanket statement about my past? Tell me what you need and we'll figure this out."

She rolled her eyes and groaned. "*No.* That's not

what I want. I'm just...I feel like I'm going to come apart at the seams. I'm so frustrated. Every time I turn around someone's whispering or wondering out loud how we got together or what I'm doing with you. What about *my* reputation?"

"Let's take a deep breath and think this through. You're stressed, baby. It's understandable. We've gone through so much in the past week, and this movie is *so* important for your career. I think you're overthinking this. They're *gossiping*. No one here really cares what we do or who we sleep with. They care about the movie."

"This is my career, Boone. This is what I live for. I do not want to end up defending myself in some gossip magazine."

"Don't you think that's a little far-fetched? We're out in Hurricane, West Virginia. We've gone out in town. You've seen how close to under the radar we're flying."

"All I know is that I feel like I'm ready to explode. I worked hard to prove myself as a serious actress, and just like that, in one day, everyone out there—all those people who know me as a professional—are tossing around barbs like I'm Lindsay Lohan."

"No one thinks you're Lindsay Lohan. That's ridiculous. I really think you should just pretend as though you don't hear it and let it blow over. You know what I'm really like, and that's all that should matter. It's not like we're making out on set or throwing our relationship in their faces."

Ronnie and April came through the door and Trish

withdrew her hand from his, which annoyed the hell out of him.

"We don't have to throw it in their faces. All it took was that one kiss," she whispered. "I can't pretend!"

"*Pretending* is what you do for a living," he reminded her more calmly than he felt.

**

THE SET WAS silent, save for the wind whispering through the long grass, where Trish spun like a child dancing through a meadow. Only she wasn't a child, and she was so pissed off about the gossip and what Boone had said, she couldn't concentrate. *Pretending is what you do for a living.* His tone, and his expression, had turned cold when the others had walked into the trailer, and the icy barb had hit its mark. Jared was the worst of them all. He didn't even have to say anything. Just the way he looked at her and Boone made Trish want to knee him in the groin. She was already on her fourth take of a scene she should have been able to do in her sleep.

The crew was exhausted and anxious to leave. Tension crackled in the air, as dark and present as the night sky. How was she supposed to portray Delia, hyped up on crack, when she wanted to run away, to cry, scream, and tell the crew they could kiss her ass? How could she maintain the image of not being mentally present when her thoughts were standing sentinel at the forefront of her mind? Everyone knew her as an A-list actress who never let anything come between her and acting, and here she'd broken her own rule and not only slept with her co-star, but she'd slept with the one co-star whose image was the polar opposite of her own. And worse, she hadn't just slept with him. She was falling in love with him.

She dropped to the ground as the camera on the crane overhead came into view, forcing into place the vacant stare she'd perfected.

Had she made a mistake? Gotten swept up in a fantasy like so many actors did when filming emotionally intense movies? In her heart she knew that wasn't the case, but Boone wanted her to *pretend*? How could she pretend not to hear and see the judgmental looks and comments? He built walls around himself as easily as she usually fell into her roles. He acted like he didn't care what anyone thought about his reputation. Only he did care! He cared enough to carefully manipulate and create his public image with purpose and forethought. Wasn't her reputation due the same attention? Wasn't it equally as important? Didn't she deserve for him to step up to the plate and tell all those judgmental people they were wrong? That she hadn't fallen for a womanizing asshole?

She lay nestled in the long grass, trying not to look directly into the camera, trying to maintain a blank stare, as she remembered the night of the storm. Flashes of that night raced through her mind. Memories of the passion that had overtaken them, followed by the rumors she'd overheard, swirled together inside her like a bad cocktail. She had to get through this scene and get away from the set before she heard another word of gossip. She needed to get her head on straight before talking to Boone.

She needed to get the hell out of there before she burst into tears.

Chapter Eighteen

"I STILL CAN'T believe she'd stoop so low," someone whispered behind Boone. "You know he's only using Trish."

Boone closed his eyes and fisted his hands, suppressing the urge to spin around and put the nosy, judgmental ass in their place. But doing so would ruin the scene Trish was already having trouble with, not to mention it would inspire more gossip rather than silencing it. But that didn't stop fire from searing through his veins.

When Chuck yelled, "Cut," Boone opened his eyes, sure smoke was fuming from his ears. He spun around, but whoever had been standing there was gone. *Coward.* His eyes moved over the dark fields. His pulse amped up as he scanned the crew closing up tents and shutting down equipment, but he hadn't recognized the voice of whoever had made the comment, and it wasn't like they'd have a blinking light around their neck. He had no idea what he would have said or done, but he knew it would've taken an army to keep him from blowing his top.

He turned his attention back toward the set, determined to get Trish out of there before she heard more of the same. She was already gone.

He stormed off in search of her. How could so much go wrong in one day? *She* was the actress. This was *her* domain, the place where she was respected and adored, and he'd unknowingly screwed it up.

He strode across the field, thinking of all Trish had done for him, and he'd be damned if he was going to let her down.

"Hey, great job today," one of the crew said as Boone mounted the porch.

"Thanks," he said on his way inside, focused on only two things—the emotions swamping him and finding the woman who was causing them.

He took the stairs two at a time and stood outside Trish's bedroom door. *Trish's door.* That was a weird thought, considering they'd been sharing the same bed practically since they'd arrived. He heard the shower running and headed down the hall to do the same. He opened his bedroom door and loved up Sparky. Not only had their lives been upended by the crew, but Sparky's had been, too. He showered and dressed quickly, then picked up the kitty and his guitar and went to find Trish. Her shower was still running, so he left a quick note on her bed and headed outside.

He reveled in the lack of people watching his every move. The crew had left equipment stacked on the porch, and even though there was no way it could, it seemed to suck the air from around him. He walked toward the field thinking about the day—and when he reached the edge of the long grass, he kept on walking. Irritated over what he'd heard, and angry at himself for expecting Trish to ignore such awful comments, he walked until he found grass that hadn't been trampled, where gossipmongers hadn't released their nastiness into the air. He walked until his lungs broke free from the vise that tethered them and filled with cool night air. He set his guitar case in the tall grass, realizing he was still carrying Sparky. He kissed his fuzzy head. He probably needed space as much as Boone did.

"Just stay with me, buddy." He opened his guitar case and set the kitten in the top. Then he stripped off his clean shirt, removed the guitar, and replaced it with his shirt, then set the kitten on it. As if on cue, the kitty curled up, licked its paw, then dragged it behind his ear. Guess he needed a shower, too.

Boone stood in the long grass, gazing up at Trish's bedroom window. The lights were on, the window open. Was she okay? Was she angry? Upset? Blaming herself when he deserved all the blame? He debated going back up to her bedroom, but she might need space, too—from him. Although that thought pained him, he'd messed things up for her and he owed her the luxury of time and space. He turned away from the house and gazed into the darkness. Without thought, his fingers began strumming one of his songs, but the tune ground against his nerves like sandpaper. He wanted to get as far away from himself as possible.

**

TRISH STAYED IN the shower so long her skin pruned up. She hadn't experienced this rough of a day since she'd first started acting, and even then the stress had been totally different. Back then she worried about her skills, which was something she had control over. Today was a mess of convoluted emotions and worries, and the gossip around the set only made her question herself even more. She'd always thought she was in control of her emotions, but today taught her she was nowhere near in control. At least not as far as Boone was concerned. She dressed in a pair of jeans and a tank top and sat on the edge of the bed reading the note he'd left.

Beautiful girl—Needed air. Outside. Come find me?
B.

She ran her finger over his writing. She'd been fascinated with handwriting when she was in the tenth grade, and she'd learned a lot about what handwriting said about a person. Boone's writing was dark, with large spaces between the words. The dark writing was perfectly *Boone*. He took things seriously. He was loyal, and he didn't run from commitment— that much she knew—although he didn't seem to take her worries over her reputation seriously. That gave her pause, but she had dwelled on that enough in her too-long shower. She couldn't stew over it anymore. She wasn't even sure she was in the right where that was concerned. Pushing those thoughts away, she looked down at the wide spaces between each word he'd written and recalled what it meant. He didn't like to be confined. She smiled. *Needed air. Outside.* The straight line of his *d*'s meant he was self-reliant and independent. The baseline of his handwriting was uneven, which meant he was moody and restless. That was the Boone she'd known when they'd first begun filming, although he'd become far less restless over the past ten days. She wondered if the day had gotten to him, too.

Looking down at his cryptic note again, she found the size of his writing the most perplexing. Large writing usually indicated a demand for attention, but it could also mean he needed elbow room. Boone rarely demanded attention, and his note asked her to find him, which conflicted with the idea of him needing room. She smiled at that, too. *You definitely strum to your own beat, Boone Stryker.*

She set the note beside the bed, slipped a hoodie over her tank top, pushed her feet into a pair of sandals, and went in search of the man she could not, for the life of her, stay mad at.

The sky was inky black, with few stars and a blue-gray moon illuminating the fields to the far reaches of the property. The sounds of crickets chirping blended with *ribbits* and the croaks of tree frogs, creating a cacophony of melodies, which was underscored by the faint sounds of Boone's guitar. She paused in the long grass and listened more carefully. Boone rose with the moon at his back, like an angel in the night, and the tune of "Don't Stop Believing" by Journey hit her ears. He began singing, and she laughed and cried, one hand over her heart, as he hit the high notes perfectly.

When he finished the song, he went immediately into "Any Way You Want It" by Journey, drawing her like a fish to water. She ran to him like a swooning teenager, and she danced, right there in the moonlight, waving her hands over her head, flipping her hair, swaying her hips, and singing every word with him. She felt free and alive for the first time since the crew had arrived. As the song came to an end, she didn't wait for him to sing the last note. She wrapped her arms around his neck and kissed him, long and passionately, with all the emotions she'd felt compelled to hide when they were on set and all the love she'd been hoarding in her heart.

"I am so sorry," she panted out. "I was a bitch, and you didn't deserve it. You were right. I should let the gossip roll off my back. I wasn't sure how to react to the comments, and not reacting to them was eating me alive. But I took a really long shower and thought about everything—the weirdness of having the crew suddenly barge into our lives, how it feels to know you're not the guy everyone thinks you are, and not being able to scream it from the rooftops. Which, by the way, I *do not* want to do. I'm just making a point." She was talking so fast, she couldn't stop the words from tumbling out. "But I finally realized what's really important. Your image protects your family, and it's important for your band's success. It doesn't matter what the rest of the world thinks about you or us. I don't care if I end up in rag magazines, or what anyone

.else says. I'm—"

He smothered her words with another loving kiss, and when their mouths finally parted, he framed her face with his hands and gazed into her eyes. She could feel his love enveloping her.

"You're more important to me than my reputation will ever be," he said with such certainty it felt palpable. "I was an idiot to even suggest you let the gossip roll off your back. You've worked hard, baby. I don't want to come between you and your career, and I know how highly everyone thinks of you. Including me. I'll fix this. I promise you, I'll fix this."

"No, Boone. It's not your problem to fix," she insisted. "I have to pull up my big-girl panties and get through it. I can do it."

"Well, hell." His eyes turned playful. "I was hoping you'd take off those big-girl panties a little later."

"We'll see about that." She poked his chest.

He took her hand and sank to the grass, bringing her down beside him.

"Today felt like it took a month," he said, reading her mind. "From the moment the crew arrived, I felt like our world had tilted. I've had you all to myself, and it's been incredible. Not having a second alone with you was hell, especially since I knew you were having a rough time. But what was worse was feeling like our connection, our relationship, was being dragged through the mud. I'm used to ignoring the gossip that comes with being a celebrity, but tonight, when I heard those comments directed at you, about me using you..." His jaw clenched, and he shifted angry eyes away. "I was ready to kill someone. No one talks about my favorite girl behind her back." He kissed her softly, and her heart squeezed with the intimate endearment. "I'll straighten this out."

She loved that he wanted to protect her, but she needed to learn to deal with this on her own. "Boone, you don't need to. Didn't you hear anything I said?"

"Of course I did." He cupped her face, gently brushing his thumb over her cheek. "But this time you need to trust me. You're on my list, remember? Right at the top. That means I take care of you."

"As much as I love hearing that, I'm not a damsel in distress."

"You're right. You're my girlfriend, which means I get to protect you, and I get to be a bit of a caveman where other people are concerned."

She rolled her eyes. He was nothing if not painfully honest. How could she deny him the thing he did best? "Please tell me you're not going to get in people's faces and do something stupid. I really think we need to play this cool and not flaunt our relationship in front of everyone."

"I won't need to be a caveman. Promise." He kissed her again. "But you'd better give me an idea of what *not flaunting* our relationship means."

"I don't know. We didn't flaunt it today. Just not a lot of PDAs, I guess. You know what I mean. Whether we like it or not, this is our workplace, so we have to keep a level of professionalism."

He mulled that over. The idea of holding back his emotions wasn't one he liked, but she was right. This was their workplace, and more importantly, her career. He had no desire to mess that up any more than he already had.

"Okay, we can try that. But don't think for a minute that I don't see that you were protecting me by not telling everyone that my rep isn't real. I appreciate that. But from now on, if we have to behave on set, I need to know that if you feel like you need to say anything at all to protect yourself, you'll say it. I can deal with the fallout. *You* are important to me, and I never, ever want to cause you heartache, okay?"

"No way. I'm not throwing you under the bus to save myself."

"Trish," he warned.

"I can't do it, Boone. The same way I know you could never say something that you know might hurt my career."

"But it was tearing you up not to, and that's not good for you or your career."

She huffed out a breath. "Well, I won't do it."

"Then I won't play any more of your music," he challenged.

"That's not fair," she complained. "Although I was surprised to hear you playing the songs you tease me about."

"I was playing your favorite songs because I felt far away from you and I wanted to be closer. I was trying to give you space, and figured you'd come out if you wanted to. And if not, then at least you wouldn't feel suffocated by the guy who was fucking up your world."

"Fucking up my world? Is that what you thought?" *Is that how I made you feel?*

He shrugged. "How could I not? Before me, no one talked crap about you, and then I made that stupid comment about ignoring it all. And our scenes? You knew your lines inside out and backward, but today you had a really hard time with some of them. That had to be my fault."

"That's not true." She swallowed hard, knowing that wasn't quite true either. "Okay, the part about no one talking about me on set might be true, but the trouble I'm having acting wasn't because of you." She took both of his hands in hers. "I wanted to feel *everything*. The emotions I feel for you, the fear Delia felt on the cusp of Rick's life-changing events, the sadness she felt for letting him down. Her helplessness, the way the drugs numbed her, leaving her barely present. But I couldn't get there because everything around me felt wrong. You said our world tilted when the crew showed up, and you were right. In my head, and in my heart, this place had become *ours*, and suddenly not only was it invaded by noise and lights and people, but some of those people were saying things I didn't like, and I wanted to kick them off the property."

"But they said things because of me, baby. Don't you see that? Any way you cut it, it's because of me."

She shook her head and climbed into his lap. "Because of *us*, but that's not the part that matters. It doesn't matter if they were saying things about us, or about my acting, or my *hair* for that matter. The point is, I'm used to not putting up with crap from anyone, but I lost sight of where that stops. I blurred the lines between reality and fiction. This house *isn't* ours. Those people *weren't* our guests. We're living on a film set. No matter how much it feels like it's ours when we're the only ones here, it's not. I lost sight of that. Just like I lost sight of how little what they said should matter. I let it eat away at me and I couldn't concentrate. That's *my* issue. I wanted to blame you, or them. But come on, Boone. I can no sooner do that than if you went onstage at a concert and forgot the words to a song and blamed me."

He winced. "That would suck."

"Yes! Exactly. I let it all affect me and I shouldn't have. I'm an actress—and I *do* pretend for a living. I was pissed when you said that, but it is true. I walk on set and pretend to be someone else. That doesn't mean it's not important work. And today reminded me of just how hard it is to do what I do, because suddenly I *couldn't* do it well enough to feel worthy of the role."

"Trish—"

"Shh. Let me finish, please? I'm not as tough as I pretend to be. And honestly, I'm not as tough as I thought I was. It turns out I've got more vulnerable girl in me than I'd like to admit."

He laughed and tightened his hold around her waist. "I really like the girl in you. Tough, vulnerable, awake, sleeping. All of you."

For a guy who came across so tough, he was a big softie when it came to her, and she loved that about him as much as she loved the alpha badass rocker in him.

"Thank you. I've never been tested like this before. It's new and scary. But I realized that I like this girly side of myself because I worried that I wasn't feminine enough in some ways. So today was an exercise in self-growth and modesty."

She wrapped her arms around his neck. "So you see, Mr. Stryker. The gossip about you was just a path to the rest of the chaos in my head. But tomorrow I'm going to blow them away."

"That's my girl." He embraced her, and it was exactly what she needed. To be held, not judged, not protected from anyone else, just held by Boone.

"Will you do me a favor?" he asked.

"Anything."

"Dance with me?"

She wrinkled her brow. "There's no music."

"I'll sing for you, but I need you in my arms. I had my own epiphany today." He lifted her from his lap and followed her to his feet, gathering her against him. "Throughout the day I was *feeling* Rick, just as you said I would. And I understand the thrill of it now. I understand how you get so into your character, she feels real. Not that I'm one-one-hundredth as good as you are, but I understand the addiction, the all-consuming feeling of being possessed by someone else."

He began to slow dance. She moved with him, feeling safe and loved and present. So very present.

"As awful as today was, it made me realize how much I care for you, Trish. When you hurt, I hurt.

When you smile, I feel it in my heart. I'm falling so hard for you, and I never want this, *us*, to end."

It was all she could do to smile and not cry. She managed, "I want that, too," and they both fell silent.

Serenaded by nature, and the steady beat of his heart, all the upended pieces of her life fell into place. And when he began singing "Can't Fight This Feeling" by REO Speedwagon, her love for him glued all those pieces back together.

Boone gazed into her eyes with more love than she'd ever imagined possible. As he sang about being unable to fight his feelings, or remembering why he was fighting them in the first place, and bringing his ship in to shore and throwing away the oars, she felt tears tumble down her cheeks. He wasn't saying he loved her, but he was telling her something just as meaningful, and she wanted to capture each word and bronze them. Keep the song, his voice, and the way he was looking at her frozen in time so she could come back to them time and time again. His voice wound around them, drawing them closer, binding them together, so nothing, not even a rumor, could come between them.

Chapter Nineteen

THE NEXT MORNING, before the sun came up or the crew arrived, when the dew-fresh air blew through the open window and the house breathed tranquility into their lungs, Boone lay awake. He thought about Trish and how selfless she was. He thought about Jude and his stints in rehab, and he thought about Lucky and the example he was setting for him. One by one he ticked off each of the people he was close to, and he began to wonder why he'd ever agreed to keep up the ruse of his reputation. He'd bought into the advice of public relations and marketing reps, and he'd thought the badass rocker image was necessary for his career—and maybe it had been. His music was dark, born from the world he grew up in. The only thing that saved his music from being too dark was the love his family had drenched him in. It was an inescapable force and a great equalizer to the surroundings of his youth. Luckily, it conveyed in his music, as well, softening the bleakest lyrics. Now he wondered if his reputation did more harm than good to the people he loved most. When he'd stopped boozing and sleeping around, if he'd allowed the media to catch wind of who he really was, would his career have suffered? Would the band have faded away? Was his career really that tenuous? Was his music not the driving factor in his success?

He rolled onto his side. Sparky yawned and stretched beside his pillow, then jumped down to the floor.

"Sorry, buddy," he whispered, and gazed down at Trish sleeping peacefully beside him. She'd become his world. She accepted him *despite* his reputation, and yesterday she'd *protected* him. Just as she'd done with Chuck before they'd come to the farmhouse. It was a strange feeling, knowing she'd stepped up for him. He didn't see himself as a man who needed protecting. But what Trish did, she did with her heart, and even if he didn't think he needed protecting, he loved her even more for doing it. She wasn't afraid to stand up and be her true self. His eyes moved along her naked curves. *Not in bed and not in life.* Not many people could do that.

Including me.

Trish's eyes fluttered open, and a sleepy smile slowly awakened.

"Hi, baby," he whispered, and kissed her cheek.

She glanced at the window; darkness smiled back at her.

"It's early." He gazed into her eyes and his body

flooded with love. "I couldn't sleep. I was just lying here thinking about you, about us. I want an honest life with you, and part of that—a big part—is protecting you above all else. From this day forward, no more PR tricks. No more games."

"Oh, Boone," she said with a sigh. "As much as I appreciate that, you can't do it. What about your band and your family?"

"Baby, look at Jude. He's in rehab again. My rep perpetuates that lifestyle, and that can't be helpful. Without realizing it, I'm sending the message that we need to be partiers in order to succeed. I might have believed that when I was eighteen, but not now. It's a different world than it was back then, and more importantly, I'm a different person. I'll talk to the band and my family. It's not like we play the media card more than a few times a year. It was a ploy we came up with years ago and I never thought twice about it. But now, with you in my life, I want to be the best man I can be."

He kissed her cheek, knowing he was doing the right thing. "This is the right decision, Trish. I know it is. And as far as my family goes, I've been thinking a lot about Lucky. He's twelve years younger than me, and he grew up in a different world than I did. Cage and I make sure he and my mom and Mags are looked after and have the things they need, but until now I never worried about how any of them feel about my public image. More specifically, how it might impact Lucky's decisions. He's too smart to do drugs, but he's also too smart to waste his life going from meaningless job to meaningless job. My father would want him to find his niche. I need to get him into college, or at least hook him up with someone who can take his computer hacking skills and put them to good use. I've got a buddy, Carson Bad, who lives in New York City and runs an elite security company. He's done work for me, and I know he'd be willing to take Lucky under his wing. I've just been running from one thing to the next for months and haven't taken the time to think about reaching out. It's time now."

"I know Carson," she said. "Well, I know his brother Dylan better than I know him. He owns NightCaps bar. My brothers and I go there when I'm in the city. I've met Carson a time or two."

"You look worried. Please tell me it's not because you had a thing with Carson and can't figure out how to tell me."

She laughed. "It's not. I'm worried about your mom."

"My mom? Baby, I'll never do anything that'll put her in harm's way. Look at Jagger, Bowie, the legends of rock and roll. Their families stayed out of the media without any diversion tactics. I'll hire extra security if I need to, but this isn't going to be as hard as we think."

"I don't know. Those guys' lives *were* diversion tactics. And your mom seems to like her life just as it is." She stroked his cheek, and he leaned in to her touch, reveling in the support she gave effortlessly and genuinely.

"I know she does. I'll talk with her before I do anything, but it's not my reputation that protects her.

It's the distraction methods my team uses to keep the attention away from where she lives when I visit. They'll just have to use different distraction methods. We'll figure that out. We have time. I'm not going back for a visit for another few weeks anyway. But from now on, no more partying images in the press, unless I'm partying with my girl. I don't want you or your integrity to come under attack."

"I want to say thank you, but that doesn't seem big enough for all the thought you've put into this." Her eyes darkened seductively.

"Mm." He nipped at her shoulder. "What did you have in mind?"

"I can't believe I'm going to do this, but..." She pushed him onto his back and moved over him, setting her legs between his. "We'll revisit your mouth on me a little later."

Her mouth came down over his, and he drank in the sweetness of her kiss, wrapping his arms around her. Her softness conformed to his hard frame. He rocked against her, and she drew her luscious mouth away.

"Don't go," he whispered.

"I promise you'll like where I'm going."

She moved down his body, pressing kisses along each pec, down the center of his chest. Her fingers trailed over his nipples, sending bullets of heat shooting through him. She followed her fingers with her mouth, licking and sucking until he was groaning with desire. Her hot, wet mouth blazed a path down his abs, licking each muscle and teasing him to near madness as she followed the flames on the tattoos across them with her tongue. He tangled his hands in her hair, fighting the urge to guide her lower, knowing by her moans of appreciation she was enjoying every lick of torture she doled out.

He shifted, propping his head on the pillow so he could have a better view of her loving him with her mouth and hands. "Baby, your mouth should be patented."

She giggled, shifting lower, her hot breath ghosting over his erection. She held his gaze as her fingers circled his cock, and she pressed a kiss to the very tip. He craved her luscious lips around him so desperately the simple kiss blew his mind. Her lips were warm, her hand was soft, but her grip was tight, and when she swirled her tongue over the swollen head, he cursed under his breath at the vision of beauty before him. Her lips curved up in a wicked smile, and she dragged her tongue from base to tip, following her mouth with one long stroke of her hand.

"Damn, baby," he hissed.

She lowered her mouth over his shaft, and he groaned at the sheer bliss of being pleasured by the woman he loved. She sucked him hard and fast, then torturously slow. His mind spun, his body hummed, and heat pooled at the base of his spine. He was close, so very close.

"Beautiful, I need all of you." He reached for her and for a condom from the bedside table at the same time.

She helped him roll it on, then straddled his hips

and sank down, her tight heat swallowing his shaft.

"Boone," she whispered, and splayed her hands on his chest as she rode him.

Feeling her body tighten around him, the sight of her hair tumbling around her pleasure-filled face, was exquisite. Her eyes were closed, lips parted, glistening and swollen from sucking him. He gripped her hips, matching her efforts thrust for thrust. But he was too far away. He wanted to possess all of her, feel every heartbeat, taste every breath. He sat up, guiding her legs around his waist, and took her in a long, hungry kiss. Her nails dug into the back of his arms, and a stream of heady moans and mews left her lungs. He loved feeling connected at every point, her body pulsing and throbbing, so swept up in their lovemaking her head tipped back and she cried out his name. He brought her mouth back to his, swallowing her cries of ecstasy as he surrendered to his own intense release.

Trish rested her forehead against his shoulder, breathing heavily. "How are we going to do this?"

"I thought we did that pretty well." He kissed her cheek, and she laughed.

"Part of why yesterday was hard was holding back every time I saw you, and I know it was for you, too," she admitted. "I could actually *feel* how much you wanted to reach out to me when we were near each other. Think we can make it through the week?"

"We can make it through anything. And it seems to me I owe you a little oral pleasure." He swept her beneath him, rid himself of the condom, and shimmied down her body.

"What? No, you don't have to...Oh. *Oh, my.*" She clutched the sheets as he licked her sweetest spot. "With mornings like this, I think I believe you."

**

A WEEK PASSED with Boone and Trish focusing on filming and trying not to react to the ever-churning gossip mill. After their talk, Trish had managed to push the whispers aside enough to excel at acting again, but it hadn't been easy. She called Fiona to vent instead of burdening Boone with it.

"Have you ever noticed that whispers can be the sweetest, hottest, most meaningful things, or they can be the most hurtful?" Trish pressed her cell phone to her ear and glanced at herself in the mirror. It was six o'clock in the evening, and Chuck had arranged for a special dinner with the cast and crew. He made a point of taking everyone to local restaurants in the small towns where he filmed. It was his way of thanking the community for putting up with them. Unfortunately, it was also his way of gaining press, which Trish was not looking forward to, especially given the churning rumor mill.

"Sure. If you think about it, lots of things are that way. Glances." Fiona sighed. "I love when Jake glances at me from across the room and there's that moment when nothing else exists and my heart races with anticipation."

Trish smiled and sank down to the edge of the bed

and petted Sparky. "I love that, too. Boone's got the most soulful eyes. I'm really falling for him, Fi, and it hurts to hear the things people are saying."

"I'm sorry you're dealing with that. Do you want me to take a few days off and come see you? *You* might have to be professional, but they don't know me from Adam. I can make snarky comments right back at them. And then I can tell Boone all your secrets and be the third wheel when the crew leaves at night and it's just you two."

"Snuggle up between us in the bed," Trish teased.

"I hear showers for three are in now."

"I miss you, Fi. Thanks for letting me vent. I always feel better after talking to you, but I'm never letting you shower with my man."

Fiona laughed. "Don't worry. Jake is more man than one woman should be allowed in a lifetime. I'm happy for you, though. Who would have thought your crush would end up being Mr. Wonderful?"

There was a tap on the door, and Boone peeked in. He mouthed, *Can I come in?*

She waved him in. "Fi, I have to go. The hottest man on the planet just walked into my bedroom. We might have to be late for dinner. Love you."

She set the phone on the bed and rose to her feet, feeling that moment of heart-thundering attraction she and Fiona were just talking about. Was it possible for clothes to make a person look even hotter? Her mouth went dry at the sight of Boone clean-shaven, in a white button-down and dark slacks. The musky scent of his cologne reached her at the same time he took her hand in his, and she grabbed him with two hands.

"My God, baby. You are stunning. Do I really have to share you with everyone tonight?" He leaned down and kissed her cheek. "And you smell incredible."

"I was thinking the same thing about you. The last thing we need is a press event, but I wouldn't give up one second of seeing you look like this."

He wrapped his arms around her waist and drew her against his hard body—and it took only a few hot kisses for him to get even harder.

"We don't need a night out to dress up," he said against her neck. "Anytime you want to role-play, I'm game. French maid comes to mind."

She let her head fall back, reveling in his luscious lips on her neck. "Oh, this could be fun! A fireman?"

"Sure, if you'll wear nothing but the boots." He kissed her again.

"Cowboy?"

He pressed feathery kisses along her plunging neckline. "Mm-hm, anything you want, baby."

"Construction worker? Lifeguard? Fighter?"

"Yes, yes, and *hell no.*"

Laughter burst from her lungs, and he gave a half scowl, half smile that made him that much hotter. She reached up and grabbed his cheeks. "A wrestler?"

He tackled her on the bed and tickled her ribs. She squealed with delight.

"No fighters?" He laughed and tickled her harder as she futilely tried to escape his relentless tickles.

"Stop! Stop! My dress! Okay! No fighters!" She

gasped for breath between bursts of laughter.

He stopped tickling, and she tried to catch her breath. "You push all my buttons."

"I can't help it. It's so fun to tease you." She lay back with an arm over her stomach and a smile plastered across her face.

He flopped on the bed beside her, breathing as hard as she was. "You're a bad, bad girl."

"Can I at least call you Cage?" She squealed as Boone's large hands trapped her beneath him and the tickle torture began anew.

**

MAIN STREET WAS lined with cars, and a mob of fans in front of the restaurant waved papers and CD cases, screaming for autographs. Chuck stood by the entrance talking with a reporter, along with the other cast members. Burly security guards stood sentinel in front of the excited crowd.

"This isn't the sleepy little town we've been staying in, is it?" Boone said from within the safety of the car. He could hardly believe the difference a few phone calls could make.

"Chuck wanted press," Trish reminded him.

Camera flashes lit up like fireworks as Boone and Trish stepped from the car.

"Boone! Trish! Over here," a blond reporter yelled, causing a number of other reporters to gather around, taking pictures and peppering them with questions.

Boone kept a hand on Trish's lower back and

eagle eyes on the crowd. He wanted to wrap Trish in his arms and shelter her from the lustful stares and handsy guys pushing against the velvet ropes they used for crowd control. But they'd agreed not to flaunt their relationship, which meant he couldn't do a damn thing other than cast a few harsh stares and stay appropriately close. After dealing with gossip for days on end, he was about done with the fine line they'd drawn between their professional life and their personal life. Jared was riding his last nerve, making innuendos that were clearly meant to undermine their relationship. But Boone respected Trish too much to make a statement without her approval.

"Boone! How do you like acting?" a balding reporter asked.

Boone flashed a smile and slipped into his rocker persona. "It's cool, dude. Difficult for sure, but awesome to work with the stunning and talented Trish Ryder."

Trish turned a warm gaze on him as she stepped forward, surrounded by eager fans and media.

"Trish, what's it like working with Boone?" the reporter asked.

"He's incredible to work with. Very intuitive and creative." She rose to the occasion full of grace and professionalism, and Boone couldn't take his eyes off of her. "I can't wait for fans to see Rick and Delia's story. Boone really brings it to life."

In the car, Trish had told him how nervous she was, but she impressively didn't miss a beat. She held her chin up high, kept perfect eye contact, and the things that rolled off her tongue pulled at his heartstrings.

A female reporter thrust a microphone toward Trish. "What's next for you?"

She smiled brightly. "I'm not sure. I might take a little time off to enjoy myself before my next film. Visit with my family and friends."

The fans erupted with dismay, and all Boone could think about was how he couldn't wait to spend that time with her.

Trish laughed and said to the crowd, "Okay, maybe just a week!"

The crowd cheered.

"And you, Boone? What's next? When's the next Strykeforce tour?"

Trish looked up at him with a question in her beautiful eyes. He and the band had been talking about doing a tour next year, which would require months of preparation. At the time his decision had been dependent upon a number of factors, most recently, Jude's addiction. Now, he realized, his decision would be most greatly impacted by his relationship with Trish, their schedules, and how they, as a couple, wanted to live their lives.

He pressed his hand more firmly on Trish's back, hoping she'd read his silent message of wanting her input. "We'll announce it as soon as we have a firm date."

They answered a number of other questions and then signed autographs. The excited fans encroached, their arms reaching over the velvet ropes, separating

Trish and Boone. The beefy guards watched on, shoving a hand between the fans and Trish when needed, and Boone tried to keep an eye as well, but in the flurry of signing autographs among screams and waving hands, and the crowd pushing forward, he could only catch glimpses of her. A young woman tore her shirt open and thrust her lace-covered breasts forward. Boone was used to full frontals, though she was wearing a bra. He signed her chest, but not without a wave of guilt passing through him. He turned and caught a glimpse of Trish rolling her eyes before she ducked into the restaurant.

He nodded to the security guard, indicating he was done, and followed her in. The restaurant had rustic charm, with barn-wood walls and faux-candle chandeliers. The scent of starchy foods, grilled steak, and comfort hung in the air, which Boone preferred to the snooty smell of overpriced restaurants where customers paid for taking up space rather than good food. That was the Bronx boy in him. Anyone with money could take up space, but it took a great deal of care to cook a meal that tasted like his mother had cooked it.

"You okay?" he whispered in Trish's ear.

"Of course, but we should have a little chat about signing body parts." She laced her fingers with his, which surprised and pleased him, given that they were not supposed to be flaunting their relationship. "I'm thinking mine are probably enough."

He was glad to see she handled jealousy as gracefully as she handled the media, and he added that to the long list of things he loved about her.

"Agreed. I'm sorry. I was just playing the part." He thought back to the Rum Hummer and the way Trish had acted out of jealousy when he'd signed the waitress's shirt. Things were different then. *Now we're a couple.*

The hostess appeared, and Trish released his hand. His stomach plummeted like a little boy who'd lost his baseball. As they followed the hostess to the private dining room, Trish flashed the warm, sexy smile he'd noticed she shared only with him and whispered, "You can make it up to me later," taking away a modicum of the sting of her releasing his hand.

Dinner was even better than the aroma promised. The conversation was light, and mostly about the movie. Besides a few sideways glances, the gossipers among the crew had wisely kept their comments to themselves. Boone sat beside Trish, holding hands under the table. He wanted to drape an arm around her, but things were going smoothly and he wasn't about to rock the boat.

After dinner everyone hung around for drinks, milling about in the private dining room making small talk.

Chuck raised his glass and cleared his throat, quieting the din of the group. "I'd like to take a moment to thank each and every one of you. It takes a grand effort to make a movie, and I couldn't be more pleased with the progress we've made so far."

He shifted his gaze to Trish and Boone, and Boone squeezed Trish's hand. He was so proud of her. She'd pushed past the discomfort and frustration of the gossip and she was back to acting even better than ever. She was so believable as Delia, he was starting to get nervous about their pivotal warehouse scene. Now more than ever he didn't want to mess that up for her.

"Trish, Boone," Chuck said with a wry smile. "Ten days in Hurricane, West Virginia, has done wonders for you two. I'm considering sending all of my starring actors away together before filming."

There was a wave of appreciative laughter. Boone tried to ignore the hushed whispers that came on the heels of the laughter, but when Jared scoffed, Boone couldn't resist sending him a look he knew clearly relayed, *Careful, asshole.*

Chuck lifted his glass higher and said, "Let's take Rick and Delia to the Oscars!"

Everyone cheered.

Boone clinked glasses with Trish's and said for her ears only, "You've got this, beautiful."

Chuck joined them a moment later. "Boone, would you mind if I swept your leading lady away for a moment?"

"Not at all, and thank you for the compliment earlier."

Chuck patted his shoulder. "You two deserved it." He guided Trish to a quiet corner of the room.

Jared sidled up to Boone with a drink in his hand and a challenging glint in his eyes. "She deserves an Oscar for most of her performances."

"Agreed." Boone tried not to hit him with an icy stare, but he feared he failed.

"I've worked with Trish quite a few times, and she's never had issues like she has recently." Jared sipped his drink, eyeing Boone snobbishly. "One can only assume the time alone with you didn't do quite as much good as it did harm."

Suppressing the urge to tell the asshole where he could take his opinion, Boone curled his fingers tightly around his glass. "That so?"

Jared shrugged. "What can I say? It kills me to see someone as beautiful as Trish with someone as emotionally ill equipped as you."

Boone stepped closer, his voice dead calm, his stare lethal. "Do you believe everything you read?"

"I'm her friend. I'm just watching out for her." He glanced at Trish across the room. "She's a fine piece of ass. She deserves better."

Boone set his drink on the table, buying himself a moment to regain control of the urge to throw the asshole against the wall. He closed the gap between them, and Jared took a step back. Boone took great pleasure in his smirk morphing to fear.

"Well, pretty boy. You're obviously as bad at being a friend as you are at reading people. Friends don't talk shit behind their friends' backs, and they don't refer to each other as a 'fine piece of ass.'" He stepped even closer, his chest brushing against Jared's. "And a real friend would know Trish is far more than a fine piece of ass. It doesn't take a genius to see she's smart and strong and has more talent and couth in her pinky than you will ever possess. And as far as what I am or am not equipped to handle, you're not nearly enough man to make that determination."

He reached up and patted Jared's cheek, smiling with his mouth but leaving no room for misunderstanding in his steely gaze. "The shit you're pulling stops here and now. And I assure you, I'm well equipped to deal with pretty boys like you."

He turned and found the whole room had gone silent. All eyes were on him.

Chapter Twenty

THE WALLS PRESSED in on Trish. Chuck had just finished telling her how proud he was of her and how thankful he was that she'd agreed to help Boone. He'd said Boone had turned his acting around and proven to be as talented and capable as Trish had indicated he could be. He'd ended that brief conversation with, *Pay no attention to the nonsense on set. If you're happy, that is all that matters, and it's obvious that you two have a deep connection that goes well beyond acting.*

What was Chuck thinking now? She'd only caught the tail end of what Boone had said to Jared, but from the wide-eyed looks of everyone else in the room, it appeared she hadn't been the only one. *The shit you're pulling on the set stops here and now. And I assure you, I'm well equipped to deal with pretty boys like you.* Lord, she'd never seen anything hotter than calm and domineering Boone standing up for her. Though she was certain he'd probably made things worse, she couldn't help feeling proud and even more in love with him.

Boone draped an arm around her shoulder and flashed a smile that looked as relieved as it did confident.

"Well." He sighed and said to the leering crowd, "That was unexpected."

"What just happened?" Trish whispered through a feigned smile.

His eyes sailed over the room, and then he turned an apologetic gaze to her.

"Sorry, beautiful. I think I mentioned I'm not very good at pretending, but perhaps I failed to mention I'm also not very good at ignoring a direct confrontation that involves us." He looked out at the others and flashed a proud smile. "That's right, folks. Trish and I are a couple, and we've had our fill of the rumor mill, so from now on, if you have something to say about my past or about Trish dating a guy who's not worthy, please come see me."

Oh. My. God.

He crossed the room to where Chuck stood, bringing Trish along with him.

"Chuck, I'm sorry to have disrupted this wonderful event, but a man can only take so much before he's got to stand up for the woman he cares about. I can assure you, as far as my relationship with Trish goes, it won't interfere with filming."

Breathe. Breathe. Breathe.

"Don't worry about me. This kind of stuff happens all the time." Chuck finished his drink and set his glass on the table. "I'm just wondering what took you so long."

The air left Trish's lungs in a rush of relief. She heard the others beginning to fan out and mingle again, relieving a little more of her tension.

"These people need to have something to talk about." Chuck smiled at Trish. "You're not used to being the center of it, though, are you?"

"Not at all. I'm sorry, Chuck. We didn't mean to cause trouble."

"As I said, I don't have any issues with the two of you. You make a hell of a team on set. Keep that up and we'll have no issues."

Boone lowered his voice and said, "I'm not as bad as the press makes me out to be."

Chuck laughed. "Most people aren't." He glanced around the room. "Some of these guys would believe in unicorns if they were in the rag magazines."

As Chuck walked away, Boone wrapped his arms around Trish's waist and touched his forehead to hers. "I'm sorry, baby," he whispered. "I know we said we would be careful, but it turns out I'm not as strong as I thought I was."

She melted into his arms, feeling like the weight of the world had been lifted from her shoulders. "You're ten times stronger. The girly girl in me loves what you did."

He cocked a brow. "Really?"

"It was hot." She trapped her lower lip between her teeth and smiled up at him.

"What do you say we get out of here and take a

walk?"

"A walk? What about the press?"

"What better way to set everyone straight than to start with a little press?"

"You realize we'll be in every gossip magazine tomorrow."

"Would you rather not? I'm cool either way. We can go back to the house and take a walk around the fields, if you'd rather. I just thought it might be nice to spend an hour or two like a semi-normal couple."

She wanted that more than she realized. "I haven't told Shea, my PR rep, about us yet. I should text her. Don't you want to alert your PR team?"

Boone guided her away from the others to give them a little more privacy.

"I'm done manipulating my image. But go ahead and text her. We have plenty of time." He reached into his pocket for her phone.

Her stomach churned nervously. She should reach out to Shea, but what did that say about Trish? Wouldn't that convey the very clear message that she worried more about what people thought of Boone than what she thought of him?

"No," she said. "Let's just be ourselves and see what happens."

His brows knitted. "You sure? If the gossip around the set was any indication, the media is likely to stir up more of the same. Shea could protect you from some of that, or at least be prepared for damage control."

"You're right. She deserves a heads-up. I'll text her and tell her what to expect, but I'm going to tell her not to issue any statements. I want those to come from me. And, Boone, I want you to know, I care about what we think of each other above all else. I'm sure you know that, but I wanted to say it so you had no doubts."

"I know. Don't worry about me. I read everything I need to know in those beautiful eyes of yours." He gave her a chaste kiss and handed her the phone.

She sent off a quick text to Shea and at the last second she added her agent as well, and sent it to both of them.

You may have already heard from Fi that I'm dating Boone Stryker. He's not what the press thinks, so don't freak out. But we're about to be caught in the tabloids, and I didn't want to blindside you. Please don't issue any statements without my consent. Thanks!

Boone reached for the phone, and she hesitated. "This is going to seem weird, but do you mind if I also text my family?"

A warm smile spread across his face. "Baby, they're more important than anyone else."

"Thank you." She looked around the room, and sadness rolled in. "It's a shame that so many people don't know what an amazing man you are."

"All that matters is that you and your family know," he assured her.

God, I love you. She bit back the confession, and as she sent her family a group text strikingly similar to the previous message, the confession lingered.

I wanted to let you guys know I'm dating Boone Stryker. He's not what the press thinks, so don't freak out. We'll probably be in the tabloids tomorrow, and I didn't want to blindside any of you. I promise you'll love him! Love you all!

She powered off the phone and handed it to Boone.

He looked at the dark screen. "You sure you want it off after sending those loaded messages?"

"That's *why* I want it off."

They made their way around the room, saying goodbye.

"You guys are cute together," Zoe said to them. "I'm sorry I asked what I did that first day we arrived, Trish." She glanced up at Boone. "It was nothing personal, Boone. I've worked with Trish many times, and her co-stars are always trying to get her attention, which means you're either packing a monster in your drawers or you're a really special guy."

"Zoe!" Trish gaped.

Boone and Zoe both laughed.

"I'm kidding!" Zoe pushed her blond hair over her shoulder and said, "If that's all you were interested in, you would have taken Vin Diesel up on his offer."

Trish shook her head and said to Boone, "There was no offer. Just a little flirtation."

He laughed. "I'm not worried, baby. You're with me, not him."

"I'm happy for you guys," Zoe added. "And half the people here who are gossiping are protective of Trish. The other half just love to gossip. You'll be yesterday's news soon enough."

Trish hugged her. "Thank you, Zoe."

"Thanks, Zoe. I appreciate your support." Boone lowered his voice and said, "Just for the record, aka rumor mill, Vin Diesel has nothing on me."

"Oh my God. You're such a guy." Trish dragged him away and was surprised when he extended a hand to Jared.

"See you on set tomorrow?" Boone said with an unexpectedly kind smile.

Jared gave one curt nod and shook his hand.

As they made their way through the restaurant toward the entrance, she asked, "What did Jared say to you, anyway?"

Boone's jaw tightened. "Nothing worth mentioning."

"Obviously it was something rude. So why were you so nice to him just now?" She waved to a little girl watching them walk by. Boone waved, too, which melted her heart a little more.

"The guy's an idiot, but it doesn't mean I have to be. I set him straight. That's enough." He kissed her cheek as he pushed open the restaurant door, and camera flashes lit up the night.

Boone kept her tucked tightly against his side as the cameras flashed and reporters showered them with questions.

"Are you two dating?" a reporter asked.

"Yes," Boone said with a proud smile that made Trish's heart race.

"How long have you two been an item?" another reporter asked.

"Long enough to know it's real," Boone answered

smoothly.

"Boone, does this mean you're off the market?"

Boone gazed into Trish's eyes and said, "Absolutely."

"Trish, are you going to quit acting and travel with the band?"

"Do you have plans for future movies together?"

Between the bright flashes, the barrage of questions, and Boone whispering in her ear, "See, beautiful, we've got this," Trish couldn't form a single answer. Thankfully, as they pushed through the crowd, Boone took care of it for both of them.

"She'd never let her fans down by quitting," Boone assured them. "And we need to get through our first movie before we can think about doing more together. But I'd gladly work on any project with Trish."

"Trish, why Boone?" a female reporter asked.

Boone raised his brows, giving her the floor. She gazed into his loving eyes and her heart thundered. She didn't want to overthink her answer or give the most professional or appropriate answer. She wanted to tell the world what she really thought of her man.

"Because he's the kindest, most sincere, loyal, and loving man I've ever met." She wound her arms around his neck, and with a half dozen cameras aimed at them, she pressed her lips to his. And when he dipped her like the famous V-J Day Times Square kiss, she held on for the ride.

A SENSE OF freedom and pride filled Boone as he and Trish signed autographs, passing smiles to each other as they did. Trish's eyes beamed with happiness. Who would have thought that something as small as admitting to being in a relationship could make two people so happy?

He reached for Trish's hand and said to the crowd, "Thank you all so much for your support, but if you don't mind, I'd like to take a walk with my gorgeous girlfriend."

They headed down the small-town street trailed by shouts of gratitude and, thankfully, no followers. Eventually the din of the fans gave way to the quiet of two lovers' footfalls on concrete.

"And so it begins," Trish said, sliding her arm around Boone's waist and snuggling in closer. "Tomorrow should be interesting." She gazed up at him with a curious look in her eyes. "What's the worst that can happen?"

"Let's see...In about fifteen minutes websites will start buzzing, and rumors will spread faster than weeds. Tomorrow morning we'll be on the front page of gossip magazines, and shows like TMZ will be chatting us up. Headlines will ponder what famed and talented good-girl Trish Ryder is doing with bad-boy womanizing Boone Stryker. Our PR reps will wonder what hit them, and on set everyone will be watching me and Jared to see if we flip out." He cocked his head. "Does that sound about right?"

"You left out the best part. Tomorrow morning we'll wake up in each other's arms, and until we turn on our phones or the crew arrives, we'll still be in this happy little bubble."

"You're right. That is the best part." He waved his hand at the quaint street, where no two buildings were the same. "And right now we're in Small-Town, USA, taking an evening stroll. Without cameras, without fans or the crew, or anyone else to scrutinize us. More than anything, what I want is to just be *us* for a little while, without worrying about what will happen tomorrow."

"I'm all for that."

They came to Main Street Music. Like several other shops on the street, the building looked like a house, rather than a store. The lower half was tan brick, with large picture windows, and the upper half was covered in white siding and hung three or four feet farther out than the brick, creating a natural cover from the elements.

"This reminds me of a music shop back home. Want to sit for a minute?" Boone smiled with the memory of sitting out front of the local music store with his friends when he was younger. "We used to sit on the steps and play our guitars, and people would stop by to listen. It was nice."

"Do you ever miss the simplicity of not being a star?"

"Yeah, all the time. But I don't pay as much attention to the crap that comes with fame, so it probably doesn't bother me as much as it does other people." He draped an arm over her shoulder and kissed the top of her head. "Actually, that's not true. It bothers the hell out of me now that we're together. But before us?" He shrugged.

"When I visit my parents, I love the simplicity of just being *Trish*. I live my life the way I want to for the most part, and I don't worry about dressing a certain way, as you saw by my airport attire. But there's something wonderful about visiting my hometown and knowing the people who knew me as Trish, the Ryder boys' baby sister, don't expect me to be someone else."

"Hometowns are the great equalizer. It's easy to get an inflated ego when you're surrounded by people who make a buck off of you and build you up all the time and fans who are in awe over your fame and the person they think you are."

His mind traveled down all the usual paths when he thought of home—family, friends, Harvey, Epson, and finally circled back and settled on his father. "When I was a kid, I used to follow my dad around the house when he fixed things. He was a mechanic, and he could fix just about anything. We'd be fixing the furnace, or repairing a leak under the sink, and I'd try to learn from what he was doing and focus on his storytelling at the same time. I can still hear his voice and see him lying on his back beneath the bathroom sink, working as he spoke. He had the type of voice you wanted to snuggle into: calm, steady, with a rough pitch to it. God, baby. I really miss him."

Trish put her head on his shoulder and held his

hand. He loved that she knew when to push and when to give him silent support.

"He used to say it was easy to look like a diamond on a sunny day, but it's how you act on the darkest days that matters."

"There's so much truth to that statement, isn't there?" Trish asked.

"Yeah. I wish so badly that he could meet you." He pressed his lips to her temple and closed his eyes, sending a silent sentiment up to his father. *I miss you, Dad, and I hope I do you proud.*

He opened his eyes and breathed deeply. "If that's the measure of a person's true inner spirit, then my parents deserve the highest accolades. Their lives weren't easy. Their parents basically disowned them when my mom got pregnant, but they didn't give up on each other. They found ways to make it on their own. I hope I can be half the man my father was."

Trish's expression turned serious. "You're so much more than that."

The door to Main Street Music opened, and they both turned. A guy with longish brown hair, wearing cargo shorts but no shirt, with a guitar strapped to his back, was locking the door. He turned and his brows drew together.

"Oh, hey. How's it going?" The guy pulled his guitar strap off and sank down to the steps next to Boone with a warm smile. He had a dark tan, which surely didn't come from working in a music store. "I'm Carey. Helping my buddy out with his store this week."

Before Boone could say anything, Carey did a

double take and said, "Boone Stryker. Rad, man. I heard you were in town." He leaned forward looking around Boone at Trish. "And you're the actress. Man, this *is* my lucky night."

"Trish Ryder. Nice to meet you," Trish said sweetly. "I hope you don't mind that we're sitting here."

"No, babe, it's cool." Carey began playing his guitar. "I'm not used to things shutting down so early. It's nice to have people to hang with."

Boone listened to him play for a minute, his fingers itching to strum as well. "You're good. Do you play in a band?"

"Nah. But my buddies have a band back home and I play with them when they practice." He held the guitar out to Boone. "Wanna jam?" He hiked a thumb over his shoulder and rose to his feet. "I'll grab another guitar."

"Do it," Trish urged. "It'll be fun."

"Sure." Boone took the guitar from Carey. "Thanks."

"Cool." Carey went into the shop, retrieved another guitar, and sat beside Boone again.

"Where's home?" Trish asked.

"Cape Cod," he said. "This shop belongs to my buddy Drake Savage. He and a few of our other buddies bought a resort on the bay in Wellfleet. Drake's up there fixing up the resort and opening another shop, which is why I'm here helping out until the manager comes back from vacay."

"My brother Blue lives on the Cape," Trish said.

"Blue Ryder. Maybe you know him?"

"Dude!" Carey laughed. "Everyone knows Blue. You must know Leanna Bray? Um, Remington now. Married Kurt Remington, the novelist. Man, I love his thrillers. Leanna's a good friend of mine. We both have space at the Wellfleet Flea Market every summer."

"Here, baby, switch places with me." Boone moved to Trish's other side so she could chat with Carey about their mutual friends.

Boone quietly played the guitar as the two of them caught up. Not for the first time, he recognized Trish's adoration for her brothers in the light in her eyes and the joyful tone of her voice as they talked about them. Carey played his guitar on and off as they talked, and when their conversation came to a natural lull, Boone and Carey played together. They hung out for a long while, and before heading back to the farmhouse, they exchanged phone numbers and promised to try to connect at the Cape sometime soon.

Later that night, Boone and Trish lay in bed with Sparky curled between them.

"I don't think I've ever seen you as relaxed as you were tonight with Carey," Trish said with a sleepy smile.

Boone kissed Sparky's belly and moved him beside the pillows, then pulled Trish closer. "I'm sure it had a lot to do with how easygoing he was, but truthfully, it also had to do with the fact that I don't feel like we're hiding anymore. And I have to admit it felt good to say something to Jared and to stop acting like we don't hear the gossip. I'm not a kid, Trish. I'm a thirty-year-old man who has no place in his life for that kind of nonsense. But I am worried about how the fallout will affect you. So I need you to know, I'm here for you. You can lean on me. I want it all. The laughter, the tears, the frustration. Whatever you feel, I want to know so I can enjoy it with you, or help fix it. And as far as my past goes, I'll handle it in whatever way we both think makes sense."

She pressed her lips to his and sighed. "I've been holding you back, haven't I?"

"Holding me back? You've set me free."

"No, I mean from being the badass boyfriend you want to be." Her eyes lit up with the tease.

"Maybe a little, but I get it. There's a proper way to act in your workplace. And then there are assholes, like Jared, and 'proper' needs to be kicked under the carpet for a little while." He kissed the tip of her nose. "But I didn't go all caveman on his ass. I think I was pretty restrained."

"And hot. Don't forget hot." She scooted even closer, bringing their bodies together. Her breath whispered over his lips. "I don't think we need to address comments about your past. I think we should let our relationship stand for itself." She reached over him and clutched his butt.

Boone swept her beneath him and nipped at her lower lip. "And what do you think they'll see?"

"Something beautiful and sexy that can handle anything that comes its way."

"I sure hope so, baby, because I can't imagine not having you by my side." He brushed his lips over hers.

"Or in my bed." He laced their hands together and held them beside her head. "I'm falling so hard for you, Trish. Can you feel it? Can you feel how much I care for you? Can you feel the way my heart goes crazy when we're together? Can you feel how much of me you already own?"

"Yes," left her lips like a secret, and he sealed that secret with a kiss.

Chapter Twenty-One

TRISH AWOKE AT five o'clock the next morning to the delicious scents of cinnamon and coffee and to an empty bed. She pulled on a T-shirt and padded downstairs. Boone sat in the kitchen with the phone pressed to his ear and the kitten cuddled against his bare chest. In the center of the table was a plate of cinnamon rolls, fresh steam curling in the air above them. Trish's mouth watered at the sight. She was counting down the days until she could eat real food again.

Boone smiled and mouthed, *Mags*, then patted his thigh for her to join him.

She loved how he always wanted her close. She walked around the table and saw he was wearing only his boxer briefs and waggled her brows. She reached for the kitten and he pulled her down to his lap with a sly grin.

"I talked to Benny and Harvey an hour ago," he

said into the phone. "The rehab center wants me to wait to talk to Jude in person, so I'll go see him when we're done filming." He smiled and said to Trish, "Mags said hi and that she sent you a text at three in the morning, too." Boone pointed to her phone on the kitchen counter, where he'd set it last night when they got home.

"Hi, Mags," she said loudly enough for his sister to hear. She got up and turned on her phone. It went off like a vibrator on speed as messages poured in. While Boone said goodbye to Mags, Trish scrolled through them, wondering if everyone in the world had stayed up all night reading online gossip.

She reached for a cinnamon bun and Boone set his phone on the table and laughed.

"That bad?" He pulled her onto his lap again and kissed her.

"It's five in the morning, you *baked*, and I have about twenty messages from my family. At *five in the morning!*" She bit into the cinnamon roll and closed her eyes. "Mm. It's like an orgasm for my taste buds."

He chuckled and kissed her. "Mm. You're like an orgasm for my taste buds."

She set the delicious pastry on the plate and wiped her hands on a napkin. "You were too nervous to sleep?"

"Just restless. I wanted to have a talk with Benny and Harvey, so they know what to expect and how things are going to change publicity-wise. I got a few emails from my PR rep and told him not to make any statements, as we discussed. And Mags said she was up all night working on new recipes and saw a clip of us on an entertainment channel. She said we looked adorable and happy."

"We are adorable and happy." She kissed him again. Her phone vibrated and she sighed. "Ugh. If I'm going to make it to the set on time, I'd better get started answering messages."

She moved to her own chair and Boone pushed her plate in front of her.

"Thanks, but I can't finish it. I only have a few more days of filming. I can't start putting on the pounds yet."

His eyes went serious. "I worry about you. Last night you hardly ate at all. Can I at least make you egg whites?"

"Yes, thank you. I love how you worry about me, but this not eating is short-lived. As soon as I'm done filming, I'm digging in to a juicy cheeseburger. I told you I love to eat." She leaned in and kissed him again, and she wanted to kiss him again and again and again, but her phone vibrated with another text, reminding her of how much she had to do. "You might not like me as much ten pounds heavier."

"Baby, I'd like you no matter how big or slim you are. It's who you are that I'm attracted to. Your looks might have lured me in, but it's who you are—your generosity, strength, intelligence, that hooked me hard." He brushed his lips over hers and whispered, "Oh, and the great sex helps."

Laughing, she smacked his arm.

"In all seriousness, I hope you know, even if you

could never have sex again and you gained a hundred pounds, I'd still be totally into you." He got up to make her eggs.

"Not me. I'd kick you to the curb," she teased. "So you'd better keep doing whatever it takes to maintain that hot body of yours."

"Lots of sex, beautiful. Lots of sex."

She laughed.

Trish answered some of her messages as she ate. Fiona sent her a high-five emoticon, with a side note from Jake that said he was glad he didn't have to kill Boone, because he liked his music. Shea was on board with not responding to comments and said she was a little jealous, given how hot *and* talented Boone was. She even thought Boone's tougher image might give the public pause about how goody-two-shoes Trish really was. They both saw advantages to that, given that Trish was hardly a goody-two-shoes, even though she was careful about who she dated.

She showered and dressed before answering her family's messages. As she descended the stairs, she spotted Boone in the living room playing his guitar. What a sight he was, cradling the guitar so naturally it looked like an extension of himself. *Like when you hold me. I feel like that, too.* Every few beats he'd jot something down in his notebook.

She took a picture with her cell phone, so she would always have it on hand. She knew they were only playing house here on the set, and her heart ached at the prospect of returning to their real lives. She realized she didn't even know where Boone lived or what his practice schedule with his band was like. How much did he travel? What was his *real* life like?

Boone looked up from his notebook and caught her staring. "Hey, beautiful. We only have a few minutes before the crew arrives." He patted the seat beside him.

"A few minutes? I need to call my family." She hurried down the stairs and sat beside him. "Group Skype, here we come."

"Okay," he said curiously.

"Twenty-two messages from them now, Boone. *Five* brothers *and* my parents. You have no idea what they're like. Sometimes I think Duke forgets I'm an adult. He means well, but he worries."

Boone slid a hand to the nape of her neck and drew her closer. Her body went warm as she melted against him. The feeling had become so familiar, she'd come to expect it. Understanding and compassion hovered in his eyes.

"And you love it, baby, as you should. It would be worse if they didn't care."

I love you was on the tip of her tongue, but he hadn't said it yet, and with her realization that they had so much more to learn about each other, she fought hard to hold the words back.

He kissed her tenderly, making her wish they could just lock the doors and hole up for the afternoon. She wanted to sit right there on the couch listening to him play the guitar while his soulful voice sank into her bones. She imagined curling up beside him reading. It felt like forever since she'd had a chance to dive into a Kristan Higgins or Diane Chamberlain novel. Her phone vibrated, pulling her from her reverie—and from their toe-curling kisses.

She showed Boone Duke's name on the screen, then sent a group text to her brothers and parents. *I'm in a hurry. Group Skype? Don't text back unless you can't Skype. I'm logging on now.* She grabbed her laptop from upstairs and settled in beside Boone again.

"You're doing it here? Don't you want privacy?" He pushed to his feet, and she pulled him back down.

"I'm doing it here because I don't want privacy. Do you mind staying? Please?"

"Sure, but as a guy with a sister, I can tell you that your brothers probably won't say what they want to in front of me."

"Trust me, they won't hold back. Besides, I'm proud to be your girlfriend. I have nothing to hide." She signed onto Skype and snuggled in beside Boone, trying to hide her nervousness. She wasn't afraid of what her brothers would think of Boone, but the last time she'd introduced a boyfriend to them all at once was back in high school, and it hadn't been her choice. She'd made the mistake of telling Jake the name of the guy she was dating, and that weekend all five of her brothers had shown up at their parents' house and demanded to meet him. The relationship didn't last through the weekend. But now she was an adult—an extremely busy adult—and she had no choice but to answer them all at once. The crew would be there any minute, and leaving her brothers hanging after they'd sent so many messages would only lead to a string of texts and lengthy explanations later.

Her parents' faces appeared on the screen. They were sitting at the kitchen table. Her father had one arm draped over the back of her mother's chair.

"Hi, baby girl," her mother said with a warm smile. She had the same sandy-blond hair color as Cash and Gage. Duke's was similar, though slightly darker.

"Hi, Mom. Dad." Both of her parents wore glasses; her mother's were amber, and her father's wire-framed. The hipster trend made them look younger, too.

"Hi, pumpkin," her father said. He was big and broad-chested, with dark hair peppered with gray. His silver soul patch gave him a youthful look. If he were in the same room, he'd have given Trish a big, warm hug.

"'Pumpkin,'" Boone whispered.

Before anyone could say a word, each of her brothers' handsome faces appeared on the screen in quick succession.

"Hey, sis," Duke said with a serious face, making her heart race even faster.

"Trishy, how's it goin'?" Jake's face was going in and out of focus. "Can you see me? I'm on a mountain."

"Yes," Trish answered. "You're shaking, but I can see you. Are you on a rescue?"

"No. Just out for a hike," Jake said.

"For the record," Blue said, pointing at the monitor, "Boone, I would have preferred to meet you in person." All her brothers were built like their father, but Blue also shared his dark hair.

"I haven't even introduced him yet." Trish leaned to the side, giving Boone more room. "Boone, this is my family." She pointed to each of her brothers as she introduced them. "Duke." Duke nodded. "Gage."

"Hey, sis. Hi, Boone," Gage said. "Nice to meet you. Ignore Duke's scowl."

"I'm not scowling," Duke said.

Cash laughed. "Dude, you're scowling. Boone, I'm Cash. I'd prefer to shake your hand, too."

"Hopefully we'll be able to do that soon," Boone said.

"Mom, Dad, this is Boone," Trish said with a wide smile. "Boone, Andrea and Ned, my awesome parents."

"Sorry we're not there to greet you properly," Andrea said. "But it's a pleasure to meet you."

Her father waved. "Nice to meet you, son."

Trish's chest warmed at the unexpected endearment.

The sounds of car doors alerted them to the arrival of the crew. "I have to hurry. The crew is arriving, but I wanted to introduce you guys to Boone." She leaned back and motioned to Boone, who smiled and waved. "And to tell you not to worry about what the press says about his background. He's not the guy they all think he is."

"What kind of guy *are* you, Boone?" Duke asked.

Boone gazed at Trish with an easy smile, like it was the simplest question he'd ever heard. "The kind of guy who adores your sister." He turned back to her family and said, "And the type of guy who's also close to his family."

"Uh-huh," Duke said skeptically. "And while you're with Trish, you're done with the other women?"

"Duke!" Trish chastised him at the same time his fiancée, Gabriella, peered over Duke's shoulder.

"Hi, everyone. Boone, I'm Gabriella. Please ignore my overprotective fiancé. He's hardly one to talk."

"Seriously," Jake said, his face bouncing in and out of the frame. "Who cares what he was like before Trish? This is real simple. You hurt Trish, we hurt you."

"Boys," Ned said in a firm voice.

"That's okay," Boone assured him. "I've got a sister. I get it. I have no intention of hurting Trish."

Several crew members came in through the front door, bringing a cacophony of commotion with them.

"We have to go. The crew has arrived." Trish rose to her feet, bringing the laptop with her.

"Wait, Trish," Blue interjected. "How long are you in West Virginia?"

"Two weeks," she and Duke said at the same time.

"How'd you know?" Trish asked.

Duke's sly grin gave his answer. Her eldest brother had connections in every industry. He'd probably already done a full background check on Boone.

"Duke, seriously?" She shook her head.

Her mother laughed. "Oh, honey, he worries about you."

"Boone? Chuck's looking for you." Zoe's voice entered the room before she did. Her blond hair was pinned up in a messy bun. She touched her headset and spoke into it. "Got him. We're coming."

"Guess I've got to run. It was nice meeting you all," Boone said to her family. "After we're done filming, let's try to grab dinner or something?"

"Looking forward to it," her mother said sweetly.

"Thanks for taking the time to meet us, Boone," her father chimed in. "Good luck on the movie. Trish, we have to sign off, honey. We've got breakfast with the Wilkinsons in ten minutes."

"Okay. Love you guys," she said to her parents.

"See you later." Boone gave Trish a quick peck on the cheek and followed Zoe out the front door.

Trish carried the laptop upstairs as she spoke. "Sorry, guys, but I have to get out there, too."

"Wait, Trish. How serious is this?" Cash asked.

Serious enough that I should thank you for the first-aid kit. If she told them the truth, they'd ask her ten more questions. "I don't know. Pretty serious." She set her laptop on the bed and slipped her feet into a pair of sandals.

"Why this guy?" Duke asked. "You can have any guy. Why do you want the one with the troublesome past?"

"Sorry, Trish, but I've got to chime in here," Cash said. "What makes you think he'll treat you any differently than any of the other women he's been with?"

"You guys haven't even met him in person yet," Gage said to their brothers.

"He's right," Blue added.

She heard the front door open and footsteps on the hardwood floors.

"Trish, makeup is looking for you," Zoe called from the bottom of the stairs.

She bent to look at her brothers. Jake was still going in and out of focus. Gage and Blue were looking at something off camera, and Cash and Duke were watching Trish like a hawk.

"Trish? Costume needs you before makeup!" a male voice called up the stairs.

"I'm sorry. I'm running late. I don't have time for these questions right now. Love you, but I have to run." She signed off before they could protest, feeling guilty for cutting them off but relieved at the same time. As she hurried downstairs and out the front door, she wondered if she'd been conditioned after all these years against feeling the *brother guilt* as strongly as she once had.

Chapter Twenty-Two

THE NEXT FEW days flew by in a flurry of nonstop filming, with meetings that carried over well into the evenings. Chuck worked them at a breakneck pace, and it paid off. They'd cut a full two days off of their filming schedule. He'd shocked them all when he'd decided to relocate the warehouse scene to the farmhouse because he said Boone and Trish's on-screen connection was too strong to chance losing it by flying back across the country to film. Boone couldn't argue that filming here with Trish felt more natural by the minute.

Boone sat beside Trish in the makeup trailer while Ronnie and April worked their magic.

"I told you you'd get used to this," April said, waving a makeup brush across Boone's forehead.

"Not like I have a choice." He winked at Trish and reached for her hand. "Three more days for you."

"I can't believe this is your last day of filming. You

have been amazing, Boone. Are you ready for this scene?" Trish faced straight ahead as Ronnie made her hair look like she'd spent a week sleeping in a gutter. April had already done an incredible job of making Trish's skin look ashen and filthy. She had on the requisite dirty yellow dress, and despite the filth, she looked stunning.

April pulled back and smiled. "Even if he's not ready, at least he'll look hot."

"That would be thanks to you, April. Thanks for making me look good and for putting up with a guy who's not into makeup." He turned to Trish, whose hair was practically dripping with whatever they were using to make it look greasy. "Now, if Ronnie would stop making my girlfriend look like she washed her hair with baby oil, we'd be all set."

He kissed the back of Trish's hand, and April *aww*ed.

"Don't you have someone else to torture?" he teased.

"Why would I do that when it's so fun to torture you?" April set her makeup brush down and leaned against her supply table. "Besides, you're way more fun than working on schedules with Jared. I was glad you gave him a good talking to. He bugs me."

Boone tried to steer the conversation away from Jared. He wasn't about to get caught gossiping about a guy whose biggest faults were an inflated ego and one too many asshole genes. "To answer your question," he said to Trish, "I'm ready, beautiful. Thanks to you. Nervous as hell, but ready."

The trailer door opened and Zoe poked her head inside. "We're ready in five."

"Okay, *beautiful*," Ronnie said to Trish with a wink. "Only you could make dirt and grime look this good." He stepped back, giving Trish room to stand up. "Whatever you do, don't touch it."

"Thanks, Ronnie." She and Boone headed out of the trailer, where Zoe was waiting.

"Oh good," Zoe said. "Boone, if you nail this, I'll give you a million dollars."

"I'll do my best," he assured her, then turned to Trish. "Hear that? A quick mil if I nail it."

"I should say, if you can nail it in less than five takes, because I have a date tonight," Zoe explained. "So if you need fifty takes, you'll have the guilt of ruining my date with a hot country boy on your shoulders."

"Whoa, that's a lot of pressure."

"Oh no. Not as much pressure as that's going to be." Trish pointed to the driveway, where Duke, Cash, and Gage were getting out of an SUV. "What the heck are they doing here?"

Boone was amused and impressed by the sight of her three surprisingly large brothers standing shoulder to shoulder like a cavalry. They probably thought they'd scare him off, but seeing them had the opposite effect. He loved knowing they cared enough to get involved, regardless of whether Trish was an adult or not. Without having ever shaken hands with these men, he already had a great deal of respect for them.

Zoe smoothed her shirt and threw her shoulders back. "What I said? Forget it, Boone. Take as long as you need. I had no idea Trish's brothers were coming. Gage *is* still single, right?"

"Yes, but not really. He's just too bullheaded to do something about it."

"Bummer. Okay, my date is back on," Zoe said. "Go quick, or you know I'll be hollering for you again."

Trish looked at Boone. "Ready to be grilled?"

"Why not?" He followed her across the yard.

Duke helped a tall, dark-haired woman from the vehicle, and Boone recognized her as Gabriella from their Skype call. Cash helped another woman out of the backseat, and Boone knew by her pregnant belly that she was his wife, Siena. Siena grabbed Gabriella's hand, and the two women hurried up the hill toward them. Trish glanced at Boone with wide, excited eyes.

"Go," he said with a laugh.

"Thank you!" She ran down the hill with her arms out to her sides, yelling, "Don't hug me! I'm in full makeup! Don't hug me!"

Mags would love these girls. When Boone had talked to her the other morning, Mags had raved about how much she liked Trish. She and Trish had been texting each other since their visit, and Mags had confided to Boone that she'd always wondered what it would be like to have a sister. She said Trish was the first woman she'd felt that kinship with. Not that he needed his family's approval to fall in love, but hearing that from his sister had further confirmed how right he and Trish were together.

The girls jumped on their tiptoes inches from each other. The air beat with their excitement *and* with the willpower it was clearly taking for them not to give in and hug each other.

Boone waved to them and continued down the hill toward the men to face the firing squad.

**

"DUKE WAS HELL-BENT on coming out here and meeting Boone face-to-face," Gabriella explained, shaking her head. She was tall, with an olive complexion that gave her a sun-kissed glow even in the winter. In her sundress and sandals she looked more like a college girl than the family law attorney she was. "Blue and Jake tried to talk him out of it, but you know Duke. You'll be fifty and he'll still think of you as his baby sister."

"He's such a pain sometimes." As irritated as Trish was by her brothers' need to barge into her life unannounced, she couldn't deny that the little sister in her secretly reveled in their protective nature.

She smiled at Siena and Gabriella. "At least you guys are here to run interference with me."

"You didn't think we'd let you face them without us, did you?" Siena said to Trish. She set one hand on her baby bump. "Lizzie was upset that she and Blue couldn't make it, but Blue is knee-deep in renovations on a huge project. But you know Blue. Duke will do whatever he has his heart set on doing, and Blue would probably rather meet Boone under less stressful circumstance."

"Duke's in for a surprise," Trish said sharply. "It would take more than the three of them to intimidate my man."

Gabriella's and Siena's eyes widened and they both said, "My man?"

"I have been dying to hear you say that about a guy!" Siena said to Trish as they headed down the hill toward the men. "This must be serious."

Trish slowed her pace and lowered her voice. "It is. I mean, I think it is."

"Think?" Gabriella asked.

"I mean, I know it is, but we haven't talked about the future or anything." She took a deep breath. "Okay, girls. This is it. Who's the biggest alpha?"

They exchanged smiles and said in unison, "Mine is."

Boone stood facing her brothers with his back to the girls. His arms were crossed, his legs planted firmly, hip distance apart. Even from the back Trish could see it was a defensive stance. Duke slid one hand casually into the pocket of his dark dress slacks. His expression was nearly unreadable, but there was a shimmer of appreciation and respect in his eyes. It was so slight, if Trish hadn't been his very perceptive sister, she might have missed it, which meant Boone probably had. Cash stood much the same as Boone, arms crossed, jeans-clad legs planted like tree trunks. *I am man, hear me growl.* She giggled inside at the ridiculousness of them. Thankfully, Gage, her most passive and reasonable brother, stood between them in a pair of cargo shorts and a shirt emblazoned with the name of the youth center where he worked as a sports director, No Limitz. His easy smile contrasted sharply with her other brothers' serious expressions. Despite all their chest-bumping, feather-ruffling posturing, she adored them.

But now was not the time for little-sister Trish to appear. She tucked away those tender feelings and listened as she approached, but the men had either silenced when they'd noticed the three of them, or they were having some sort of stare down. A shiver ran down her back at the thought.

She walked between them and Boone, eyeing each of her brothers. "I'd hug you guys, but that would only encourage this behavior. Besides, I'm in full body makeup, so I can't." She glared at Duke, fighting the smile tugging at her lips. "You are the most ridiculous brother *ever*." She smiled with the half-truth, and so did Duke. "And, Cash?" She held her palm up toward the sky. "Really?"

"What I don't understand is why you would think I *wouldn't* be here?" Cash asked.

Siena and Gabriella went to Cash's and Duke's sides, each resting a firm yet gentle hand on their man's arm. Trish's heart squeezed. She knew they were doing that for her, silently reminding her brothers that there was more to this conversation than assessing the worthiness of the man Trish was falling for. They were reminding her brothers that just as it wouldn't have mattered what anyone had said about the women they'd fallen in love with, Trish was an adult, and she would give her heart to whomever she wished. *As if I have any control over my heart. It belongs to Boone no matter what you guys think.*

Siena glared at Cash, and his gaze softened.

Gage laughed.

Trish rolled her eyes at Cash and stood in front of Gage with her hands on her hips. "And you're here to keep the peace, right? All the way from Colorado?"

He shrugged. "Someone's got to pull the reins." He leaned forward and lightly kissed her cheek. "You're my sister. Of course I'm here."

"Thanks, Gage." She glared at Duke again and sidled up to Boone, whose face was a mix of amusement and seriousness. How did he do that?

"Fill me in. What kind of ridiculous things have already been said?" she asked Boone, but before he could answer, she turned her gaze to her brothers. "This is the absolute worst time for you to come in here all Neanderthal and protective. We're about to film Boone's toughest scene."

"I'm sorry about the timing," Duke said calmly. "We've been trying to reach you since this morning, when we finally got our schedules together."

"That's true," Gabriella added. "We've been blowing up your phone."

"Boone! Trish! Two minutes!" Zoe yelled from the top of the hill.

Boone gave Zoe a thumbs-up, then set a supportive hand on Trish's back.

"We've been filming since seven." Trish pointed to her greasy hair. "I'm sorry, but I don't check my phone until after we're done for the day."

"Right," Duke said, and rubbed his chin. "Sorry. We didn't think that part through. All we really wanted to do was take you two out to dinner, get to know Boone."

Uh-huh. If by get to know him *you mean grill him until you know everything from his birth weight to his blood type.* She glanced at Boone, both apologetically and curiously. She'd leave the dinner invitation up to him.

"Sounds good to me." Boone smiled at her brothers, which impressed Trish, because she might not have been so casual if she were on the other side of the fence.

"Look," Boone said. "We all know you came here to check me out. And from what I know about you, Duke, you've probably already done so."

Gage covered a chuckle with a cough.

"I have nothing to hide. You can ask me anything after we do this scene." Boone turned a confident, warm gaze on Trish. "But right now your sister's Oscar is at stake." He shifted his gaze to Duke again, then slowly to the others. "And nothing is worth screwing that up."

Lacing his fingers with Trish's, he kissed the back of her hand, despite the makeup. "She deserves more than an Oscar. She deserves the world at her feet."

"Boone," she whispered, touched by his sweet words.

Duke's brows knitted, as if he were picking apart every word and deciding whether he wanted to believe them. Gage nodded and smiled at Trish. She knew Gage felt Boone's love and already had his answer. Cash's expression was somewhere in between Duke's skepticism and Gage's acceptance. Gabriella and Siena *awwed* and sighed the sighs dreams are made of. Just like Trish was doing inside.

Chapter Twenty-Three

TRISH AND BOONE headed up the hill. The set had been built on the edge of the woods at the far end of the property. They'd brought in old crates, broken bottles, and other paraphernalia, transforming the edge of the field into a dump, which they'd cut into other scenes to appear as if it was located next to the abandoned warehouse as originally planned. April and Ronnie were waiting for them by two director chairs for last-minute primps. Cameramen and crew members were moving about the set, getting ready for Boone's toughest scene. Trish heard her brothers talking as they followed them across the field. Gabriella and Siena were laughing about something. She imagined her brothers looked like an entourage of security guards and was glad the girls had come. For all their brawn, her brothers were softies when it came to the women they loved, and she knew that would help ease the tension later when they all had dinner together.

She knew her brothers meant well, but she was nervous for Boone about his performance, not about the familial nonsense. That just added pressure to an already stressful situation.

"Are you okay?" She searched his serious expression, and her stomach twisted and burned. "I'm so sorry about all of this."

"Your brothers are doing the right thing," he said without looking at her. "They love you."

"But you look stressed. Do you want me to ask them to leave and we can meet them later? I'm sure they won't mind. Believe it or not, they do understand how difficult this will be."

He stopped walking far enough away from the crew that they wouldn't hear what he had to say, but her family was on their heels, and they stopped a few feet behind them. She gave Boone a questioning look, hoping he knew she was asking if he wanted privacy for whatever he had to say. He glanced at Duke, who smiled and looked away, offering them a modicum of privacy. Gage nodded knowingly in their direction and took Cash by the arm, turning him away. Gabriella and Siena immediately sought Duke and Cash's attention the way only the best girlfriends would know to.

"Baby," Boone said softly. "I don't think I've ever been this nervous, and it has nothing to do with your family. I'm glad they're here. They care so much about you I can feel it from here. I'm nervous because you've worked so hard to help me bring my acting up to par, and I don't want to let you down."

She slid her fingers into a belt loop on each of his hips. "You could never let me down. Even if we have to do a million takes."

"But this is your shot, and you've worked hard to get here." The sincerity in his voice slid into her chest and cradled her heart.

"So have you," she reminded him. "If there's one thing in life I've learned from my parents"—she looked at Duke, standing with his arms around Gabriella, and Cash, whispering in Siena's ears, and at Gage, who was texting—probably Sally, because she was always on his mind—"and my family, it's that things like awards are for egos. My ego doesn't need filling up, but my heart is a different story. Knowing you're giving your all to this film, that you care about me, that's *everything*." She went up on her toes and kissed him. "The best things in life aren't *things* at all, Boone. They're this moment right now and when we were down the hill and you said I deserved the world at my feet—which I don't, but the sentiment meant so much to me. Even if I never get an Oscar, this film brought us together. Those are the things that matter."

"Guys!" Zoe interrupted, strutting toward them with a clipboard in one hand and a stern expression on her face. "Chuck is stressed, and when Chuck is stressed, we're all stressed. Can we please get moving?"

"Sorry!" Trish smiled up at Boone. "You'll do great."

Fifteen minutes later, Trish was lying on the ground among the rubbish, staring blankly up at the clear blue sky. Cameras moved overhead, but her stare remained vacant and distant. Her brothers and the girls had seen her act before, but it didn't lessen the sense of pride she felt knowing they were there. It didn't matter that this scene only required her to be drugged out and wouldn't show her range of emotions. It took immense skill to zone out the way she needed to and to go lifeless when Boone would eventually lift her into his arms and carry her away.

She thought about Boone and all the other stuff going on in his life—Jude going to rehab, his worries about Lucky, outing their relationship to the press, his confrontation with Jared, her brothers showing up, his upcoming performance. Even with all of that, he was focused on Trish and how his performance might affect her chance at notoriety. If that didn't tell her brothers everything, she wondered if anything could.

**

BEFORE EACH PERFORMANCE with his band, Boone centered his mind by mentally ticking through all the steps it had taken him to achieve the level of success he had. Doing so made him even more appreciative of the opportunities he had been given and drove him to give his fans the best damn show he could. Now, as he stood on set preparing to give his most critical performance, he tried using the same tactic to calm his racing nerves. But his nerves were more fried than ever. To make matters worse, he wasn't sure exactly why he'd gone from feeling more confident with each scene they'd filmed to suddenly feeling as though he were standing in quicksand.

In seconds they would begin filming and all eyes would be on him. He could do this. He'd been acting all week without issue. Soon he'd face Trish lying lifeless before him. His chest constricted, but not in the same way it had before he and Trish had worked through his past. This feeling of suffocation had nothing to do with *detaching* from his feelings and everything to do with how deeply he cared for her.

Her brothers and their significant others looked on from the fringes, wearing expressions of rapt anticipation. This movie had the power to launch Trish's career to a higher level, and despite what she'd said, he knew damn well how important it was to her. That had to be what had him feeling as though his lines were sinking into the muck, and he had to use that knowledge as motivation to pull his shit together. *Fast.*

The first assistant director yelled, "Roll sound."

The set fell silent.

Deep breaths. One. Two. Three.

The boom operator hollered, "Sound speed."

I can do this. For Trish, I can do anything.

He listened as the next few directives were announced.

"Roll camera."

"Camera speed, hit it."

An assistant stood before the cameras, called out the scene designation, and clapped the slate. Boone's pulse skyrocketed, and he took in the rubbish-littered grass and finally allowed his eyes to drift to Trish lying on her back, staring absently up at the sky. Her arms were tracked with needle marks, her fingers angled limply upward. Dark moons shadowed each beautiful eye. Her wrinkled dress was bunched up over her bruised thighs. The makeup was so real he could feel the pain of every bruise, every scar, every bad decision. No longer was he experiencing flashes of his past or anger at Destiny's parents. No, those emotions had been unearthed, laid bare, and he'd mentally done exactly as Trish had suggested. He'd forgiven the weaknesses and failures of Destiny's parents. He'd moved on, and in doing so, he was weighed down by new, even more powerful emotions: earth-shattering, chest-constricting, overwhelming love for the woman lying on the ground.

Someone yelled, "Set."

This was it.

Chuck yelled, "Action," and Boone's breath caught in his throat.

He knew the scene by heart. Crouch beside her and say, *What do you expect me to do now?* But those words were all wrong. He would never think of himself at a time like this.

Fear and urgency sent him across the field. He fell to his knees beside Trish. "Delia! Delia. Delia." Trish and Delia were intertwined like ghosts fading into each other, feeding his fear, rage, and confusion with every frantic beat of his heart. His knees dug into the earth as he hovered over her, trembling, his eyes burning with tears. His lines washed away with the scent of Trish, the woman he loved, hovering on the brink of death.

"Baby! No, baby. No!" He took out the prop phone he wasn't supposed to use until the end of the scene and instinctively punched 911 and balanced it between his shoulder and chin as he lifted Trish's limp body, cradling her against his chest while he rattled off the fictional address to the nonexistent emergency services at the other end of the line. The phone dropped to the ground as he rose to his feet with Trish's lifeless body.

He brought his face to hers, speaking through gritted teeth. "Don't die on me, baby. Don't you die on me." Tears streamed down his cheeks, dripping onto her skin. "I love you, baby. You're the reason I'm here. The reason I *breathe*."

His eyes darted over the set, a rush of emotions swamping him. Everything blurred together. "Keep breathing. Breathe, baby, breathe." He stared out at nothing and yelled, "Where's the fucking ambulance?"

With his heart in his throat, he turned his face up toward the sky. "Take me!" he screamed through his sobs. "Please! Take. Me."

Trish's arm fell limply toward the ground. Her head lolled back over his arm, and he pressed her prone body to his chest. Sirens sounded in the distance.

He took a step and his knees weakened. He stumbled, swaying as he tried to regain his footing from the bone-deep fear coursing through him. He fell to his knees again, cradling her safely against him as the sirens neared.

"You're good, baby. Good and smart and beautiful, and I love you. I love you so damn much. Don't give up. Don't you dare give up, baby."

Sirens blared, and as he fell back on his heels, paramedics rushed to claim her. He held too tightly, couldn't let go. A paramedic grabbed his shoulder, but all Boone saw was Trish's glassy eyes staring into a world of nothingness.

"We've got her. Sir, let go. We've got her."

He felt her weight leave his arms, and a flurry of activity ensued, but Boone was in a fog, lost between reality and fiction. He was vaguely aware of movement and voices, but he was frozen in place. Silence fell over the fields, competing with the rush of adrenaline flooding Boone.

Boone turned toward heavy footfalls off to his left, and his mind slowly came back to the moment. Blurred faces came into focus. Trish stood, slack-jawed, beside Duke. Boone felt every eye on set boring into him with shock and worry. Panic surged through him, sending him to his feet. He stumbled again, trying to ground himself as the horror of the moment hit him like a gale-force wind. He'd royally fucked up. He'd unintentionally *improvised*.

Chuck's pounding, angry steps closed in on him like a death sentence, dark and powerful. Jaw clenched, eyes narrow, he said, "This is a *Chuck Russell* film. We *do not* improvise."

Silence nearly suffocated him as he choked out,

"Yes, sir."

He looked around the set and seethed, "Do we improvise?"

A series of *no, sirs* rang out, and Chuck returned his attention to Boone. "Do you know why we don't improvise?"

"Because you purchased the script for the way it was written. I'm sorry. I just..." *Lost my fucking mind?* He had. He'd lost touch with reality. "I apologize. I'll get it right next time."

Chuck stepped closer, bringing a wave of tension with him. "There won't be a next time."

There was a collective gasp around them.

Boone's eyes shot to Trish. Her hand covered her mouth, and fear shone in her wide eyes. He mouthed, *I'm sorry,* his heart shattering into a million little pieces.

"Because that was damn perfect," Chuck said, and slapped Boone on his back, throwing him off-balance. The interminable silence of the crew continued.

"Wh..." Boone shook his head, sure he'd heard him incorrectly. "What?"

Thunderous laughter burst from Chuck's lungs. "We don't improvise. We will *never* improvise ever again. But we're keeping that scene. That was magnificent! You are one hell of a lucky man."

A rush of relieved expressions sounded around them at once, followed by applause and cheers as Boone tried to wrap his head around what Chuck had said. And then Trish was hugging him and the crew and her family were slapping him on the back, showering him with compliments, embracing him.

Knowing he hadn't screwed things up for her put all those shattered pieces of his heart back together. "It was all you, baby," he said to Trish. *When I said "I love you," I meant it.* "You drew me in, and I hope you never let go."

Chapter Twenty-Four

TRISH AND BOONE were still buzzing with excitement over Boone's incredible performance as they settled into a table at the Greenhouse of Teays Valley Bistro with Duke, Gabriella, Cash, Siena, and Gage. The distinctive restaurant was the perfect backdrop for what promised to be an intense dinner. Dark wooden bookshelves littered with gourmet sauces, jams, jellies, rubs, and salsas lined red walls. Tables displayed a plethora of decorative vases, books, T-shirts, and flip-flops for sale. In the back corner of the restaurant were a number of shiny black grills, all of which were also for sale. The host had told them that the owners gave grilling lessons on the weekends and had begun selling grills a few years earlier at the customers' requests.

The initial tension Trish felt when her brothers had arrived had dissipated for the most part, but a thread of uncertainty lingered. She felt like that teenage girl again, worrying about her brothers driving Boone away. It was a silly thought, she knew. Everything Boone said, the way he looked at her and the way he touched her told her that no one, and nothing, could come between them.

They sat at one of the round tables, of which there were several, though none were the same size, and the chairs were mismatched. Each table was covered with a shiny green tablecloth, the same shade as pool table felt. The restaurant had a low-key, homey feel, and smelled like spices and grilled meats. Boone stretched an arm across the back of Trish's chair, and she instinctively leaned in to him.

"It smells so good in here. It reminds me of home," Gabriella said.

Duke slid his hand beneath Gabriella's dark hair and around her shoulder, drawing her closer. "Gabriella grew up off the East Coast on Elpitha Island, in a big family where everything is cooked with love. Right, babe?"

"Cooked with love, served with love, eaten with love." Gabriella turned to Boone. "My father is Greek and my mom is Southern, so..."

"Sounds wonderful," Boone said with an easy smile.

"Trish said your family's in New York," Cash said to Boone. "Is that where you live, or are you out in LA?"

"I've got a place in LA, but I consider the Bronx home."

"Cool," Cash said. "And you said you're sticking

around here until Trish is done filming?"

"That's the plan," Boone answered.

"But he gets to sleep in tomorrow," Trish reminded him. "I have to get up at the crack of dawn. I'm filming at four thirty a.m., and I film straight through until four or five in the afternoon. The day after tomorrow we film at four thirty a.m., then I have the afternoon off, and we film at sundown. We have a weird schedule for the next few days because Delia's character is a night owl."

"At least you two will still be together," Siena said. "That's what matters."

"Remember when Mom used to tell us nothing good happens between midnight and five a.m.?" Gage said, which started a round of *Remember when...*

Trish and Boone exchanged a heated glance. *Mom was so wrong.* Every time he looked at her she felt like she might go up in flames. She was surprised neither of the girls had called her on it yet.

A jovial-looking man with wire-framed glasses, thick salt-and-pepper hair, and a welcoming smile sidled up to the table. "Howdy, folks. Welcome to the Greenhouse. I'm Eric, the owner, and I'll be serving you tonight."

"Now, that's service," Cash said.

"There's a barn bash over at Millie Sipher's place tonight, and what kind of boss would I be if I didn't let my staff take off for the fun?" Eric said *Millie Sipher's* like they knew who she was, and it made him even more charming.

"Now, *that* sounds like home," Gabriella said. "I'm

from Elpitha Island, and we were just talking about how it smells so good in here it reminded me of home. My brother owns a restaurant there, and he does the same thing for his staff. It's rare, meeting a business owner who cares as much about their staff as they do about their business."

"In Hurricane, family comes first," Eric said. "My wife and I visited Elpitha about a decade ago. Sweet little island. I'm going to ask my brother Joe, our executive chef, to cook you up something special. Galaktoboureko?"

Gabriella's eyes widened. "I haven't had that in months." She looked around the table and explained, "It's Greek crème brûlée in phyllo, and it's to die for." She got up and hugged Eric. "Thank you! I'd go right back into the kitchen and hug your brother if I wasn't afraid he'd think I was crazy."

Everyone laughed as she took her seat.

"Thank you. You've just made my fiancée's night. Next time you and your wife want a weekend away, you can stay at one of my resorts." Duke took out his wallet and handed Eric a business card. "Visit that website, pick a location, and tell them Duke and Gabriella sent you."

"Thank you, Duke," Eric said. "My wife will be thrilled, but you know, this is one dessert, and what you're offering is worth so much more. I'll comp the whole group. Every time you come here."

"No need. It's our pleasure," Duke assured him.

Trish wished Duke had welcomed Boone as graciously as he did strangers, but she knew his abruptness with Boone wasn't really about Boone. It was about protecting Trish, his not-so-little sister.

"Have you lived here your whole life?" Trish asked.

"Good gosh, no," Eric said with a laugh. "We're typical West Virginians. When you're twenty-five, you can't wait to get away. We headed south and took up residence in Florida to live *the good life*. Like most people from around here, when we got old enough to sprout some gray, we couldn't wait to get back home." He lowered his voice like he was sharing a secret. "Wisdom really does come with age. Turned out the good life was right here waiting for us."

They chatted for a while longer. Eric took their drink orders and returned with them a few minutes later.

Duke eyed Boone's soda. "You're not drinking?"

Trish's nerves flared at her brother's nosy question. *And off we go...*

"I rarely do," Boone said.

Duke and Cash exchanged a curious glance. They'd obviously been influenced by Boone's reputation.

"We lost my father to a drunk driver when I was a kid," Boone explained with a solemn expression. "It's not that I don't drink. I have a drink now and then, but when I'm out, I typically go for soda or water."

"I'm sorry to hear that," Duke said sincerely. "That must have been very difficult for you and your family."

Trish was surprised Duke didn't already know that about Boone. He must not have looked into his background as deeply as she'd thought. That pleased her, because it had to mean that he was backing off, at least a little. She wondered if she'd misjudged his surprise visit. Maybe he really was here only to get to know Boone better and he just hadn't quelled the overprotective, scrutinizing side of himself yet.

A girl could hope.

"It was. It is," Boone admitted. "I'm not sure you ever really get over losing your parents, no matter what age you are when it happens."

"Boy, isn't that the truth." Gage took a pull of his beer. "My close friend Sally lost her husband when her son was a teenager. It's been several years and they both are doing well, but sometimes her pain is right there on the surface."

Trish patted her brother's arm, feeling like she'd just been given a glimpse as to why, after years of attraction between Gage and Sally, they still hadn't gotten together.

Gage smiled. "Then there are the times when Sally lights up with a happy memory, and it makes her whole world seem brighter. Is it like that for you, Boone?"

"Yup," Boone said casually. "So many things can spur a memory, and when it happens it's like riding a roller coaster in blinding darkness. You never know what to expect."

"Maybe that's why you were so good today in that final scene," Siena chimed in. "You've lost someone you loved, so when you looked at Trish, you felt it all come rushing back. When I model, depending on what the client is going for, I have to pull from memories or images to get into the right frame of mind."

Boone's eyes fell on Trish. "I had no choice this afternoon. When I saw Trish lying there, the words just came."

"You were in the zone," Trish said softly.

"I'm still in it." He leaned in and kissed her.

She felt her cheeks heat up, and Duke cleared his throat.

Boone shifted his eyes to Duke. "Sorry, Duke, but I'm not going to apologize for kissing your sister."

Duke laughed. "No, but I'll apologize for coming across a little harsh. Look, Boone, I won't beat around the bush. Let's just get everything out in the open."

"This is so ridiculous, Duke," Trish said. "When you brought Gabby home, and when Cash met Siena and Blue fell for Lizzie, none of them had to go through inquisitions. We just loved them, because you did. Why can't you do the same for me?"

Duke's face went even more serious, and everyone fell silent.

Gage leaned closer to Trish and whispered, "I think you failed to mention you were in love with him during our Skype chat."

"What?" She looked around the table. Gabriella and Siena flashed wide eyes and wider smiles. Boone looked completely and utterly shocked. "Ohmygod. I said I love you. Oh my God. It just slipped out."

A slow smile lifted his luscious lips and crept all the way up to his eyes. Trish trapped her lower lip between her teeth to keep from laughing, crying, kissing him...She heard Siena and Gabriella whispering, but she was too nervous to focus on anything except the man reaching a hand to the nape of her neck and drawing her closer. He smelled like love and lust and everything good in the world, and he was looking at her like she'd just told him he'd won a prize.

"Baby." His warm breath whispered over his lips. "I adore you. I've been trying to hold back from saying I love you, but it's been killing me. When I said it in the scene, the words were meant for you. I love you, beautiful girl. I love you so much I ache with it."

He pressed his lips to hers, and Gabriella and Siena both sighed.

Boone framed her face with his hands and gazed into her eyes. He was all she saw, all she smelled, all she heard. He was all she needed.

Duke's hand landed on Boone's shoulder and they both turned.

Her brother smiled down at them, and Boone rose to his feet as Duke said, "She'll always be my little sister, so you know that thing Jake said to you over Skype? It pretty much says it all."

Everyone laughed, and Duke embraced Boone. Trish's throat thickened.

"I'm not who the press thinks I am," Boone assured him.

Duke took Trish's hand and helped her to her feet. "It wouldn't matter if you were," he said to Boone. "As long as that's not who you are with our sister." He smiled at Trish and said, "Can you forgive me for being pushy? You're right, sis. I have no right to question your choices, and I'm sorry. From now on I'll think before I act."

"Thank you." Trish soaked in his warm embrace. "But we both know you won't."

Everyone laughed again, and the air around them lightened. The rest of the evening was lighthearted and fun, the way Trish was used to feeling when she was with her family. She and Boone held hands and kissed throughout dinner. Gabriella and the others enjoyed their special dessert. Duke teased Trish about not eating. *Wait until she's not filming, Boone. Hide your fingers at dinnertime, because she eats as much as we do.* She told them about Boone's extravagant breakfasts and teased Boone about needing to find things to make him edgy so she could have them once a week.

Since Boone's work on set was done, and Trish had three more days of filming, her family decided to stay for the night and hang out with Boone tomorrow while she worked. It filled her with joy to see Duke let Boone in and to see everyone else accept him so easily. By the time they went their separate ways, it was as if they'd known Boone forever.

As they pulled up to the farmhouse, Trish said, "Thanks for hanging in there with Duke. He means well, even if he's...*Duke.*"

"He's cool. Stop worrying so much. You should ask Mags what I've put her boyfriends through in the past."

"No way were you as aggressive as Duke. Where do you think I learned it from?"

"Darn," he said with a laugh. "I knew I forgot to thank him for something."

"Boone, I'm sorry I blurted out my feelings like that." She'd been thinking about the way the words had come without warning. They felt so right, she didn't regret admitting she loved him, but she worried that he might have felt put on the spot. "I didn't mean to put you on the spot."

He cut the engine and leaned across the console, taking her chin between his finger and thumb, and kissed her. "I love you, baby. I've wanted to tell you several times over the last few days, but I fell for you so fast and so hard, I was afraid I might scare you off. I *want* to be put on the spot as long as that spot is with you."

Chapter Twenty-Five

TRISH REACHED FOR her phone and silenced the alarm. Three forty-five was too early for any sane person to be awake. She yawned and rolled over, reaching for Boone. Her eyes came open at the feel of the empty bed, and she listened for sounds of him in the bathroom, but the only noises came from Sparky purring beside Boone's pillow, crickets outside, and a gentle breeze floating in through the open window.

She sat up and listened intently, but the house was silent. She threw on Boone's shirt from last night and went to his bedroom to see if he was there. Finding it empty, she hurried downstairs, hoping he wasn't stressing about their declaration of love last night. But the kitchen was empty. Panic bloomed in her chest. She peered out the back door into the darkness, hoping he was sitting on the porch. Her stomach plummeted at the sight of the empty porch. Her pulse raced as she headed for the front door, telling herself to calm down.

The front door was locked. She pulled it open, and her eyes sailed over the trailers and canopies, to the empty driveway. Goose bumps climbed up her limbs. She searched her mind for something, anything. A comment about him needing to be somewhere? She'd remembered he'd gone to get condoms one morning when she was still sleeping and headed upstairs to shower, thinking he'd probably been unable to sleep and had gone to run an errand.

At three forty-five.

He could have.

Maybe?

She flipped on her bedroom light and spotted a note on the bedside table. She snagged it and read it. Twice.

Beautiful, had an emergency. Knew you had to film. I'll be in touch. Love, B.

What the heck?

"Seriously? You couldn't have woken me up?" she said to the empty room, and picked up her phone to check her messages. None from Boone, although she had messages from Fiona, Shea, and Siena. She called Boone, breathing so hard she felt like she might explode. What kind of emergency? She thought of Jude and Lucky, but surely he would have just written that in the note, wouldn't he? The call went straight to voicemail. *Great.*

"Hey, it's me. Where are you? What happened? I love you, and I hope you're okay. Call me."

It was almost four and the crew would be there

soon. She took a quick shower and dressed, then tried his cell again. The call went to voicemail.

The front door opened and she ran to the top of the stairs. "Boone?"

Zoe stared up at her. "You lost your boyfriend?"

She rolled her eyes and tried to hide her frustration and worries. "No. He had to take care of something. I'll be right down."

"Better hurry. You know how Chuck is about getting the perfect lighting," Zoe called after her.

Yeah. Tell me something I don't know. She didn't usually bring her phone on set, but today it would take an act of God to stop her. She left it on silent and checked it between every scene. She was so worried about what was going on with Boone she could hardly concentrate, but thankfully her rote acting skills took over.

Her brothers and the girls showed up around nine, and she remembered they were supposed to spend the day with Boone. After she wrapped her scene, she asked Duke if any of them had heard from Boone.

"No. Why?" Duke asked.

"He was gone when I got up. He left a note that there was an emergency he had to take care of, but I haven't heard from him." She spotted Jared coming her way and cringed. He was the last person she wanted to talk to right now.

"Trish," Jared said with a hint of arrogance.

"Hey, Jared." *Please go away.* Siena must have noticed her discomfort, because she took up residence beside her, and like birds of a feather, her family gathered around.

"Guess Boone blew out of here first chance he got, huh?" Jared looked down at his phone. "Sorry he screwed you like that."

"Hey," Duke said, stepping between them. "What's your problem?"

Jared held up his hands in surrender. "I've got no problem, but your sister might."

He thrust his phone toward Trish, showing her an image of Boone with an arm around a gorgeous brunette on Perez Hilton's website, with the caption LOOKS LIKE STRYKER'S DONE ACTING. Trish's heart stopped cold.

"That doesn't mean a damn thing," Siena said, putting an arm around Trish. "You know that, right? I saw the way he looked at you last night. There's no way those pictures are real. Trust me, if anyone knows how to read fake pics, it's me."

"The press will try to break you up now that they know you're a couple," Cash added. "We've seen it happen to Siena's friends."

Duke ripped the phone from Jared's hands, ignoring his protests. His eyes swept over the article and he pushed it into Jared's chest. "This is bullshit. Get out of here."

Gage took Trish by the arm and guided her away from Jared. Disconcerting thoughts raced through her mind. She didn't believe Boone was with anyone else, but that didn't stop jealousy from piercing her heart.

"Trish, what the hell was that all about?" Duke

asked angrily.

"Jared's an ass. He's been talking crap about me and Boone since we first started filming, and Boone set him straight. Boone uses the press for distractions. But he said he was done with that. You can't say anything to anyone about his using the press for distractions. It's important to keep his family out of the limelight."

"Then that's what this has to be. A distraction," Gabriella said.

"He's got to be with Jude or his mother. Or maybe his brother Lucky." Her mind raced, and the words tumbled out fast. "If he is, he needs me." She scrolled through her contacts, looking for Maggie's number.

"Trish," Duke said gently. "Wouldn't he have told you if it was a family emergency?"

"You don't know Boone. He's used to dealing with *everything* on his own. When his friend was in trouble, he didn't even stop to talk about it. He just packed up his stuff and was ready to race out of here." She remembered his surprise when she wanted to go with him. "His note," she said absently. "It was cryptic, but for Boone, it was a huge deal, even if it seems minuscule to us. He doesn't slow down when his friends are in trouble. He goes."

"Okay, I get it." Duke took out his phone.

"Who are you calling?" Trish asked, raising her phone to her ear as she called Maggie.

"My assistant. I'm going to have her call all the hospitals around the Bronx and see if he's there."

"Rekyrts, that's his mother's name." Maggie

answered the phone, and Trish held up a finger to Duke. "Mags? It's Trish. Have you heard from Boone?"

"Yes, he's here at the hospital with us."

Trish grabbed hold of Duke's arm. "What happened?"

"Our mom had chest pains again," Maggie explained. "She was rushed in in the middle of the night. Didn't he tell you? He said he left a note. We can't use cell phones in the hospital. I'm surprised you caught me. I was just coming outside to call the school and let them know she wouldn't be in tonight to clean. Boone and our brothers are in with her now." She told Trish which hospital they'd taken her to and she sounded just as frazzled as Trish would expect her to.

"Thanks, Mags. He did leave a note, but he didn't say where he was. Sorry to bother you. Please give your mom my love." She ended the call and said, "I have to talk to Chuck. Duke, how fast can you get me to New York?"

"Faster than you can drive, that's for sure. I'll get a plane." He was already calling as she headed up the hill.

"What can we do?" Gabriella asked.

"Can you get our kitten, Sparky? He's upstairs in the bedroom. And ask the girls to throw some of my clothes into a bag? Please? I have to tell Chuck I need to leave." *And he's not going to like it.*

She ran across the field toward Chuck without waiting for a response. Her heart beat frantically. What was Boone thinking? He should have told her. He didn't need to handle everything on his own. What was wrong with him? She had no idea how long she'd be gone. She should have asked Maggie for details, but she was too focused on getting there to think straight.

She paced, waiting for Chuck to finish his conversation with the cameraman and hoping Raine was going to be okay.

"Chuck," she said when the cameraman walked away. She stepped in too close, and Chuck stepped back. She didn't want anyone to hear what she had to say, so she stepped closer again.

"Chuck, I would never ask this of you if I didn't have to, but I need to leave."

"Leave?" His face twisted.

"Yes. Boone's mother is in the hospital, and I need to be there. I'm sorry. I don't know what's wrong, or how long I'll be gone, but he shouldn't have to face that alone. I need to be there. I—"

"Whoa. Slow down." Chuck's expression turned solemn, like her father's had when he'd told her their dog had died when she was thirteen. "I got the part about Boone, but you know Jared's flashing pics around of Boone in LA with some woman. The cast is all hot under the collar about him hurting you. You can tell me if that's what's really going on."

"Oh my God! Seriously?" She threw her hands up in the air out of anger. Boone's mother was in the hospital and everyone thought he was with another woman?

"Those pictures are—" She stopped before saying more and drew in a deep breath, forcing herself to regain control. "I'm sorry, Chuck. You didn't deserve that. I need to be with him. Can I please go? I will work extra hard when I get back. I'll even pay for whatever you want me to, the crew's time. Whatever." She lowered her voice and said, "I'll do anything. I just need to be with him."

His face grew serious. "You're willing to risk walking off the set for Boone Stryker?"

She swallowed hard. She knew this could cost her the chance to ever work with Chuck again, but the best thing in her life needed her. Her answer came easily.

"Yes."

"You really fell for him, didn't you?"

She shrugged and smiled. "How could I not?"

"I've been married for twenty-five years. Believe it or not, I get it. Your priorities are where they should be. You want to be with him in his time of need." He set a harder, assessing gaze on her. "And you really believe that's where he is?"

"Chuck!" she snapped. "I'd bet my life on it, and you know if I'm willing to put my career on the line for him, I believe it with all my heart."

"Okay. You can go."

She threw her arms around his neck. "Thank you! Thank you so much!"

"One day, Trish. That's all I can give you. Tomorrow morning at six, cameras are rolling."

"Six. I promise. I'll be here." She took a step away as horrible thoughts crept in, and she turned back. "Wait. Chuck, I don't know what shape his mom is in. What if...?" A lump formed in her throat at the thought of something horrible happening to Raine.

"Trish, Go. I'm a director, not a monster. Use good sense and keep me in the loop."

She stared at him for a long beat, trying to figure out how to say what she knew she needed to. She lowered her voice again and said, "He's worked for years to keep the press away from his family. Is there any way I can get you to not dispel the rumors about Boone and those pictures? Not to tell the crew where I'm going? I know it's a lot to ask."

He pressed his lips together, and then his gaze softened. "Honey, I've been in Hollywood long enough to know it's necessary. I've got your back. Just make sure you've got mine. This movie's got a chance to move mountains."

"I promise."

She hurried inside, scrubbed off her makeup and changed her clothes faster than she ever had in her life, and rushed out front, where Duke was waiting. Everyone else was already in the car.

"You okay?" Duke asked. "The plane's all set. The girls got your clothes and your kitten. You have a kitten?"

"Yes." She took a deep breath and smiled. "*We* have a kitten. Me and Boone. We found him in a parking lot." Her eyes filled with tears. "Duke, I know it must seem like he's not right for me in lots of ways, but he is. I know the secrecy and pictures make it looks like I'm a fool, but I'm not. He's as right for me as Gabriella is for you. And I met his mom. She's amazing. If anything happens to her..."

Duke gathered her in his strong embrace and held

her tight. "Shh. It's okay, sweetheart. We'll get you there as fast as we can. And as far as Boone goes, don't worry. I knew the minute we met face-to-face. The first thing he said to us was that he was glad we'd come. He said he felt better knowing your family loved you enough to put you ahead of everything else, and after our dinner together, it's easy to see how much he cares for you."

Trish leaned back and looked at her brother. "He said that to you?"

"Yes. Now, let's get you to him."

Chapter Twenty-Six

"SOMETHING HAS TO change," Boone said quietly but firmly to Lucky. "Mom can't take the extra stress of worrying about what kind of trouble you're going to get into next." He and his siblings were in the waiting room at the hospital as their mother went through more tests to figure out what was causing her chest pains.

"It's not like I'm a felon," Lucky snapped. He ran a hand through his thick dark hair and crossed his arms, eyeing his siblings.

"Nobody is saying you are," Cage said. "Look, Boone's right about stressing out Mom. Between coming in and out at all hours, going from job to job, and skirting the law, Lucky, she worries. We all do."

"I put a call in to my buddy Carson Bad," Boone told Lucky. "He's the one who owns an elite security firm. He's willing to talk to you about putting your computer skills to good use, and he's just as brilliant as you are. He'll make sure you're never bored. Chances are, you can work whatever crazy hours you want because half the IT staff works at night."

Lucky rolled his eyes.

"If you're dead set against going to college," Cage added, "then at least consider talking to Carson. Get a job that can lead somewhere. Get your own apartment."

"Start growing up," Mags added. "Oh my gosh. We sound like Mom and Dad. Remember when we were kids and Dad would get mad because we were horsing around and he'd say, 'You're not little kids anymore. Act your age.'"

"Yeah." Boone smiled with the memory. "And we'd crack up because we *were* kids."

"Half the time Mom would end up laughing, and then Dad would laugh and call us fools," Cage said with a smile.

They fell silent, each lost in their own memories.

Lucky sighed. "See? You guys were lucky. You only had two parents. I've got four."

Boone draped an arm over his youngest brother's shoulder. "Buddy, if there were any way for me to bring Dad back, we'd back off in a heartbeat. You definitely missed out, because he was frigging awesome. But since he's not here, and we all love you despite your need to be a smart-ass, limit-pushing pain in the butt, you're stuck with us trying to help you find your way."

"Think of it as our way of helping you make Dad proud," Cage suggested.

"That's just it," Lucky said. "I think Dad would be proud of me. I don't want to move out. Mom *needs* me there. You guys are there when I'm in trouble, or when Mom needs you, or for quick visits, but I'm there when she gets up at three in the morning because she can't sleep. Or when she's reading that shoe box of letters from Dad and cries."

"She still reads those?" Cage asked, exchanging a concerned glance with Boone.

"I'm not denying that I'm all those things you said," Lucky explained, "but I don't *just* add stress to her life. I make sure she has her favorite books. We go out to dinner sometimes, and I'm always there to talk about Dad, because she needs that. She needs to know she can talk about him without making everyone sad."

"He's right," Mags said softly. "She's pretty careful about how often she talks about him to me."

Boone had to admit he'd noticed that, too, but Lucky staying with her was a double-edged sword. He couldn't fault his brother for acting eighteen. Lord knew the rest of them had had to grow up fast after they'd lost their father. He had to find a way to protect both his mother's health and Lucky's ability to gain the freedom an eighteen-year-old needed to grow up and learn responsibility.

"Lucky, Mom's not your responsibility. Are you staying just because she needs you? Do you want your own place? If so, then that's what we have to work on, so you can start to have a real life and take on responsibilities that are more appropriate for a guy your age. If Mom needs us around more, we can do that. I'll make sure I'm around more."

"I see her all the time because we work together, so I'm pretty sure I'm around enough," Mags said.

"I'll make a bigger effort," Cage offered. "I've been hammered with promoting my fights lately, but it's no excuse. I'll step it up."

"Do you guys hear yourselves?" Lucky's face went serious. "Mom's not my responsibility, but I'm the one stressing her out? Do I want my own place? Y'all are ready to drop everything to fix me *and* to make sure she's okay, which is awesome. Seriously, I'm not complaining about how much you love us, but you're totally missing another point."

"What do you mean?" Boone asked.

"She's lonely," Lucky said. "She's a forty-seven-year-old woman. Surely you get this. She's our mom, but she's a woman, too. She has needs that aren't being satisfied, and I don't mean just sex. She needs adult companionship. A man to tell her how beautiful she is, to go out with, to make her feel special in ways that none of us can or should."

Lucky shook his head and turned a compassionate gaze to Boone. He looked so much like their father at that moment that Boone got a chill.

"Boone, you're a great protector, and you fly home to fix anything and everything the minute there's trouble. Mags, you're there for her in more ways than you probably realize. And, Cage? You and Mom have this incredible bond over all things Dad related. But she needs *more*. You saw the way Officer Payne looked at her and how she reacted. That wasn't a one-time thing, Boone. He's asked her out a number of times, and I've asked her why she won't go. She's got a million excuses, but I think she's worried about you guys being okay with it."

"What?" Boone didn't know if he was upset that she'd think that or upset that he actually might not be.

"Lucky's right," Cage said. "It's been a hell of a long time since we lost Dad. She had us to keep her busy when we were younger, but she deserves more. She deserves a full life, and if she thinks we're holding her back, then we have to let her know we're cool with it."

Boone scrubbed his hand down his face, trying to get past the juvenile ache of not wanting that spot his father had held for all these years to change. "Can we please deal with one tough issue at a time? Let's make sure she's healthy before we go marrying her off."

"No one's marrying her off, but she deserves to be happy," Mags said. "And now that I think about it, when we cater parties, guys are always showing interest in Mom. I thought she was blowing them off because she was at work. But, Lucky, I think you see what I haven't wanted to."

She put her hand on Boone's shoulder. "Mom being alone won't bring Dad back. She deserves to be loved, doesn't she?"

Boone thought about all the feelings he'd kept bottled up about Destiny and wondered if his mother had imprisoned herself in a similar yet different type of hell. He'd needed to forgive Destiny's parents, if even in his own mind. What if his mother needed him—them—to forgive her in a different way, for allowing herself to move forward?

"Yes," he answered quietly. "She deserves the best of everything. If she wants to date, we should let her know we're behind her."

"Boone?"

He spun around at the sound of Trish's voice. "Baby? Duke? What are you doing here? You're supposed to be filming."

"Filming?" Trish's face scrunched up with disbelief. "While your mom is in the hospital? How is she?"

"They didn't find any issues with her heart, so they're running more tests. They think it might be a GI issue. I can't believe you're here."

"Thank God it's not her heart." She wrapped her arms around him and said, "Filming comes third on my list. You're first, family and closest friends are second, and work comes third." She drew back and gazed into his eyes. "Why didn't you wake me?"

"You had to be on set at four thirty and I got the call at two thirty. I had no idea what we were dealing with, and I didn't want to put that kind of stress on you until I had a handle on things."

She frowned. "Your stress *is* my stress. Why didn't you tell me where you were going in your note? I didn't know if something had happened to Jude, Lucky, your mom..."

"I'm sorry. This film is your big chance, and I didn't want you stressing out until we knew if there was something to stress out over. I've been watching the clock. I would have called at five, right after you were done filming."

She banged her forehead against his chest, then gazed up at him with warm, loving eyes. "You didn't want me stressing out? If you're stressing out, I want to be with you. That's how relationships work. You made me *more* worried, and Jared showed everyone pictures of you and some girl God knows where."

"What?" His chest constricted.

Duke stepped closer. "She's right. I saw the pics."

"Boone, did you tell Tripp to cancel the hospital directive?" Cage asked.

"Aw, hell. No. I forgot about that. When Lucky had his appendix out a few years back and I had to cancel a tour and fly in, we set up a system with the hospital. If any of my family members are admitted, they notify Tripp, my PR rep. Then Tripp releases pictures of me anywhere else but here. I forgot to address that. I'm sorry, Trish."

She shook her head and smiled. "Well, this time I'm not. It made me realize I should call Mags."

"Uh-oh." Maggie winced. "I might have forgotten to tell you she called. Sorry, Boone."

"No worries," he said to his sister, then to Trish, "I'm sorry, beautiful. I'll make that call as soon as we're out of here."

Cage reached out a hand to Duke and pulled him into a manly embrace. "Hi. I'm Cage, Boone's brother. He's a little too sidetracked to introduce us properly."

"Duke, Trish's brother. Nice to meet you."

Lucky embraced Duke. "I'm Lucky, another brother."

"Great to meet you, Lucky," Duke said. "We'll have to get our families together soon."

Mags hugged Trish. "I'm so glad you're here. Sorry I forgot to tell him you called."

Boone warmed at the love passing before him. He'd never imagined wanting to let anyone into his inner circle like this, but Trish and Duke and the rest of her family felt like they were already part of his family.

"That's okay. I'm just glad I caught you when your phone was on." Trish introduced Duke to Maggie. "Duke chartered a plane so we could get here fast. My family was in West Virginia with me. The rest of them went home, and Siena and Cash have Sparky, but I asked Duke to come with me. I hope you don't mind."

"Your family is always welcome," Boone said.

Cage opened his arms and embraced Trish. "Nice to see you again. You will forever be known as the woman who made my brick-wall brother go soft."

"Hey, there's nothing soft about me," Boone said, and pulled Trish close again. "I'm really sorry about not filling you in sooner, but I didn't want to come between you and today's filming."

"I get that you were trying to protect me." She reached for Duke's hand and guided him beside Boone, then looked lovingly at both of them. "There are times when I need protecting and there are times when it's nice, as a woman, to feel protected. But things have to change. Duke, if you had called and spoken to me before showing up, I would have been less annoyed, regardless of whether you were checking out Boone or not. Okay?"

"You've got it. I learned my lesson." Duke smiled and added, "From now on I should listen to my soon-to-be wife. She told me the same thing."

"See? There's another reason I love Gabby." Trish turned her attention, and her beguiling eyes, to Boone.

His insides went soft, but he wasn't about to admit that to Cage, who was watching them with an awestruck look on his face, alongside Mags and Lucky.

"And you." She grabbed Boone by the collar, her lips curving up in a sweet, loving smile. "You, my badass rocker, need to understand that when I said I loved you, and when I said you were on top of my list, I meant it."

Her brows knitted, but when she spoke, even trying her hardest to sound firm, he heard the undercurrent of love loud and clear. "I know you want to protect me, but you're not alone anymore, and when you're in a relationship, you don't get to make all the decisions. There is no choice between family and work, and when your family is in crisis, I get to be there for you. I get to make that decision. No questions asked."

"Okay, beautiful." Boone slid his gaze to Duke. "I understand I get to thank you for her pushiness."

Duke shrugged. "I can't even begin to deny it."

Trish pressed her hand to Boone's cheek and guided his eyes back to hers.

"Now, about your cryptic note-writing skills..."

**

LATER THAT EVENING, after Duke left and Raine was discharged from the hospital, they tried to relax before Trish had to pick up Sparky from Cash and Siena in the city and then catch her flight back to West Virginia. Raine's tests revealed a severe case of esophagitis, caused by acid reflux. The doctor assured them that with proper diet and medication, Raine would heal.

"Esophagitis," Raine said for the third time in the last hour. "I still can't get over how inflammation of the esophagus can cause so much pain. I really thought I was having a heart attack. I feel so bad for taking Trish away from filming, and, Cage, you missed your radio interview."

"Don't be silly," Trish said. "I'm just happy you're okay."

"You did me a favor." Cage got up and hugged Raine. "I hate radio interviews."

Boone walked in from the kitchen and sat down beside Trish. "Mom, I put your medicine on the counter, along with the directions the doctor gave us. I also printed out a few articles on esophagitis and bookmarked a few recipe sites that might help with the reflux."

"Thank you, Boone." Raine's eyes moved over each of the children's faces. "What are you not telling me?"

Boone and his siblings exchanged looks Trish couldn't read.

"Boone gave me a guy's number for a computer job," Lucky said. "I'm going to call him tomorrow."

"Really?" Raine's eyes widened with delight. "That's wonderful."

"Yeah, I figure it's time." Lucky glanced at Boone, who smiled appreciatively.

"And I'm going to make you lots of reflux-friendly foods and freeze them," Mags said. "I took tomorrow off so I can clean out your fridge from all those chocolate truffles you've been hoarding."

A knock sounded at the door, and Boone got up to answer it. Officer Payne stood on the steps in a pair of jeans and a crisp white button-down shirt, holding a bouquet of flowers.

"Officer Payne," Boone said in a much friendlier tone than he had spoken to him the last time he was there. "So nice to see you."

"Hi. I heard your mom was in the hospital and thought I'd stop by and see how she was doing." He smiled as he stepped inside, and his eyes went straight to Raine.

"Patrick," she said a little breathlessly.

Trish recognized the look of attraction. Raine was looking at Patrick the same way Trish had first looked at Boone.

"Hi, Raine." He knelt beside the couch where she sat and handed her the flowers. "I brought these for you. Are you feeling okay?"

"Yes. They're beautiful. How did you know I was in the hospital?" she asked.

"Oh. I..." Patrick looked at Boone, and Trish swore she saw Boone shake his head. "I heard the 911 call come through on the police scanner, but I was on duty and couldn't get away until now."

"It's nice of you to come by." Boone walked behind Cage and Lucky and discreetly touched their shoulders and cocked his head toward the door. Each of his siblings began murmuring about needing to be somewhere.

"We'd better pick up Sparky and get to the airport," Boone said to Trish.

She started to protest but quickly realized Boone had set up the whole thing. Rising to her feet, she whispered, "You did this for her?"

He gathered her in his arms and pressed his cheek to hers. His hot breath sent shivers down her spine as he whispered, "My smart girlfriend taught me that we can't have a future without first putting our pasts to rest."

Her heart swelled with love. But she also knew her man well enough to realize how difficult this must be for him. "You sure you're okay leaving? I can go back by myself and we can connect in LA after I'm done filming if you want to be here for your mom."

She watched his expression warm as he looked at his mother chatting quietly with Patrick. Raine was glowing, despite her ordeal. Patrick turned and winked at Boone. A look of gratitude passed between the two men.

Boone gazed down at Trish and said, "I think she's in good hands. Besides, speaking of LA, I was thinking you should move in with me."

Trish's voice caught in her throat and her body flooded with love. "I should...Oh my gosh, Boone? Are you serious?"

"I told you I suck at pretending." He arched a brow.

He looked cocky and sexy and so in love she wanted to climb into his arms and kiss him for hours. "That's one of my favorite things about you, but I don't even know where you live. I've never been to your house. I don't even know what your life is like off set."

"Then I should move in with you," he said casually. "Because I don't care what your house is like. I'd live in a hovel with you. And as for my life, it'll be whatever *we* want it to be. If we want to tour, we'll tour. If we want to be together while you're on location, we'll do that. If we want to give up everything and travel around the world for two years, I'm all in."

"Boone." Her breath left her lungs.

"Baby, we've *been* living together for weeks. You know what I'm like, and that's all that matters. Or is it too much too fast? *Tsk.* I told you I'd screw up."

Cage brushed by them and snickered. "He's really good at screwing up."

"He didn't screw up," she said to Cage.

"Hey, I'm the screwup," Lucky said to Cage. "He's the overprotective one."

"You're both fools," Mags teased.

Trish smiled at Boone and said, "I have a crazy idea."

"The last time you had a crazy idea, you pretended to pass out at a creek party and told strangers you were pregnant."

"She did?" Mags perked up. "I want to hear this."

"Hold on. I think we're negotiating," Boone said.

"How about if after I'm done filming we spend time at your place," Trish suggested. "Then we spend time at my place, and we can decide where we want to call home afterward?"

"Home?" Boone tugged her in closer, his eyes full of love, his heart beating sure and steady against her own. "Home is wherever you are, beautiful."

"You're moving in together?" Mags asked so loudly everyone went silent.

Raine squealed. "You are? Oh my gosh. I knew it the minute I saw the way you looked at each other!"

"Who's the pushy one now?" Trish poked Boone in his ribs. "What if I'd said no?"

"You still haven't said yes," he whispered.

"Yes, you goofball."

Boone scooped her into his arms and twirled her around. "I'll live anywhere you want. Your place. Mine. Wherever you want."

"I usually split my time between New York and LA."

"I will, too," he offered.

"I have a million pairs of shoes and two walk-in closets."

"You can have my closet."

"I eat like a pig. We're talking *big* grocery bills," she teased. "Huge. Enormous."

"Good thing I like to cook."

"How do you feel about weddings?" she asked.

"Well, we are already pregnant." He called over his shoulder to his family, "Inside joke. *Not really.*"

"Not ours! Be my date for Duke and Gabby's wedding."

His expression turned serious again. "I had to ask you to move in with me to be invited?"

"No! I just remembered. There's been so much going on, it slipped my mind."

"In that case, I'd be honored," he said with a wide grin, still holding her inches above the floor. "And for the record, I love weddings. I believe in weddings. One day I want a wedding. Our wedding."

His lips came down over hers, and as his family showered them with excitement, she fell even deeper in love with him.

"I don't really care where we live either," Trish said as he lowered her feet to the floor. "I just didn't want to seem easy."

"Baby." He laughed. "I promise you that's one thing I'll never accuse you of."

Epilogue

STRINGS OF WHITE lights stretched from one end of the bluff to the other, sparkling like a canopy of diamonds against the night sky and illuminating Duke and Gabriella's wedding reception. Duke and Gabriella had walked down an aisle lined with hurricane candles and said their vows in a beautiful gazebo Blue had made just for their special moment. The whole ceremony had a magical feel that carried over to the reception.

Dozens of round tables adorned with white tablecloths and colorful floral centerpieces dotted the lawn. Enormous vases of flowers were placed around large buffet tables and around the dance floor, where Duke and Gabriella were dancing cheek to cheek. They looked happier than Trish had ever seen them. Duke was handsome in his charcoal-gray tuxedo, holding his new bride. Gabriella's mother and aunts had made her the perfect island wedding gown. The satin and lace backless dress had spaghetti straps and a layer of chiffon over just-above-the-knee satin, giving her full-length gown glamour without the restrictions of confining layers. Behind them were streams of vertical lights hung from decorative frames, rippling like waterfalls in the breeze sweeping up the bluff. At the far end of the property, a lighthouse stood sentinel. Its light shimmered off the inky water like a glamorous carpet leading to Elpitha Island. Duke had gone all out for the wedding, and Trish had never seen anything so beautiful.

She gazed out at the water, her eyes catching on the two boats by the docks, which had been loitering for hours, and guilt pressed in on her. With all of the Oscar buzz about their performance, she and Boone had been barraged by press and paparazzi for weeks. Lately she'd realized how her priorities had shifted. She and Boone had spent time at each other's homes and had finally decided to sell both and buy one together—farther away from the masses. They'd purchased the house in Hurricane under Boone's real name and had been living there to escape the craziness of Hollywood. The community had come together and helped them live under the radar by not making a fuss when they were out. Luckily, West Virginia didn't have enough going on to deem worthy of the media shenanigans that went on in Los Angeles. They did, however, have to beef up security for the wedding to keep the press from docking and coming onto the island.

Trish looked down at Cash and Siena's baby in her

arms, Charlotte Rose—Coco—and kissed her forehead, inhaling her sweet baby scent. Across the lawn Lizzie was holding Coco's twin brother, Seth Samuel, named for the man Cash hadn't been able to save in a fire. They were only two months old and already looked so much like their parents Trish knew her brother and sister-in-law were in for trouble when these two became teenagers. They were the most curious of babies, too. When they were lying next to each other, Seth clung to Coco as if she were his to protect. *Such a Ryder man already.*

"I don't know why the press finds me and Boone so interesting when there are so many more interesting things to give attention to. Like you and your cutie-pie brother," she said to Coco. "The press is so silly."

"You have been hogging that sweet baby all evening," her mother said, reaching for Coco.

Trish turned away with a smile. "I'll give her to you in a minute." She kissed the baby again. "Right, Coco? Auntie Trish needs one more second with you before Grandma gobbles you up."

"Refusing to give up a baby is the first sign of wanting one," her mother said.

"I know," Trish confided. "My ovaries have been doing a baby dance all evening." She and Boone had talked about having a big family, and holding Coco made her want to get started right away. The breathtaking wedding had also tugged at her heartstrings.

Her eyes slid to Boone standing with her father,

Gage, Sally, Blue, and Lizzie. Boone lifted his eyes and caught her staring.

He mouthed, *Marry me.*

Her heart nearly stopped. Surely she'd misread his words. She blinked several times and met his gaze again.

He smiled and mouthed, *I love you.*

Oh God. She was losing her mind. Her head was playing tricks on her. It had to be the wedding. Sometimes she wondered if her heart would give out from the sheer depth of love she felt for him. Were hearts capable of loving this hard forever?

She shifted her eyes to Gage and Sally. They were always together, and Gage's love for her was palpable. Everything Sally did spoke of her feelings for Gage, but even now there was an invisible line between them. A sliver of space keeping them apart. Trish wondered if Sally's love for her deceased husband filled that space. On one hand, she hoped that wasn't the case, because the idea of Gage's love being unrequited forever was too painful. And at the same time, she knew how full her heart was for Boone and couldn't imagine ever loving another man.

"They're coming over." Her mother nodded toward Boone and the others heading toward them. "Maybe you should give me the baby now."

"Why is that a reason to give up the baby?" Trish kissed Coco one more time and placed her in her mother's arms. She glanced at Boone, whose eyes were locked on hers, sending familiar sparks through her veins.

"I'm just freeing up your arms to hold Boone," her mother said with a wink. "Oh good, here come Duke and Gabby, too. If we could only get Jake to stop lusting over Addy, we could make a family toast." Addy was Gabriella's best friend and worked with her at her law practice.

"They've been playing cat and mouse all evening," Trish said, needing a distraction from her crazy thoughts. "What do you think's up? Jake's usually not so coy." Addy and Jake had met when Gabriella and Duke had first started dating, and their connection was white-hot, but as far as Trish knew, they'd never gotten together.

"Isn't it obvious?" her mother asked as the others joined them. "He finally *likes* someone."

"Who's 'he'?" Blue asked, holding hands with Lizzie.

"Jake," Trish answered. Boone sidled up to her and wound an arm around her waist.

He pressed his lips just beside her ear and whispered, "Be mine forever."

Before she could say anything, he pressed another kiss beside her ear and said, "I love you."

"Are you talking about Jake and Addy?" her father asked.

Had she heard Boone right? She was vaguely aware of the conversation going on around her. She turned and looked at him, and he shrugged.

"Boone?" she whispered, earning a wide, silent grin.

"Jake's been flirting with her all evening," Lizzie

said. "Did you see him when Gabriella's brothers danced with her?"

"I did," Sally said. "He looked like he was going to blow his top."

"Jake can be a little possessive." Her mother shifted the baby in her arms.

"Jake?" Siena laughed. "All the Ryder men are possessive!"

Boone kissed Trish and whispered, "I love it when you're possessive of me. Marry me."

She shot her eyes to his and he shrugged again. "What?" she whispered, but he just smiled and kissed her again.

"If he likes Addy, he's out of luck," Gabriella said. "She's taking off for a few weeks to go trekking in the mountains. I swear she's so determined to prove her independence, she won't stop until she's conquered everything there is to conquer." Addy was the daughter of a world-renowned fashion designer. She'd broken away from her family after graduating college to get out from under her father's thumb and prove to herself she could make it on her own.

"I'm sure Jake would be happy to let her conquer him," Duke said.

Gabriella glared at him. "That's my best friend you're talking about."

"Sorry, babe." Duke kissed her and whispered something in her ear that made her blush.

"What are you going to do without her at your legal practice for that long?" Gage asked.

Gabriella and Duke exchanged smiles. "Actually,"

Duke said, "we're hoping to start a family right away, and Gabriella wants to cut back on her law practice to take care of our babies."

"Really?" Trish hugged Gabriella. "I can't wait for more nieces and nephews!"

Boone wrapped his arms around Trish from behind and whispered, "Have my babies."

Trish stood stock-still, sure she had heard him right this time—and getting more excited by the second.

"Coco and Seth need playmates," Siena said.

"I can't believe my baby is in college," Sally said. "Time goes so fast. I would have loved to have another baby." She glanced at Gage, and he raised his brows, as if that was a discussion they'd already had.

"Blue and I want a big family," Lizzie said.

"We sure do." Blue pulled her in closer.

Boone whispered, "So do we," in Trish's ear. She turned in his arms and gazed into his dark eyes.

"What are you doing?" she whispered.

"Subliminal messages," Boone answered.

"So, Blue," Gage asked. "When's the wedding?"

Trish didn't know if Blue answered Gage or not. She couldn't concentrate past her racing heart. She couldn't see past the beautiful man sinking down to one knee before her, holding her hand in one of his and a diamond ring in the other.

"Beautiful girl," he said, drawing tears to her eyes. "You've taught me how to be a better man, how to forgive and move forward."

Warm tears slid down her cheeks.

"I want to wake up with you in my arms every day and raise creative, pushy babies, or nerdy babies, or whatever-they-want-to-be babies, and show them how incredible life can be."

A sob bubbled out of her lungs, and she lifted a shaky hand to cover her mouth. Boone rose to his feet and took that hand in his.

"In my head, and in my heart, you're already mine, but I want to see you walk down the aisle and become my wife. And more than anything in the world, I want to become your husband. I'll make you proud, baby, and happy. And I promise you, I'll be the best father to our children. I had a good role model." His eyes welled with tears as he stepped closer and asked, "Will you marry me, beautiful?"

She nodded as he slid the gorgeous engagement ring on her shaky finger. "Yes. Yes, Boone. I want to be your wife more than I want my next breath." She melted into his arms—and into his kiss. Cheering and congratulations rang out around them, but they didn't stop kissing. She hoped they'd never stop kissing.

"Thank you, baby," he said against her mouth.

She blinked away tears and smiled at the man she adored. "I have a crazy idea."

He laughed and hugged her tight. "Oh, baby. This is why I love you so much. God, do I love you." He kissed her again and said, "Tell me your crazy idea."

"Let's get married right here on this glorious island. This week. Everything's already set up, and we can bring your family in. I don't want to wait."

"Already planned. I knew my favorite girl would

have a crazy idea. Within an hour of asking your father for your hand, I called your brothers. Apparently Duke knows you pretty well, and he anticipated your response, just as I did. Thankfully, he and Gabby were okay with sharing their wedding week. My family will be here in two days. You have two days to find a dress."

"You asked my dad for my hand? Duke knew I'd want this?" She burst into tears, trembling all over, and then she was engulfed by too many loving arms to tremble at all.

—Ready for more Ryders?—
Fall in love with Jake & Addison!

As the daughter of a world-renowned fashion designer, Addison Dahl enjoyed a privileged life attending the most sought-after parties, traveling around the world, and having anything she wanted. Until she broke free and went against her father's wishes, needing to prove to herself—and to him—that she could make it on her own. Now she's ready to take her adventures in a new direction and sets her sights on roughing it in the wilderness.

Jake Ryder followed in his father's footsteps as a top search and rescue professional. He spends his days saving those in need and his nights in the arms of willing women who offer nothing more than a few hours of sexual enjoyment. Just the way he likes it.

When Jake's sister-in-law calls and reports her best friend missing, it's up to Jake to find her and bring her home. But Addison isn't lost, and she sure as hell isn't going to be told what to do by an ornery mountain man with whom she'd spent one torrid night after her best friend's wedding. Jake has never left anyone behind—will Addison be his first failed rescue?

Please enjoy this preview of
CRUSHING ON LOVE (The Bradens)

STEVE JOHNSON TOOK off his sweaty shirt and guzzled a bottle of water. Nothing beat a predawn run, especially after a shitty night's sleep. He set the empty bottle and shirt on the steps leading to his rustic log cabin and crossed the yard to the chopping post, determined to work the remaining tension from his body. A six-mile run on the rough terrain of the Colorado Mountains should have worked out all his piss and vinegar, but not this morning.

Sun beat down on his shoulders as he centered a slab of wood on the tree stump that served as his chopping post, trying to ignore the reason he'd been unable to sleep last night. He filled his lungs with the scents of nature and tranquility. He knew every sound and smell of the area, could differentiate every species of animal and plant in the forest, and anticipated inclement weather well before it hit. His body was attuned to the mountains as if he were a part of them.

He hoisted the ax over his shoulder, thoughts he was trying to ignore pushing back in like adamant thieves. He swung the ax. A loud *crack* echoed in the forest—and in his head—rattling the truth of his angst free. Shannon Braden was back—and she'd come home last night wrapped around Cal Hayden on the back of his horse.

He ground his teeth against that reality and set another log in place.

Smart, sexy-as-sin, talks-a-mile-a-minute Shannon. He'd known her for years. His sister, Jade, was married to her second cousin, Rex. Shannon had spent weeks doing research on red foxes in the mountains. She'd been staying at her uncle's ranch in Weston, but he knew the company she was working with had made arrangements for her to stay at the vacant cabin just around the bend for the remainder of the project. He swung the ax, thinking of the weeks she'd spent flitting in and out of his peaceful life, full of energy and never-ending conversations—mostly one-sided, which she didn't seem to mind. Truth be known, neither did he. Listening to Shannon rattle on about *anything* was hot. She tangled up his thoughts in ways no other woman ever had, which was just his luck. Steve wasn't into meaningless hookups, and Shannon's life was in Maryland, while his was there on the mountain, which rooted Shannon Braden firmly in his off-limits zone.

The past couple of weeks had been quiet while she'd returned home to Maryland to attend her brother's wedding, and the fact that Steve had noticed, and disliked it being quiet, had thrown him for a loop.

His mind reeled back to last night again. He'd heard Cal riding back down the mountain about two hours after he'd arrived. As he swung the ax, he wondered if Shannon had done some hands-on research with Cowboy Cal last night.

He set another log in place, telling himself it was none of his damn business if she had, and split the log so hard the two halves flew ten feet from the stump. Another log, another split. And so became his stress-relieving pattern as the sun sailed higher, taking the bite off the chilly spring morning.

A mass of birds took off from the treetops. Steve paused midswing, a smile tugging at his lips. *Shannon.* He split another log, trying to ignore his accelerating pulse at the thought of her flitting back into his life.

The sweet sounds of her humming floated into his ears, and he tried harder to deny the thrum of heat racing down his spine. He heard the crunching of leaves and his smile widened further. Damn, he needed to get a grip.

"Hey there, mountain man."

He forced the foolhardy smile from his lips, replacing it with what he hoped was a less lustful one, and turned to find the all-too-chipper and insanely hot brunette. Her hair was piled on her head in a messy bun, a few dark tendrils curling past her shoulders. She held a mug in each hand. Curls of steam rose into the air. Her pink shirt hitched on her breasts, and he chalked that up to the list of things he was futilely trying not to react to. But his body wasn't on board with the off-limits plan, and it brimmed with heat. It had been a hell of a lot easier to be around her when she was staying at her uncle's house in town. At least then by the time he saw her she had a freaking bra on.

He dropped his eyes to avoid staring, but her flannel pajama pants hung low on her hips, revealing a sliver of taut skin just below her belly button. Christ, she was gorgeous. Striving for a safe view, he looked at her leather boots. Boots were safe. There was nothing sexy about boots. Bright pink laces hung loose over the dark leather, her pajama pants bunched around the tops, showing another flash of skin. He pictured her shoving her bare feet into them before jaunting out the door with her mind-blowing smile in place. There must be something wrong with him, because he found that sexy, too.

"You should lace those up." He ran a hand through his hair, grinding his teeth against the way his entire body was buzzing like a live wire.

"Well, *Mr. Safety.* I missed you, too." She thrust a mug toward him with a coy smile. "Just the way you like it. Bitter as weeds."

She was too damn cute, too damn social, and too damn temporary for the likes of him.

He reached for the mug. "Thanks, Butterfly." The nickname flew off his tongue without thought, just as it had the first time she'd flitted into his yard, turned his insides to fire, and flitted back out. He was surprised to realize he'd missed saying it while she was gone.

"No prob, Grizz."

Grizz. Hell if he hadn't missed that, too. Her eyes

dropped to his bare chest, lingering long enough for him to feel it lower. *Much lower.* Her cheeks flushed, and she slid those gorgeous hazel eyes to his ax—the one in his hand, not the one in his pants.

"Preparing for a cold night, or thinking about becoming a serial killer?"

I wouldn't have cold nights if you were in my bed. As if on cue, his body stirred again, reminding him it'd been far too long since he'd been with a woman.

"As *interesting* as a serial killer sounds, I don't think I'm cut out for it."

"Right. It would require human contact."

"I missed that smart mouth of yours," he said sarcastically. He'd been fantasizing about her full lips and sassy mouth ever since they'd reconnected at Rex and Jade's wedding, several months ago. But she was only there until her project ended, so sarcasm it was.

"Heard you ride in with Cal last night. How long are you here for?" He hadn't just heard her arrive. He'd gone out to see who was riding up the mountain and had seen her arms wrapped around Cal from behind as they rode past the overlook. In the moonlight they'd looked like a frigging Hallmark card.

"A few weeks. Four and a half, I think. Something like that." She stretched one arm, flashing even more of her midriff.

Torture. Pure, exquisite torture.

"You could have called me to bring you up the mountain." He shifted his eyes away, trying to figure out who had taken possession of his mouth. *Called me?* He had nothing against Cal. He was a nice guy and was one of the most respected horse trainers around. And he shouldn't give a shit who Shannon was with. Sure, she was hot, smart, and he liked her ballsy attitude, but he liked his life just the way it was. The last thing he needed was a social butterfly like her bringing noise and chaos into his life, telling him what to do or how to live.

"I know." She kicked at the dirt, her eyes downcast. "Treat and Max stopped by in the afternoon and I went into town with them to visit my uncle Hal and my cousins. Cal was there and he offered to drive me back, since he lives in Preston. It was only once we got back to his place that he suggested we ride up on horseback. Besides, you don't exactly love going into town."

Great, now he was stuck envisioning her at Cal's sprawling horse ranch.

He finished his coffee and handed her the mug. "Thanks. It was perfect." He turned to set another log on the stump. "You ought to be careful bringing guys up to your cabin," he said with his back to her.

"I thought I left my overprotective big brothers at home." She sighed. "I hardly think Cal is a threat. He's known Rex forever."

Steve rested the ax over his shoulder, weighing his response. The last thing he wanted to be was her big brother, and he'd known Cal forever, too. Cal wasn't the kind of guy to take advantage of a woman, but that didn't stop Steve's gut from churning at the thought of them cozied up together.

"He's a *friend*, Steve." She narrowed her eyes as he

drew the ax back. "Don't even try to pretend you don't bring women up to your cabin."

He arched a brow. That would be a big *no fucking way*. He liked his privacy.

Her jaw gaped. "What? Don't you ever get bored? Lonely?"

"Not really," he said as he swung the ax. It was a damned lie, at least since Shannon had flitted into his life, making him feel things he'd once been adept at ignoring.

"Why not? That's not normal." She finished her coffee and set the mugs on the ground as he split the log and set another one on the stump. "What do you do for sex?"

He laughed under his breath. "Seriously, city girl?"

"I'd hardly call Peaceful Harbor a city. It's a beach town, and you're avoiding the question."

"Maybe because you're asking questions you shouldn't be asking." He swung the ax and split another log.

She smirked. "Look at you, all big and brawny and afraid to talk about sex."

"What's gotten into you?" He set the ax-head on the ground and leaned on the handle. Before she'd gone home, he'd gotten away with a strategically placed *Uh-huh*. "I'm pretty sure you weren't this curious about my sexual habits the last time you were on the mountain."

Her eyes rolled over him, and he couldn't tell if she was assessing or enjoying the view.

"I don't know," she said with a mischievous grin.

"You're standing there like a lumberjack. Six...what?"

"Three," he said with a sigh.

"Right. Six three of shirtless, sweaty muscle, with your hair all tousled." She moved her hands around her head, causing her shirt to lift up again. "You haven't shaved in who knows how long, and you look like the guys on 'Seriously Sexy Hot Guys' Pinterest boards. A guy who looks like you *can't* be going without." She shrugged and her cheeks pinked up. "It made me wonder..."

"How about you wonder a little less?" *Because hearing you talk about my sex life makes me want you in it. Front and center.* "Pinterest? What the heck is Pinterest?"

Her eyes widened with disbelief. "I forgot you know nothing about the *real* world. Pinterest is this awesome social media site—"

"Never mind. That's so far from the real world it shouldn't exist. People nowadays are content to sit inside and stare at screens, talking with people they don't know instead of living their lives. Bodies are meant to *move*, Butterfly. Weather is meant to be *experienced*. If people were more like animals, the world would be a better place."

He saw a hint of hurt in her eyes and felt bad. Sometimes he forgot that he wasn't the only one protective of their lifestyle. He tried to change the subject to a lighter one.

"What are you doing out here so early anyway?" he asked.

"The company offered me a new project, and my

boss at my real job gave me a leave of absence to do it. I thought that was pretty cool of him. I'm going to be comparing the habits of gray and red foxes, and I'm here to scout the grays. You know how red foxes prefer edge habitats and grays prefer mountainous forestland?" Edge habitats were the boundary of two habitats, like field and forest. She didn't wait for him to respond before continuing with her explanation. "They're similar in life and history in almost every way, except for grays being shier and slightly smaller and where they make their dens. I'm going to study them to see if their behavioral patterns reveal reasons for the difference in habitat preference. I was hoping you'd have time to show me where I can find them."

The request took him by surprise. She'd spent weeks researching red foxes and hadn't once asked him to help her.

"No can do today, Butterfly." He had a busy day planned. He'd caught a group of twentysomethings partying by one of the rock ledges last week and he'd spotted a few of them again yesterday. He needed to make the rounds to ensure they weren't back and getting into trouble, and he had to head down the mountain to meet with his old buddies Mack and Will Cumberland. Yesterday he'd learned the Cumberland ranch was going up for sale: two hundred acres in Weston, adjacent to the national park where Steve had worked as a ranger and wildlife consultant for a decade. Steve had grown up in Weston, and though he lived two towns away now, his small-town roots ran deep. He wanted to try to convince his buddies to put the land into conservation instead of selling.

"Bummer. I was looking forward to catching up on all the crazy shenanigans you were up to while I was gone." She waggled her brows with the tease.

He smiled and shook his head. "Be careful out there. I caught some kids partying recently. They're probably harmless, but guys and alcohol...Just be careful. You got that Mace I left in your cabin?"

"That was you?" She narrowed her eyes and said, "You do realize I'm a grown woman, right?"

Christ, had he ever.

**

SHANNON WATCHED STEVE swing his ax. He was built like the very mountains he loved: strong and stable, with layers of hard-earned muscles born from honest, hard work. *Pure perfection.* And that hair? *Lord.* What would it be like to fist her hands in his hair and kiss him? To touch all those hard planes of muscle? To discover the man behind the walls? She told herself those were *wants* not *needs*, no matter how much they felt like it. *The kind of unrelenting wants that bring a girl to reach beneath the sheets and satisfy her fantasies.*

Down, girl.

Shannon had been surprised by how much she'd missed Steve when she'd gone home for her eldest brother Cole's wedding. She and Steve hadn't spent more than a few stolen moments together during the weeks she was here for her first assignment. Usually she'd catch him working on equipment, or in his yard, before she returned to her uncle's ranch in the evenings. He'd captivated her with his passion for, and endless knowledge about, all things wilderness related. And he was different from most of the guys she knew. He wasn't hung up on his looks or material things. He was *real*, with a strong set of values and priorities. Somehow, between their almost daily conversations and weeks of hoping she'd see him, she'd become completely and utterly taken with him.

When she'd been offered the assignment *and* the cabin, she'd accepted without hesitation. She'd missed Steve too much to deny the attraction, and she wanted to see if something might come of it.

Now that she was here, her body was thrumming at the mere sight of him. Given that she'd actually asked him about his sex life—and nearly died on the spot when the question slipped out—she desperately needed to rein herself in.

He wiped sweat from his brow, his tanned skin glistening in the morning sun. "Need anything from town?" he asked, setting another log on the stump.

She couldn't pry her eyes from his rippling abs and his bulbous biceps flexing with every move. "Town?"

He cocked a smile and hoisted the ax again. "Town. You know, the place where people who like *Pinterest* live?"

She forced her eyes away, glancing at the trees swaying in the breeze, the rocks at her feet, anywhere but at him.

"I know what town is. I'm just surprised you're going there." Everyone knew Steve hated to leave his precious mountain.

"Gotta take care of some business."

Going into town was a big deal. Unlike a quick trip to the store from her apartment in Peaceful Harbor, the drive into town took at least thirty to forty-five minutes, depending on which town he was going to. She'd realized last night she'd forgotten two very important supplies. Pop-Tarts and toilet paper. She could probably live with the single roll of toilet paper for another few days if she needed to, but Pop-Tarts were pretty much of a necessity. Besides, maybe she could convince Steve to help her scout gray-fox habitats at dusk. *Perfect!*

"Can I come with you?" she asked hopefully. "I need to pick up a few things."

"I'll get them for you. What do you need?"

She bit her lower lip, willing herself not to fib. But if she asked him to pick up what she really needed, he'd leave and she'd have to go searching for habitats by herself. Now that she'd thought about going later with her yummy mountain man, she'd already settled on it in her mind.

"It's girl stuff. You won't want to get it." So much for not fibbing. "Can I please go with you?" She gave him her best pleading look. "I promise not to talk your ear off." *Fib, fib, fib!* She had no control over what came out of her mouth, especially around him.

He muttered under his breath and set the ax against the stump. "I'm not making a hundred stops."

She leaped with delight and ran over to hug him. Her heel slipped out of her boot and she stumbled into him in a half hug, half full-body-draped-over-Steve embrace. His skin was hot, his body was hard, *and getting harder by the second.* He smelled like man and musk, and...she was still plastered against him.

She cleared her throat and managed, "Thank you." Using his chest for leverage—*yum, yum*—she found her footing and pressed her heel back into her boot. "One stop. That's it. Promise."

"You're excited to get those supplies." He picked up the logs he'd chopped and piled them on his forearm like they were toothpicks.

"I'm just excited to be back. Maybe at dusk you can help me map out the habitats? It'll be fun to scope them out together."

He gave her a curious look. "Haven't heard anyone describe hanging out with me as fun in a long time."

"Then you're hanging out with losers, and I'm taking that as a yes." She grabbed the coffee mugs, unable to stop smiling.

"I'm leaving in twenty minutes."

"I'll be back lickety-split." With a bounce in her step, she headed toward her cabin and heard him mutter, "Lickety-split," followed by a chuckle.

—End of Sneak Peek—
To continue reading, buy CRUSHING ON LOVE
(The Bradens at Peaceful Harbor)

Please enjoy this preview of
WILD BOYS AFTER DARK: LOGAN

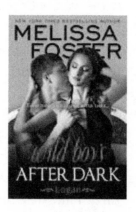

BACHELOR PARTIES WERE the worst. Stella Krane couldn't understand why guys needed a wedding in order to go to a bar, drink their asses off, flirt with strangers, and talk about it for the rest of their lives. *Remember when...?* It was like a rite of passage for uptight businessmen. *Real* men took it to a hotel room, hired strippers, and fucked the hell out of them in ways their pretty little wives wouldn't ever let them. She cringed at the thought. She wouldn't want a man who did that. God, what was going on with her?

There was a time when Stella had dreamed of being someone's pretty little wife, but that was before Carl Kutcher. Her gut twisted with the realization that he was getting out of jail in four days. The man had stolen every dream she'd ever had—and who knew when he'd steal her life. She no longer held on to the fantasy of a doting husband, a few kids, and a white picket fence. Now she was just happy to be alive.

"Hey, sweetheart, how about a little sugar with my drink?" drunken asshole number six asked as he leaned over the bar. He was with the bachelor party and had been drinking for the past few hours. Five guys with wedding rings pawing, groping, leering, making lewd comments, and trying their best to live out a stilted fantasy.

Stella eyed his wedding ring. Damn, she needed to get off tonight—and she wasn't thinking about getting off work. It'd been too many months since she'd gotten laid, and she'd had it up to here watching everyone else play out their dirty fantasies. She longed for the feel of a man's hands on her ass while his cock drove hard and deep inside her, allowing her brain to escape reality for a while. Stella wasn't *really* a one-night-fuck type of girl—but right then, boy did she wish she were. She missed the feel of a hard chest pressing against her and the deep, naughty whispers of a man telling her how much he wanted her. She'd never been that down-and-dirty girl until Kutcher. He'd sparked a side of her that she hadn't known existed, a dangerous, rebellious side that turned her on in ways she never imagined possible. But that was before things went bad and Kutcher showed his true colors. *The bastard.* She refused to even think of him as *Carl* anymore. Now he was just *Kutcher.* Kutcher had taught her many things, like that men pretty much suck. They lie, cheat, and sometimes...they beat the hell out of you.

She narrowed her catlike green eyes at the mildly attractive, dark-haired sure thing before her and practically purred, "How about I get you another drink and you go home and fuck your wife's sugar-coated pussy?"

Jaw slack—check. Eyes wide—check. Oh, look, a bonus. Mr. I Want Some Sugar backed away from the bar.

Some days she felt like a babysitter and a whore at once, but hey, working at a bar in New York City might not be like running her own interior design business in Mystic, Connecticut, but it kept her alive. She missed Mystic. She missed the harbor, the safety of the small town, her friends. She missed her mother most of all. Her mother was battling cancer, but like everything else in her life, she'd had to sever all ties with her mother in order to keep her safe from Kutcher.

Stella had lived in Mystic her whole life. Until Kutcher. *Fucking Kutcher.* Slick-tongued, hard-bodied, and unfortunately, hard-fisted Kutcher. She'd dated him for only a few months before he showed his true colors. His possessiveness knew no boundaries, and she'd barely escaped with her life. No, this might not be Mystic, and she might have had to leave everything she knew and loved behind, but at least she'd survived—even if she had to spend the rest of her life pretending to be someone she wasn't.

She felt the eyes of the man at the end of the bar on her again. He wasn't part of the bachelor party—at least that was a plus. He'd come in an hour ago, ordered a Jack and Coke, and hadn't moved anything but his piercing blue eyes—which had tracked her every move—since. He wore an expensive suit coat over a white dress shirt open at the neck, exposing a swath of sexy chest hair. Perfect for running her fingers through when she straddled him.

Lord.

What had Kutcher done to her? How had she gone from being a proper Wesleyan girl to a slutty-minded runaway? She'd met Carl Kutcher at a party for one of her interior design clients. He was tall and dark with a trim beard, eyes as black as night, and a quiet confidence that gave him an aura of importance. Stella had learned too late that there were two sides to the man who seemed too good to be true. He moved like the sea, calm and alluring one minute, angry and dark the next. His moods changed with the wind, and when they did, he left no room for escape.

Stella pushed thoughts of Kutcher away and tried to concentrate as she served up two more drinks, feeling the heat of Mr. Blue Eyes rolling over her breasts as she leaned down to wipe the bar. Hell if it didn't make her entire body go hot. She'd been through enough over the past few months and knew better than to let a man intimidate her, but every time she tried to meet his gaze, she couldn't do it. He *was* intimidating, in an edgy sort of way. Everything about him, from his thick dark hair and chiseled features to his iridescent baby blues, screamed sex, power, and intensity. Even his scent was musky and sensual, like liquid amber. She'd like to roll around in his scent, revel in the feel of his big hands on her breasts, her rib cage—

What the hell am I thinking?

She was pretty sure that her landlord, Mrs. Fairly, wouldn't be thrilled with a midnight romp in her basement bedroom. Stella wasn't exactly the quietest of lovers. She'd been lucky enough to find a place to stay where she could pay cash for rent and didn't have to provide her social security number for the lease. She had to be completely untraceable, which meant no credit cards, no checks, and never using her ATM card. Fucking Kutcher had tracked her down everywhere she went, which was why she'd finally left Mystic and come to the Big Apple to disappear.

So far so good.

A large hand landed on the bar just beneath her chest, fingers splayed. No wedding ring, soft, unmarred hands, manicured fingernails. The hand of a wealthy man, that much was for sure. Her eyes traveled up to a thick, masculine wrist, suit jacket stretched tight across flexed biceps, to the piercing blue eyes she'd been fantasizing about. Her breath caught in her throat at the intensity of his stare. He circled her wrist with his index finger and thumb, drawing her eyes downward and sending her heart into panic mode. She'd been here before, restrained by Kutcher, unable to break free.

She forced her mind to function and pulled her arm free, rubbing it as if it had been burned.

"Sorry, darlin'. I didn't mean to frighten you." His deep voice slithered over her skin as his gaze softened, penetrating in a different way. Not intense and threatening, but the kind of heated gaze that felt safe and seductive at once.

Stella swallowed her initial fear, gathering her wits about her. She wasn't a meek girl. At five foot five, a hundred and twenty-five pounds, she was curvy and solid, and until Kutcher, she'd had the confidence to match her strong body. Now it took a few minutes to reclaim that confidence. She hated that even after a few months Kutcher's memory could still swamp her.

"Just one of those nights." With her words his eyes went from seductive to assessing, his dark brows knitted together, and he lifted his hand from the bar and rubbed the sexy scruff peppering his chin. A slight smile curved his full lips as he glanced over his shoulder at the loud bachelor party, then turned and lowered his voice.

"Yes, I can see it is." He held up his glass. "When you have time?"

"Sure." She picked up on a faint Midwestern twang that came and went and pictured him in tight jeans, cowboy boots, and a Stetson. She turned to mix his drink, thinking about the man behind her whose eyes burned a path through her back. She wondered what he did for a living, dressed like that and alone at a bar on a Friday night. A man with eyes like Chris Pine's, a face like Channing Tatum's, and a voice like melted chocolate, which made her want to lick him from head to toe. Unaccompanied on a Friday night? *Gay?* No way. Not with the way he'd been eye-fucking her all night. *Freak?* Probably.

On that lovely thought, she turned and pushed his drink across the bar. "That'll be—"

He placed his hand over hers, stopping her cold

and making her body hum and rattle with fear in equal measure.

"I know how much it is, darlin'. Thank you."

She withdrew her hand from beneath his, instantly missing the connection. It'd been too damn long. She just might have to break out her battery-operated boyfriend tonight and satisfy the itch she'd been ignoring since arriving in the city.

He handed her a twenty. "Keep the change. You're new here." He sipped his drink, eyes locked on her.

She worked the register, trying not to think about the man behind the generous tip. *Yeah, right.* She wiped the bar to give her hands something to do besides wanting to touch his again, and eyed him warily.

"I started a few weeks ago."

"That explains it. I've been in and out of town the last few weeks. Where'd you work before this?"

She leaned one hand on the bar, finding her confidence once again. It came and went like the wind these days, and she was glad when it decided to blow back in. The guy's eyes turned sultry, and a rush of excitement heated her insides. It'd also been a long time since she'd been *properly* flirted with.

"Around," she answered, toying with him.

A blond guy leaned in over Midwestern hottie's shoulder. "Can I get another gin and tonic, please?"

She took his glass and turned away to mix the cocktail.

"She's so fucking hot," the tall blond said. Stella hoped to hell he wasn't talking about her. She'd heard enough about her ass, her tits, and her fuckable mouth for one night.

She handed him his glass and he shoved a ten across the bar with a wink. A fifty-cent tip. *Jesus Christ.* She used to earn six figures, and now she was schlepping drinks in a bar for peanuts.

The familiar mantra played in her head like a broken record, giving her strength and perspective.

At least I'm alive.

I'm alive. I'm alive. I'm alive.

—End of Sneak Peek—

To continue reading, buy WILD BOYS AFTER DARK: LOGAN

Be sure to check out these two new stand-alone romance novels from Melissa Foster

TRU BLUE

He wore the skin of a killer, and bore the heart of a lover

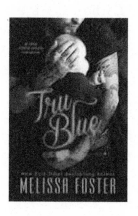

There's nothing Truman Gritt won't do to protect his family—Including spending years in jail for a crime he didn't commit. When he's finally released, the life he knew is turned upside down by his mother's overdose, and Truman steps in to raise the children she's left behind. Truman's hard, he's secretive, and he's trying to save a brother who's even more broken than he is. He's never needed help in his life, and when beautiful Gemma Wright tries to step in, he's less than accepting. But Gemma has a way of slithering into people's lives and eventually she pierces through his ironclad heart. When Truman's dark past collides with his future, his loyalties will be tested, and he'll be faced with his toughest decision yet.

Tru Blue conquers darker topics than Melissa's other contemporary romance novels and is written in the same loving, raw, and emotional voice readers have come to love. Set in Peaceful Harbor, with cameos from Jillian Braden (The Bradens at Pleasant Hill) and the Whiskey family, who were introduced in River of Love (The Bradens at Peaceful Harbor).

TEMPTING TRISTAN
A M/M Contemporary Romance

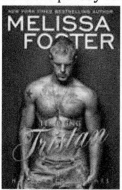

***AUTHOR'S NOTE: If you have never read a M/M book,
rest assured this is one of my favorite romance novels,
written with the full range and depth of emotions as all
of my M/F romance novels.***

Fresh off the heels of yet another bad relationship, Tristan Brewer is taking a break from men to try and figure out where he keeps going wrong. He knows his biggest fault—he leads with his heart, not his head—and that's never going to change. But after several introspective weeks, he's beginning to get a handle on things. That is, until badass heartthrob Alex Wells walks into his bar...

Alex has spent eight years in the Army, months in a hospital bed, and far too long hiding his sexual identity. He's guilt-ridden, damaged, pissed off, and up for a Silver Star—for the incident that nearly cost him his life, and kept him from his grandmother's funeral. But all he wants to do is forget his stint with the institution that *allows* but doesn't necessarily *accept*, and live the life he's always dreamed of.

The chemistry between Tristan and Alex ignites from the moment they meet, and the more time they spend together the hotter the flames become. But the closer Tristan gets, the more Alex's walls go up, and when the two walk onto a military base, Tristan finds out Alex's physical scars aren't the ones that run the deepest.

Read the entire LOVE IN BLOOM SERIES

SNOW SISTERS
Sisters in Love
Sisters in Bloom
Sisters in White

THE BRADENS
Lovers at Heart
Destined for Love
Friendship on Fire
Sea of Love
Bursting with Love
Hearts at Play
Taken by Love
Fated for Love
Romancing My Love
Flirting with Love
Dreaming of Love
Crashing into Love
Healed by Love
Surrender My Love
River of Love
Crushing on Love
Whisper of Love
Thrill of Love

THE REMINGTONS
Game of Love
Stroke of Love
Flames of Love
Slope of Love

Read, Write, Love
Touched by Love

SEASIDE SUMMERS
Seaside Dreams
Seaside Hearts
Seaside Sunsets
Seaside Secrets
Seaside Nights
Seaside Embrace
Seaside Lovers
Seaside Whisper

THE RYDERS
Seized by Love
Claimed by Love
Chased by Love
Rescued by Love
Swept into Love

HARBORSIDE NIGHTS SERIES
Includes characters from
Love in Bloom series

Catching Cassidy
Discovering Delilah
Tempting Tristan
Chasing Charley
Breaking Brandon
Embracing Evan
Reaching Rusty
Loving Livi

AFTER DARK SERIES
Wild Boys After Dark
Logan
Heath
Jackson
Cooper
Bad Boys After Dark
Mick
Dylan
Carson
Brett

Stand-Alone Novels by Melissa

Tru Blue (contemporary romance)
Chasing Amanda (mystery/suspense)
Come Back to Me (mystery/suspense)
Have No Shame (historical fiction/romance)
Love, Lies & Mystery (3-book bundle)
Megan's Way (literary fiction)
Traces of Kara (psychological thriller)
Where Petals Fall (suspense)

SIGN UP for Melissa's newsletter to stay up-to-date with new releases, giveaways, and events

NEWSLETTER:
www.melissafoster.com/newsletter

CONNECT WITH MELISSA

TWITTER:
www.twitter.com/Melissa_Foster

FACEBOOK:
www.facebook.com/MelissaFosterAuthor

WEBSITE:
www.melissafoster.com

STREET TEAM:
www.facebook.com/groups/melissafosterfans

Acknowledgments

I had a blast writing about Trish and Boone and learning all about Hurricane, West Virginia, although I have taken fictional liberties with the town, the people, Main Street Music, and Greenhouse of Teays Valley restaurant. Heaps of gratitude goes to Eric Reckard, the owner of Greenhouse of Teays Valley, and his brother, Joe, the executive chef, for allowing me to bring them into our fictional world.

Several characters in Chased by Love are from other series in the Love in Bloom big-family romance collection. You'll read about Drake Savage and Carey in my upcoming Bayside Summers series (releasing 2017). The Ryders were introduced in The Remington series (FLAMES OF LOVE, Cash Ryder and Siena Remington, and READ, WRITE, LOVE, where you meet Blue Ryder), and you learn more about them in the Seaside Summers series. Find out more about The Remingtons and Seaside Summers on my website. www.MelissaFoster.com

A special thank you to my fantabulous street team member, and friend, Alexis Bruce, and to my friends Nina Lane and Clare Ayala, for brainstorming at a moment's notice. If you haven't joined my street team yet, please do! www.melissafoster.com/ST

The best way to stay abreast of Love in Bloom releases is to sign up for my monthly newsletter (and receive a free short story!) www.MelissaFoster.com/Newsletter

Follow me on Facebook for fun chats and

giveaways. I always try to keep fans abreast of what's going on in our fictional boyfriends' worlds. www.Facebook.com/MelissaFosterAuthor

Thank you to my awesome editorial team: Kristen Weber and Penina Lopez, and my meticulous proofreaders: Jenna Bagnini, Juliette Hill, Marlene Engel, Lynn Mullan, and Justinn Harrison. And last but never least, a huge thank you to my family for their patience, support, and inspiration.

www.MelissaFoster.com

Melissa Foster is a *New York Times* and *USA Today* bestselling and award-winning author. Her books have been recommended by *USA Today's* book blog, *Hagerstown* magazine, *The Patriot*, and several other print venues. She is the founder of the World Literary Café and Fostering Success. Melissa has painted and donated several murals to the Hospital for Sick Children in Washington, DC.

Visit Melissa on her website or chat with her on social media. Melissa enjoys discussing her books with book clubs and reader groups and welcomes an invitation to your event.

Melissa's books are available through most online retailers in paperback and digital formats.

CPSIA information can be obtained at www.ICGtesting.com
Printed in the USA
BVOW08s1253280716

457178BV00001B/1/P